"My dear Miss Hart."

Lord Winston moved to the chair beside her, took her hand and brushed his thumb across her damp face. "It was my privilege and honor to shield you." His green eyes shone with an ardor she had never imagined she would receive even in her most sublime girlhood dreams.

The footman cleared his throat, the sound of it holding a slightly menacing hum.

Lord Winston blinked, grinned sheepishly and sat back in his chair. "There is another matter in the book that disturbed me."

Catherine inhaled deeply to recover herself. "And that is?" The words came out on a breathy sigh.

This time, Lord Winston had the grace to ignore her discomfiture. "I cannot think well of Edward Ferrars because of his secret engagement. He was living a lie, which no gentleman should ever do if he expects to be highly regarded. I simply cannot tolerate a liar."

As if cold water had been dashed in her face, Catherine's mind and emotions cleared, and her giddy, girlish sensibilities yielded to good sense.

Books by Louise M. Gouge

Love Inspired Historical

Love Thine Enemy
The Captain's Lady
At the Captain's Command
*A Proper Companion
*A Suitable Wife
*A Lady of Quality

*Ladies in Waiting

LOUISE M. GOUGE

has been married to her husband, David, for forty-eight years. They have four children and seven grand-children. Louise always had an active imagination, thinking up stories for her friends, classmates and family, but seldom writing them down. At a friend's insistence, in 1984 she finally began to type up her latest idea. Before trying to find a publisher, Louise returned to college, earning a B.A. in English/creative writing and a master's degree in liberal studies. She reworked that first novel based on what she had learned and sold it to a major Christian publisher. Louise then worked in television marketing for a short time before becoming a college English/humanities instructor. She has had thirteen novels published, several of which have earned multiple awards, including the 2006 Inspirational Reader's Choice Award. Please visit her website at http://blog.Louisemgouge.com.

A Lady of Quality

LOUISE M. GOUGE

HARLEQUIN® LOVE INSPIRED® HISTORICAL

Recycling programs
for this product may
not exist in your area.

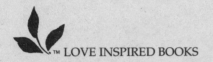 ™ LOVE INSPIRED BOOKS

ISBN-13: 978-0-373-82973-6

A LADY OF QUALITY

www.LoveInspiredBooks.com

Printed in U.S.A.

For by grace are ye saved through faith; and that not of yourselves: it is the gift of God: Not of works, lest any man should boast.
—*Ephesians* 2:8–9

This book is dedicated to my beloved husband, David, who has stood by my side and encouraged me through my entire writing career. I would also like to thank Laurie Alice Eakes, Nancy Mayer and the Beau Monde Chapter of RWA for helping with my research into the Regency era. Thank you, Ramona K. Cecil, for your invaluable critiques and suggestions. *Merci beaucoup* to Leslie Carroll for translating my French passages. And of course, many thanks to Rachel Burkot, my wonderful Love Inspired Historical editor, whose insights always improve my stories.

Chapter One

London, England
June 1814

"En garde."

Lord Winston took his position on the fencing strip and injected as much boredom and hauteur into his voice as he could without insulting his young opponent. Why Monsieur Angelus had assigned him this tall, almost gangly youth as a sparring partner, Winston could not guess. His purpose in patronizing this particular academy was to meet with London's most challenging adversaries. But today, the fencing master had paired him with someone who had the look of an untried novice, a youth so green that he wore a protective mask. When they had lifted their Italian foils in their opening salute to each other, Winston could even see a slight tremor in the boy's hand, a sure sign he would have no trouble dispensing with him.

"Mais non, monsieur." Flawless French spoken in an alto tone revealed that the youth's voice had not yet changed. What a foolish youngster to come out and play with grown gentlemen. *"Vous en garde."*

So he meant to launch the first attack. Winston smirked.

"*Très bien, enfant.* Proceed." Expecting a wild lunge, he prepared to deflect the boy's foil and make quick work of this match so he could advance to a more exciting opponent.

But the aim was steady as he thrust his sword at Winston's heart. Winston jumped back to avoid the "fatal" touch of the button-shielded weapon on his padded vest. Interesting. Now he truly was on guard, for the youth was proving to be a real adversary. Winston lunged, searching for a weakness that he usually found in an opponent's eyes. But that ridiculous mask hid such unintentional signals. No doubt he was a pretty boy whose mother demanded that he wear the unmanly protection.

The boy grunted softly as he sidestepped to avoid the touch, holding his foil in the proper defensive position. With a clink of metal on metal, their two saucer-shaped hilts caught and held, and Winston stared into the mesh of the mask, seeking a weakness in the dark, shadowed eyes. All he saw was hatred.

For the briefest instant, shock overrode his customary coolness in this sport. Why should this stranger despise him? No doubt he was a Napoleon sympathizer, bitter over his emperor's recent defeat and exile. Winston would happily teach him a lesson in British superiority. He shoved the boy away and took a more aggressive tack. Using every trick his father and Monsieur Angelus had taught him, he bore down upon his opponent with aggressive parries and rapid ripostes, at last striking the boy's right hand hard with his buttoned blade.

The lad gasped and dropped his foil, then straightened and spread his arms to accept the "fatal" touch.

Unexpected compassion filled Winston's chest. For his surprising skill, the lad deserved another chance. "Not at all, my boy." He pointed his weapon at the dropped sword. "Pick it up."

Without a word of gratitude, the Frenchman grasped the foil with his *left* hand and lunged at Winston. Another surprise from this astonishing foe. Again they parried back and forth. Their ripostes increased in speed. The metallic clink of the blades grew louder, the boy's grunts more frequent. Winston found himself breathless, as well. He became aware of other gentlemen stopping their own matches to watch. *Good.* That was exactly the kind of attention he required in his quest for political influence, especially since the Duke of Kent could be among the onlookers.

In the second it took for Winston to foolishly locate the king's son, the French youth found an opening and lunged. Warning cries went up from the crowd, and Winston saw the unshielded foil coming at his heart. Fear shot through him. Did the boy mean to kill him? No, for he hesitated, doubtless aware of the lethal—and illegal—danger he was imposing upon his opponent. Winston seized the moment to deflect the weapon and strike his own blow on the heart-shaped target on his opponent's padded vest.

"Touché." Winston straightened, unable to hide a triumphant smirk amid the applause of the other gentlemen.

The boy should have lifted his foil in a salute. Should have congratulated Winston on his victory. Should have removed that ridiculous mask to reveal his identity.

Instead, he threw down his weapon and shoved his way through the crowd, disappearing down a back corridor, utterly depriving Winston of his chance to act the gracious victor.

Catherine du Coeur thought her heart might leap from her chest. Pulling off her mask, she stumbled against the wall, but caught herself from falling as she scurried down the back corridor of Monsieur Angelus's fencing academy.

Never in her twenty years had she encountered such arrogance. True, she knew little of London's aristocracy, but Lord Winston's pride would put a peacock to shame. Vanity and conceit were written across his all-too-handsome face, which was framed with blond hair so curly she could almost envy him. Then there were those intense gray-green eyes and that straight, narrow nose he'd peered down to look at her as if she were some sort of inferior being. She could see from the way he carried himself, the way he ruthlessly defeated her, that he would have no scruples about using false evidence to send an innocent Christian gentleman to the gallows.

Perhaps she was just making excuses. God had been merciful in staying her hand when she had the chance to plunge the unprotected foil into the baron's evil heart. No, she would not be the one to kill him, merely the one to expose and destroy him for what he did to Papa.

"Very clever, my dear." Mr. Radcliff came out of the shadows at the back door and flung her black woolen cloak around her shoulders. "How did you remove the button?" He gave her arm a paternal pat. "And why did you hesitate? You could have killed Winston and been done with it."

She pulled the hood over her head. "Hurry. We must get away before anyone pursues us." To gain her admittance to the academy, Mr. Radcliff had forged a letter as if from Papa to Monsieur Angelus, who was all too willing to let his old friend's "son" fence at the Haymarket academy. She could not imagine what Mr. Radcliff included in the letter to persuade Monsieur Angelus to overlook the scandal and lies attached to Papa's name. But it would only add to her father's disgrace if that "son" was discovered to be a girl.

They exited the back door of the elegant stone building

into the sweltering heat and entered the waiting hackney. Only when they were seated and on their way could Catherine breathe out a long sigh of relief. When she inhaled, the stink of horses and sewage nearly sickened her. How she longed for her country home, but until Papa's name was cleared, she must endure the miseries of a London summer.

"I did not remove the button. It broke off when the baron knocked my foil to the floor."

"Ah." He pointed to the gloved hand Lord Winston struck. "Is the injury severe?"

"'Tis nothing at all." No doubt bruised, but fortunately, ladies wore gloves at all times, even in the summer, so she could keep the injury covered. She brushed back her hood and pulled a linen handkerchief from her sleeve to mop away the perspiration streaming down her face. "Is London always this hot?"

"It is unusually warm this year." Mr. Radcliff retrieved a black linen fan and waved it before his pale, slender face. Understanding filled his dark gray eyes, and she could see he would ask no more questions about her duel with Winston. This gentleman knew she could not commit murder. Just as Papa had always done, he was letting her learn through her experiences. And today she had learned much about Lord Winston. Now she could plot her revenge.

She gazed at Mr. Radcliff fondly across the small carriage. How like an uncle he was with his care for her family. Vaguely resembling his cousin, Lord Winston, he was perhaps five and forty years old, a little older than Papa and Mama. But he appeared much older due to his thin, frail body and wispy gray hair. The three of them had been friends long ago. This winter past, when Lord Winston had falsely accused Papa of being a Bonapartist and conspiring to assassinate the French king, who had taken refuge in England, Mr. Radcliff had helped Papa escape imprisonment. Then he befriended the family when no one else would. Now, as secretary to Lord Blakemore, he had secured a position for Catherine as Lady Blakemore's companion, providing her with fabricated references to keep anyone from associating her with someone all deemed a would-be assassin. Catherine's family owed him so much, but he asked nothing in return for all of his kindnesses.

A rush of gratitude swept into her chest. "Dear friend, I wish you could attend the marchioness's ball this evening." She gave him a playful smile, such as she might bestow upon Papa. "I would dance every dance with you."

"What?" He chuckled. "And scandalize your gracious employer, not to mention my beloved wife?" His expression fell. "No, no, my dear. Such gaiety is not for the likes of me. I had my youth. Now it is your turn."

She guessed he had suffered some great loss, but she would not ask him about it lest it remind him of his sorrows. Perhaps in helping her, he was somehow finding comfort.

The hackney wended its way through the London traffic much too slowly for Catherine's taste. Today was her half day off, and she needed to be back at Blakemore House soon to prepare for the ball. But Lady Blakemore was a tolerant employer, so she did not worry excessively. Moreover, this afternoon's charade had served an important purpose. She had evaluated her enemy and knew his greatest weakness, which was nothing short of overweening pride. How easy it would be to use that fault to destroy him or at the least force him to admit that his evidence against Papa was false.

She would somehow arrange an introduction, flatter him and win his friendship, perhaps even his love, then coax him into confessing his crime to her. Last, she would go to Lord Blakemore and beseech him to ruin Lord Winston with the information. Even though he was a peer, Winston would be punished, perhaps imprisoned. Papa would be absolved of all guilt and could return home. Only then would she be satisfied with her revenge.

A vague memory scratched at the back of her mind, a Bible verse advising that vengeance belonged to God alone. But surely the Almighty would understand she was the only one who could save Papa from execution for a crime he did not commit.

Winston surveyed the ballroom, looking for another partner. Of the three young ladies with whom he had already danced, not one excited his interest. Their mutual indifference was obvious in the way they continued to cast glances at the uniformed soldiers who dotted the room like a measles rash. Not that he would have any of the silly chits, but surely his wealth, his pedigree and his barony of writ that extended back to the days of Henry III should garner some interest among the marriageable misses in Society. No doubt it was the uniform. Had Father not forbidden Winston to join His Majesty's army to fight Napoleon, he, too, could be attracting a bevy of colorful butterflies.

What vain and foolish thoughts. What care did he have for their frivolous choices? His features and physique were passable, or at least not repulsive, yet he would much rather strengthen his inner man, his character, as Father had always instructed from the Scriptures. Likewise, in his necessary pursuit of a wife, he must search for a sensible, refined lady of good pedigree. Yet after twice losing his targets to other gentlemen, his confidence had begun to falter, especially tonight as the gallant, crimson-coated heroes forced him to the sidelines. On the other hand, what better place to observe which young ladies might have the essential character his wife must possess?

He must not make the same mistake Father made some twenty-five years ago. After burying two wives and their unborn children, the previous Lord Winston married a lady thirty-two years his junior in his final attempt to produce a living heir. Such a tenuous beginning always humbled Winston, for he and his sister would not exist had those poor souls not perished. How often he wondered if he would ever live up to God's expectations for him—*or* Father's. Certainly Mother had not. Although Winston loved her, he had long wondered what shortcoming had caused Father to banish her to their country estate some seventeen years ago, while Winston was a small boy.

But again, these were vain and foolish thoughts. He must concentrate on his search and find a sensible lady of good family and connections. Perhaps if she were plain, she would not be inclined to silliness. He would leave the silly girls to their soldiers. If this evening did not produce at least one candidate for him to pursue, he would be forced to accept Countess Lieven's invitation to Almack's tomorrow evening, a prospect he did not find agreeable, despite the countess's well-regarded political influence.

Across the room, Miss Waddington stood chatting with her mother, Lady Grandly. The young lady had the deportment required of a diplomat's wife, but she was given to occasional giggling. Winston shuddered. Perhaps he could school it out of her. With a sigh, he began his trek toward her. Although she had refused him the last time, perhaps she would look with favor on him this time.

Guests whirled about the floor in a waltz, obscuring his view of the lady, so he skirted the dancers and ambled toward her. At that moment, a red uniform bowed over her hand. Winston spun away with not a whit of disappointment. Yet when he noticed newlyweds Lord and Lady Greystone nearby, gazing at each other with obvious adoration, a surprising pang struck his chest. What would it be like to find a lady who loved him, one whom he could love in return? How did a gentleman go about finding such a jewel? Considering Father's apparent disappointment with Mother, Winston feared he would make the same mistake in his haste to wed. And wed he must. A wife was as essential to a diplomat as linguistic skills. Yet here he stood in a room full of young ladies, utterly unable even to find a supper partner, much less a candidate to wed.

He clenched his jaw. If this ball were not so important to his career, he would leave. But one simply did not leave the marquess's ball before supper. Perhaps he should give up his quest for the evening and find an old dowager to dine with. He had always appreciated the wisdom of the older generation, and most of them seemed to find his company agreeable, as well.

"Ah, there you are, Winston." Lady Blakemore accosted him near the refreshment table. "I must ask a favor of you."

At last Providence smiled upon him. "Of course, my lady." He bowed over the tall countess's hand, eager to do her bidding. Her husband was the very diplomat with whom Winston hoped to serve in France. He would gladly dance and dine with her. "Ask what you will, and I shall do it."

She took his arm and, rather than move toward the dance floor, drew him toward a dark-haired young lady seated near the wall and staring down at the skirt of her light green gown. "Winston, this is Miss Hart. I promised her the young men would be lining up to dance with her, but she has not been asked to stand up for a single set. Do save me from being a liar."

"Lady Blakemore!" Although the young lady did not look up, Winston could see that her cheeks had turned a deep pink.

Pity welled up inside him. Obviously this poor girl was the countess's hired companion and did not have the makings of any nobleman's wife, much less a diplomat's. But surely one gentleman in this room could show her a little kindness and courtesy without granting her too much consequence or harming his own interests. With no one else to fill that office, he held out his hand.

"Miss Hart, may I have the honor of this dance? You see, I have lost my partner to another gentleman, and only you can rescue me from utter mortification."

Gasping, she looked up sharply and stared at him.

For an instant, he could not breathe as a new sort of shock slammed into his chest. Never in his three and twenty years had he seen a more exquisite female face. A perfect oval, with a fetching widow's peak, though he doubted this young lady was a widow. Sparkling dark brown eyes fringed by long black lashes. He had never before noticed any lady's eyelashes. A faint pink blush of chagrin remained on her ivory cheeks, and her full, smooth lips invited— But he would not think such an inappropriate thought.

She placed her hand in his and slowly rose. Again shock pummeled him, for the graceful ascent of her slender form lifted the top of her thick, smooth coiffeur to perhaps three inches short of his own height of almost six feet. Miss Hart was by far the most elegant, dare he say *regal* lady he had ever set eyes upon. He stood staring, unable to move until she gazed up at him soulfully and smiled.

"I thank you for your gallantry, Lord Winston. Perhaps we shall rescue each other from mortification." The music of her dulcet alto voice settled into him like the purr of his favorite cat.

Catherine could hardly control her laughter. Attracting Lord Winston's interest was far easier than she had ever imagined. Spending her entire life in the country, she'd had little to do with gentlemen of her station, for when Mama married an impoverished French *comte* fleeing the Reign of Terror, her family had not entirely welcomed the alliance. Further, she had never counted her appearance as her best asset, for she was too slender, and her unusual height often brought more disdain than admiration.

But Lord Winston's awestruck expression and obvious approval revealed a certain guilelessness at odds with the arrogance he had displayed at Monsieur Angelus's academy this afternoon. In fact, she had to admit she admired him in return, at least in a physical sense. His height exceeded hers by perhaps three or four inches, and his impossibly curly blond hair had been coiffed with care, unlike the sweat-dampened coils he had sported after their match.

With a wave of her fan, she made a show of dismissing her feigned chagrin over Lady Blakemore's comment regarding her lack of dance partners. Her employer had no idea that Catherine had refused several invitations. Of course, Society decreed that once a young lady refused an offer from one gentleman, she must not accept another for the entire evening. But after they all turned their backs on Papa, she had little care for Society's dictates.

Although the dancers were assembling, the baron did not move, but continued to gaze at her, a half smile on his finely sculpted lips.

She nodded toward the dance floor. "Shall we?"

He cleared his throat. "Yes, of course." As he led her to the floor, the smile that lit his entire face gave him a charmingly youthful appearance.

Now a giddy feeling stirred within Catherine, but she forced herself to remember why she was here. This man—she would not think of him as a gentleman—was not some innocent, harmless soul. He was responsible for the destruction of her family. Even now, Mama, Lucien and Isabella lived under the constant threat of being thrown out of Mama's ancestral home, all the while suffering the indignities heaped upon the relatives of a suspected traitor and assassin.

With great difficulty, Catherine forced her mind to the present, forced her hand to relax in Lord Winston's gentle grasp as they joined other guests for a country dance. At the end of the line, he released her to stand opposite with the other ladies as more couples continued to join them. The music began, and the couple at the top of the line set out on a lively pattern of steps, weaving in and out of the lines as they moved from one end to the other.

During the dance, conversation with the baron was impossible, for everyone had to pay attention to their own movements. So Catherine spoke with her eyes. Not as the silly, simpering girls flirted outrageously with their targeted gentlemen, but with shy glances and half smiles, as if she were thanking him for his gallant rescue. She could not fail to notice that his returning glances held a surprising amount of kindness.

Again she thrust away such generous thoughts. This afternoon she had seen his true heart as they fenced. In the fierce glare in his gray-green eyes, she could see that he would gladly have killed her in a real duel, just as he had, in effect, murdered Papa's reputation. Now she would use his obvious admiration to win his affection while she searched out the secrets that would destroy him and acquit Papa.

A nagging memory surfaced. When she was a child, her governess had read her wonderful stories of heroic people in the Old Testament. While she had always imagined herself a Ruth or a Deborah, this evening the only biblical woman who came to mind was the temptress Delilah, who wheedled from Samson his deepest secret so his enemies could defeat him. For the first time in her life, she wondered whether Delilah's actions had actually been justified.

Winston did not much care for dancing, but the exercise was a necessary evil for social, and therefore political, purposes. Yet for the first time in his life, he was enjoying a dance. Miss Hart kept glancing at him in the most charming way, her lovely dark brown eyes twinkling in the ballroom's bright candlelight. Soon it was their turn to wend their way down the line, threading in and out between the other dancers. Once they successfully reached the bottom, she offered him a triumphant smirk, and he returned a little bow. Perhaps he should reconsider this matter of dancing.

Still, the set lasted far too long. He was eager to become better acquainted with her and discover her family connections. Upon further thought, he considered that as Lady Blakemore's companion, no doubt she was an impoverished lady of good family. No lady hired a companion of inferior birth, for such a woman would not be permitted into the drawing rooms of the aristocracy. Once Winston discovered Miss Hart's pedigree, he would know whether or not to launch a pursuit.

At last the music ended, and the guests applauded, then

proceeded to the dining room two by two in order of precedence, led by the marchioness on the arm of a duke.

Winston bowed to his partner. "Miss Hart, I consider myself the most fortunate of men that you will be my dinner companion this evening." He was not experienced in flattery, but apparently he had chosen the right words, if the lady's smile and blush of pleasure were any indication.

"I thank you, sir." She took his offered arm, but winced slightly when he placed his hand over her gloved one.

He quickly withdrew. "Forgive me. Did I cause you pain?"

Her eyes widened briefly, then she leaned close to him and whispered soberly, "If you promise not to tell anyone, I will confess that I was cruelly wounded today."

"What?" Winston stopped abruptly, staring down at her as rage rose in his chest. "Who would dare to harm you?" This called for swift and severe punishment. "You must permit me to call upon this person to account for his actions."

Now she laughed. "Do you like cats, Lord Winston?"

For a moment, he could not grasp her meaning. Then understanding dispelled his anger. "Ah, I see. You encountered a disagreeable feline."

She tilted her head and smiled. Great mercy, she did have a striking smile. What would it be like to see that beautiful expression every day of his life?

No, it was far too soon for such thoughts. He must not be drawn in by mere looks, which he often speculated had been Father's undoing when he wed Mother. He cleared his throat. "To answer your question—" he resumed walking, and she easily followed his lead, as if they had often walked together "—yes, I do like cats." His moment of enjoyment was cut short by a worrisome thought. "I am certain you are aware that cat scratches can lead to serious illness. Did you treat the injury?"

Again, her eyes widened, and she looked away with a frown. "Oh, yes." Another glance, another smile, and his heart tripped. "Do let us forget it."

He would be pleased to offer his physician's services to examine the wound, but that would suggest that Lady Blakemore had neglected her companion's health. "As you wish, Miss Hart."

They descended the wide, elegant staircase to the vast second-floor dining hall. Once there, and hoping to find two empty chairs near someone of influence in the diplomatic corps, Winston searched around the long table.

"May I assist you, milord?" A footman in red livery extended a gloved hand toward two vacant places.

"Will this suit you, Miss Hart?" Winston noticed the vibrant curiosity in her dark eyes. Perhaps this was her first formal outing with Lady Blakemore. And perhaps for just this one evening, he could forget his ambitions and do all in his power to ensure a pleasant experience for the lady at his side.

"Oh, yes. I thank you." She smiled at the footman who was pulling out her chair.

Winston made a mental note to explain to her that she need not acknowledge the footman. The best servants were those who received their orders and performed their duties as if almost invisible. Acknowledgments often embarrassed them. But such schooling would come later, should there be a later for himself and the young lady.

In the next chair, Lord Rettig lounged, goblet in hand, but offered them only a brief glance before sipping his wine.

Warmth crept up Winston's neck. Like him, Rettig was a baron, one with no special distinctions that qualified him to give his equals the cut. Before the footman could finish pulling the chair out for Miss Hart, Winston held up his hand to stop him so that he might test the waters.

"Miss Hart, may I present Lord Rettig." If the baron did not rise for the introduction, he would instruct the footman to find them another place.

Rettig did not rise. He merely looked the lady up and down through his quizzing glass—a despicable practice meant to put inferiors in their places—and yawned.

"Ah, yes. Lady Blakemore's...*companion.*" His tone dripped with disdain, and his lips curled into an arrogant sneer. He turned decidedly away to his own supper partner, a lady Winston did not know. Nor was an introduction forthcoming.

Winston fisted his hands at his side, longing to strike that sneer from Rettig's face. But Father's scriptural admonition echoed in his mind. *Be slow to wrath, my son. For the wrath of man worketh not the righteousness of God.* He took a quiet, deep breath and addressed the footman. "I think we would prefer—" He surveyed the table for another pair of empty chairs.

"Oh, do let us sit here." Miss Hart blinked her lovely eyes and leaned close to him, sending a whiff of rose-scented perfume his way. "The Dowager Lady Beckwith, on your left, is a dear old soul, though a bit deaf." Her whisper fanned over his cheek and sent a pleasant sensation down his neck. "Perhaps we can make her evening enjoyable." She nodded toward the lady's partner, a rakish sort obviously more interested in the pretty young miss on his other side.

Winston's heart lightened at Miss Hart's kindness. "Yes, of course." How generous and even diplomatic of her to think of an old woman's enjoyment rather than her own.

As the footman resumed his attempts to seat them, the

dowager viscountess looked up and gave Miss Hart a beneficent smile. "Ah, there you are, Kitty. I was hoping to see you this evening."

Beside him, Miss Hart jolted.

Chapter Two

Catherine could barely withhold a gasp. Ancient Aunt Beckwith had not seen her since she was fourteen and, being senile even then, had paid her little attention. Confusion still lingered in her pale blue eyes, almost as if she had no idea where she was. Catherine should have taken the opportunity to escape her scrutiny. But she could not bear to see the old dear abandoned, for all intents and purposes, by her supper companion, a gentleman whose duty it was to engage her in polite conversation throughout the meal. Yet if Aunt Beckwith truly recognized Catherine—unlikely but possible—she could expose her deception.

Even now, Lord Winston questioned her with one raised eyebrow, and she grasped for some way to deflect his curiosity and redeem her plans against him. She offered a slight smile, a ladylike shrug, a tiny shake of her head, and he nodded his understanding. How easy she found it to lie to him without saying a word. Guilt gnawed at her conscience, but to silence it, she pictured dear Papa suffering exile in some unknown place. Now she must continue to brazen her way through this situation. She leaned toward Aunt Beckwith's good ear.

"Good evening, Lady Beckwith. May I present Lord Winston?"

"Winston? Winston?" Aunt Beckwith studied him up and down. "My gracious, such a tall young gentleman, and so handsome, too." She reached out a bejeweled hand, and he gallantly kissed it. "Very much like your grandfather in his youth, if I recall him correctly. Many a young *gel* set her cap for him and no doubt will for you, as well— that is, if you are not already married." She winked at him, then stared at Catherine. "Now, who is this young lady with you?"

Catherine's knees almost buckled with relief. As she had those six years ago, Aunt Beckwith rarely kept a thought for more than half a minute.

Lord Winston glanced at Catherine, and a kind smile lit his face. "Lady Beckwith, may I present Miss Hart?"

"So pleased to meet you, Miss Hart." Aunt Beckwith patted the chair next to her. "Now do be seated so we can eat. I am fair to starving."

Catherine released a quiet sigh of relief, but caution warned her against relaxing too much. At any moment, those pale blue eyes might sharpen with recognition, and all would be lost.

Winston made certain Miss Hart was comfortably seated, then took his own chair. Lady Beckwith's confusion about Miss Hart did not put him off in the slightest, nor did her mistake about the gentleman she referred to as his grandfather. Having an elderly father had given Winston an appreciation of older people, both for the wisdom they imparted and, in Father's case, their godly character. Perhaps this evening presented an opportunity for him to learn something interesting. He was already well pleased to observe Miss Hart's kindness to the lady, a useful trait for a lady's hired companion. Or a diplomat's wife.

No, it was far too soon for such a thought. He must employ some of that patience Father had tried to impart to him. Pedigree was an indispensable trait in his choice of a wife, and he must not forget that.

While they engaged the elderly lady in conversation about the hot summer weather, an army of footmen served the first course, which consisted of a thick, creamy asparagus soup and an entrée of stuffed trout and small meat pies. Once Winston and Miss Hart determined just how much to raise their voices so Lady Beckwith could hear them, they settled down to a comfortable, if unproductive, evening. For now, he must abandon his ambitions, for not one person within the range of proper conversation could advance his diplomatic career.

The elderly dowager, loquacious in the extreme, thrice repeated a story about the time pigs invaded her rose garden. Winston bore the repetitions with good humor, helped by Miss Hart's lively interest in each telling. His esteem for her increased, especially when the dowager continued to call her Kitty. Without so much as a blink of an eye or word of contradiction, she permitted the doddering old Lady Beckwith to think she was the late Lord Beckwith's great-niece. Surely such grace would stand her in good stead as any gentleman's wife.

As the meal progressed to a lavish second course of venison, lobster and a variety of vegetables, Winston found himself admiring Miss Hart's artful manners, which were worthy of a duchess. Despite her gloves, he could see that her fingers were long and tapered, and she wielded her cutlery with grace. Perhaps she played the pianoforte, a useful skill for any lady.

Lady Beckwith nodded off between the second course

and dessert, giving Winston and Miss Hart a few moments of private conversation while the servants cleared and reset the table.

"Tell me, Lord Winston—" Miss Hart accepted a dish of cream-covered pastry from the footman, thanking him with another of her pretty smiles "—what think you of the scandal regarding Lord Cochrane's fraud against the Stock Exchange? Will he be sufficiently punished with only a year in prison and the loss of his naval rank?"

Winston caught himself before barking out his indignation over Cochrane's wicked scheme to defraud his fellow Englishmen. "Why, Miss Hart, should a delicate lady concern herself over politics and crime?"

Those dark eyelashes batted in pretty confusion several times. "Oh, my. I do not wish to venture upon ground unfitting for a lady." She glanced down the long table toward where her employer sat. "I would grieve to cause embarrassment to Lady Blakemore."

Her innocence touched a spot in Winston's heart that he never knew existed. "Well, no harm is done." A chuckle escaped him. No doubt she longed for reassurance in the Cochrane matter. "My dear lady, have no fear. The House of Lords has dealt appropriately with Cochrane and his associates. Do not give it another thought. All is well."

"Yes, of course." She gazed down at her gloved hands, which rested in her lap. The slight lump near her right wrist reminded him of their earlier conversation.

"Miss Hart, a while ago, you asked me a question. Now I must ask you one."

Her perfect brown eyebrows arched. "Oh, yes. Ask what you will, and I shall answer."

Inexplicably, his pulse began to race. With some difficulty, he cleared his throat and managed to croak out, "Do you like cats?"

Now her expression turned impish. "Why, yes, of course." She glanced around, as if checking to see whether or not anyone else was listening, then whispered, "I am convinced that only evil can come from a person who does not like cats."

Now he laughed as an agreeable sensation swept through him. "Madam, I concur with your premise whole-heartedly."

What a delightful lady. What extraordinary wit and intelligence. But he would not quickly surrender his heart as he had seen several of his peers do, to their ruin. No, entirely too much depended upon his having the right connections. Perhaps Lord Bennington could advise him regarding which items he could safely strike from his list of requirements for a wife. But until he managed to secure an appointment with his busy mentor, he would find as many proper ways as possible to spend time with the lovely Miss Hart. He did have an appointment with Lord Blakemore on the morrow. Perhaps he would see her then.

All the way back to their Mayfair mansion, Lord and Lady Blakemore laughed as they shared harmless bits of gossip. Lady Drayton had declared the night a success after no fewer than three marriage proposals had been offered. A conceited lord deep in his cups boasted that he would race his finest thoroughbred against all challengers, and a dozen or more gentlemen agreed to the contest. Their host, the Marquess of Drayton, announced that Prinny would attend the theatre with Louis, the French king, sometime during the coming week.

Catherine paid particular attention to this last bit of news. Papa had been accused of being a Bonapartist and conspiring to assassinate Louis so they could prevent the Bourbons from reclaiming the French throne. Which, of course, was ridiculous. Papa had no cause to do such a thing. He utterly disdained Napoleon Bonaparte, and his allegiance to England, his country of refuge, was unwavering.

Regarding the rest of Lord and Lady Blakemore's gossip, Catherine listened with moderate interest. At any time she might be called upon to participate in a conversation about the marquess's ball. Ignorance of the latest *on-dits* among the *haute ton* was unforgivable, even for a companion, for that would make her employer look bad.

"And what have you to say for yourself, Miss Hart?" Jolly Lord Blakemore, with his fringe of graying hair around his balding pate and his short, plump stature, made for an odd pairing with his tall, slender wife. But their temperaments seemed perfectly suited, and their household was a haven of peace in noisy, smelly London. "Did you enjoy the evening? I saw you with Lord Winston, which, I must say, is quite startling. One does not expect Winston even to speak to those outside of his small circle, much less to dine with them."

Before this evening, that description of the baron might have suited her very well. But after dancing and dining with Lord Winston, she saw no hint of his former arrogance. Instead, she had found his manners faultless and his conversation charming. Even poor Aunt Beckwith had received his kindest attentions. Where was the crack in his facade? What would prove him worthy of her revenge when added to his lies about Papa?

"You have Lady Blakemore to blame, my lord. She forced me upon the unsuspecting baron, poor man."

The Blakemores traded a look and laughed in their jovial way.

"Ah," said Lady Blakemore, "but one did not observe Winston trying to escape your company."

"But why should he wish to escape?" Lord Blakemore wiggled his wiry eyebrows in a comical fashion. "What more charming company could he ask for?"

The countess nodded agreeably. "No, he was more than pleased to spend his evening with our Miss Hart."

The familiar benevolence in her smile struck a deep chord within Catherine. No matter what her true station in life, these good people should regard her as just above a servant. And yet they had risked Society's censure by taking her to one of the most important social events of the Season, even providing an exquisite gown from Lady Blakemore's talented modiste. And what did Catherine offer in return for their generosity? Lies and deception and the risk of being accused of harboring a traitor's daughter, something that could ruin Lord Blakemore, no doubt in more ways than Catherine could imagine. Guilt ate at her until her eyes stung, and she prayed her employers could not see her tears in the dim light of the closed carriage.

"What's this?" Lord Blakemore's gentle tone did nothing to help Catherine's self-control. "Why tears, my dear? Did Winston insult you? Did anyone?" The jolly little earl's eyes narrowed. "You must tell me the truth, now. I insist upon it."

"Gracious, no." Catherine managed a dismissive laugh. "I am thinking only of how grateful I am for all that you have done for me." Not a lie at all. "You have taken me to the theatre several times to enjoy Shakespeare's wonderful plays, and tonight you escorted me to the marquess's ball. You have honored me far more than a mere companion deserves or should expect."

The earl waved his hand dismissively, but in his pleased smile she could see her gratitude was not wasted. Yet somehow she must turn this conversation back to the baron to uncover his weaknesses.

"Your comment about Lord Winston surprises me. Does he truly not mingle with anyone but a small circle of friends?" The baron had behaved quite pleasantly toward her despite his apparent assumption that she was born of the gentry.

Again the couple traded a look, and the earl nodded to his countess.

"I would not say he is overly proud," she said. "Of course, he holds to our views regarding the classes. We know God has ordained that the aristocracy should rule and manage the affairs of mankind. But we are expected to do so benevolently." She patted her husband's hand and gazed at him fondly. "Why, just these past weeks, Lord Blakemore has joined with Lord Greystone and Mr. Wilberforce to propose laws restricting the use of small children as chimney sweeps."

"That is most commendable, my lord." How could Catherine return the conversation to Lord Winston without exposing how deeply she was interested in him or causing them to think that interest was romantic? "Surely not every aristocrat is so benevolent." She had seen sufficient poverty in London to know the wealthy could and should do more to help them.

"Ah, but we were speaking of Winston." The earl chuckled in his endearing way, almost as if he could read her thoughts. "You may be interested to know, Miss Hart, that earlier this month he accompanied Greystone to a disreputable tavern on the Thames and helped to rescue two kidnapped climbing boys. Just think of it. Two peers taking on such a dangerous adventure to save chimney sweeps, the lowest of the low."

"Indeed?" Catherine's heart warmed briefly before she dismissed such a favorable emotion. Perhaps the baron could be kind to poor children and elderly ladies, but that did not excuse his evil lies about her father.

"Indeed," Lady Blakemore said. "Quite commendable."

"Tell me, my dear." The earl addressed his wife. "What did you hear from Swarthmore about the Cochrane affair?"

Catherine watched with interest as the countess detailed Lord Swarthmore's opinions regarding the complicated scheme Lord Cochrane and his cohorts had perpetrated against the Stock Exchange. Like Papa, not only did Lord Blakemore listen attentively to his wife, but he respected her opinions, which she sprinkled liberally throughout the discourse.

And yet Lord Winston had refused to discuss the affair with Catherine. Apparently, he found her too naive to be informed about important matters of the day, as though she had no intellect or fortitude. That suited her plans quite well, for if her enemy underestimated her, so much the better.

"By the by, my dear." Lady Blakemore addressed her husband, but something in her tone alerted Catherine and interrupted her musings. "At what hour is Winston arriving tomorrow? I should like to be at home and have tea with him. You do not mind, do you, Miss Hart?"

Catherine's thoughts raced. She would have to enlist Mr. Radcliff's help to arrange an encounter with the baron during his visit. For now, she schooled her face to suggést polite indifference. "My lady, you do not require my approval to entertain whom you will."

Lady Blakemore traded another of those conspiratorial glances with her husband. "But my dear, he does require *my* permission to have tea with *you*." She laughed softly. "I do hope you are not disappointed that I granted it."

How hard it was for Catherine not to smile, not to crow with victory. The path to bringing Lord Winston down was proving to be all too easy.

Chapter Three

"Come in, Edgar." Winston beckoned his cousin Radcliff into the sunny breakfast room of his Grosvenor Square town house. "Have you eaten? My cook has laid out far too much food for one person." He selected eggs, rolls and sausages from the oak sideboard and moved toward the head of the table. Last night at Lord Drayton's ball, he had been too occupied with Miss Hart to have much appetite. Now his stomach rumbled in complaint over such neglect.

"Good morning, Winston." Radcliff's tone, always cheerful, sounded particularly good-humored this morning. "Did you enjoy last evening?" He took a plate and studied the selection of food.

"A very grand affair." Winston hesitated to mention Miss Hart, lest nothing come of his interest in her. As charming as the young lady had seemed last night, this morning his father's admonitions came to mind, warning him against haste in forming any alliance. Still, he looked forward to this afternoon when he would visit Blakemore and have tea with his wife *and* her companion. He considered asking Lady Blakemore's permission to take the young lady for a drive, but decided such a move would have to wait until he learned of her family connections. And he really must do that today.

"Meet anyone interesting?" Edgar took the chair adjacent to Winston's and laid a linen serviette across his lap. He leaned toward Winston and arched his eyebrows to punctuate his question, as if he knew the answer.

Winston almost choked on his buttered roll. Edgar had always seemed able to read his mind. To deflect the question, he eyed his cousin's plate, which held a single sausage and one roll. "Is that all you want?" As sanguine as he felt this morning, he would gladly feed the world. After months of fruitless searching for a wife, perhaps he was close to achieving his goal.

Edgar accepted a cup of coffee from the footman. "I never know whether Blakemore will invite me to join him for breakfast or not." He sipped his beverage. "It's always best to arrive for work a little hungry so as not to offend him. Unfortunately, I cannot depend upon his feeding me, so I must eat something." He emitted a rueful chuckle.

"Indeed?" Winston grimaced at the thought. His cousin was as thin as a banister spindle and could ill afford to miss a meal. As Blakemore's secretary, surely he had the liberty to nourish himself in the kitchen in the course of a day's work. "Well, you must eat your fill here as often as you like before going to work."

"I thank you for your generosity. But let us not dwell upon my eating habits. Must I repeat my question, cousin?" Edgar gave him a knowing smirk. "Did you meet anyone interesting last evening? A young lady, perhaps?"

Winston bit into a sausage to avoid answering, savoring the blend of spices with which his chef had seasoned it. How annoying that Edgar was so persistent. But then, this was his dear cousin, who had known him all his life. Surely he could confide in him.

"Very well, yes, I did meet a young lady." He waved to the footman to refill his coffee cup, then made a great ceremony of adding sugar and cream before taking a sip. Then adding more sugar.

Edgar laughed. "You know I will not leave until you tell me everything."

Winston's heart lightened at this prompting. Edgar cared deeply for him, even though his birth had displaced his cousin as Father's heir. Any other gentleman might resent it, but Edgar had never appeared to covet the title or the wealth, even though he had been relegated to the edges of Society and forced to earn his living, a shame for any aristocrat.

"Her name is Miss Hart, and she is Lady Blakemore's companion." There. He confessed it. Now he sat back and waited for the honest opinion that would doubtless be forthcoming.

Edgar gaped at him for a full ten seconds. "That chit? Why, my dear, naive cousin, I never would have imagined that quiet little mouse would dare to set her cap for a peer of the realm." He snorted out his disgust. "Why, she has no family to speak of. No name, no dowry. Why would you permit some scheming girl like that to engage your heart?" He rose from his chair and paced the length of the table and back. "Well, then, go ahead. Fall in love with her. But do not speak of marriage. Set her up in her own house and…you know."

For several moments, Winston could only watch his cousin in stunned silence. Then heat blasted up his neck and into his face. He stood and slammed his serviette down on the table. "You will not speak of her in that manner. I am convinced she is a lady. Do you even know her?" Hands fisted, he took a step toward his cousin.

Edgar blinked but did not move. Then his breath

seemed to go out of him. "Forgive me, cousin." He set a hand on Winston's shoulder. "She and I are employed in the same house, but we have barely spoken two words to one another. And I must admit that I have never observed anything but proper comportment on her part." He gave Winston a sad smile. "Please permit me to explain myself. I wish only the best for you. With your ancient and well-respected title, you could marry an earl's daughter, even a duke's, someone to advance your position in Society and give you connections and influence in that diplomatic career you aspire to. Perhaps even snare that earldom Old Farmer George promised your father. Why choose a girl who is doubtless a mere gentlewoman and can provide none of that?"

Despite his disapproval of Edgar's impertinent reference to their poor, mad sovereign, Winston's anger evaporated, replaced by gratitude for his cousin's concerns. "I cannot disagree with what you say. Be assured that I am not in any hurry to marry Miss Hart after chatting with her for a single evening. I merely find her appealing. And, after all, one does hope to possess some degree of affection for his wife, as you feel for Emily."

Edgar's expression seemed to twist into disgust, and he turned away. Had Winston been mistaken about Edgar's love for his wife? Yet when his cousin faced him again, his genial smile had returned. "Yes, one does wish to love and be loved. So what is your plan to woo this little…this young lady?" His words dispelled Winston's concerns.

"After my appointment with Lord Blakemore, for which I thank you, dear cousin—" he punctuated his gratitude with a nod and received one in return "—I will take tea with Lady Blakemore and Miss Hart. If all goes well and Miss Hart's family connections prove acceptable, I may ask the countess for permission to take her for a carriage

ride. That is, if you do not think it too soon…or improper…
for such an outing."

"You may be certain that Lady Blakemore will decide
what is proper regarding Miss Hart. But you must remember that ladies hire companions to keep at their sides for
their own convenience, not to marry them off." Edgar
blew out a sigh of apparent frustration, and Winston felt
for a moment like a foolish schoolboy. "But if you insist
upon this plan, which carriage will you take? What have
you purchased since coming to London?"

Consternation swept over Winston. "I never thought to
purchase a new carriage for town. Father's old ones stored
in the mews could use some repair, but—" He had already
spent a large sum to replace the roof of this town house,
which had languished uninhabited for six years during
Father's final illness.

"But nothing!" Edgar huffed with indignation. "How
can you take a young lady out for a drive in a shabby
conveyance? You would become Society's laughingstock.
No, no, you must postpone your outing until you have a
new one. A landau, a barouche, a coach. No, not a coach.
It must be an open carriage to protect the young lady's
reputation. You must have a landau. And a matched pair
of horses, of course. You do have a matched pair?" He
clasped his hands behind his back and resumed his pac-
ing across the parquet floor, as if the fate of England depended upon the matter.

"Yes, of course. Some of Father's best cattle from
home." Winston scratched his chin, partly amused by
Edgar's antics, partly chagrined by his own lack of fore-
thought. "But there's no time to order a new landau. My
appointment with Lord Blakemore is in a few hours, and
Lady Blakemore will expect me to stay for tea, as I promised. Perhaps I can borrow Mrs. Parton's new landau."

Edgar chewed his lip. "Yes, that's just the thing. You must send her a note straightaway, and I'll wager she will give you whatever you wish. All of our relatives have always done that, have they not?" A hint of pain clouded his thin features, a haunted look that often appeared when they discussed their family.

Winston never knew how to answer his cousin in this matter. In truth, Mrs. Parton, their distant relation, *had* spoiled Winston, except in the matter of Lady Beatrice, for whom she had favored Lord Greystone. But she had also been kind to Edgar. Perhaps Edgar feared Winston would neglect their friendship if...*when* he married.

His cousin's ingratiating smile canceled such concerns "Now, what about your clothes?"

Winston looked down at his black suit, which was miraculously free of cat hair thanks to the labors of his valet and the footmen keeping Crumpet out of the breakfast room. The little rascal was an excellent mouser, but he did love to get into mischief and was not always easy to apprehend when he escaped Winston's suite. "Yes? What about them?"

"Dear boy." Edgar posted his fists at his waist. "Why do you insist upon wearing this somber black all the time?" He waved a dismissive hand toward Winston's suit. "You have the appearance of a country vicar."

Winston endured his scolding with good humor. "As I have told you before, because this blond hair gives me the look of a sixteen-year-old and black makes me look older." Never mind his annoying curls, which his valet had given up trying to control.

"Boring, actually." Edgar waved a hand in the air. "Too late to do anything about that for today, but you must see your tailor soon and get some color into your wardrobe."

"Yes, Edgar." He had no intention of changing his wardrobe.

"Well, I must be off. Blakemore does not abide tardiness." Edgar snatched a roll from the sideboard and stuck it into his pocket as he walked from the room.

That simple gesture, coupled with his cousin's genuine concerns for him, stirred Winston's soul and caused him to love Edgar all the more. How he wished Father had not thought so little of his former heir, but perhaps Winston could somehow make it up to him in the years to come.

A hearty sneeze in the hallway interrupted his trip back to the breakfast table.

"Get that beast away from me." Edgar's angry words shattered the usual calm of the town house.

Winston hurried to the door in time to see a footman seize Crumpet the instant before Edgar's violent kick could make contact with its furry rump. Crumpet twisted in the man's hands with a hiss and swung a paw at his cousin, claws extended.

"Sorry, sir." John Footman grimaced as he caught sight of Winston. "Sorry, m'lord. He got away from me." He clutched the golden creature and murmured, "There now, laddie, shame on you for botherin' his lordship's guest."

Edgar gave another violent sneeze, glared at Crumpet, swung a grimacing smile at Winston and hastened down the front stairway.

"Sorry, m'lord," the footman repeated.

"Never mind, John." He took Crumpet from his servant and cradled him against his chest. As if blown by the wind, golden cat hairs instantly appeared on the front and sleeves of his black jacket. But Crumpet's purring soothed away any concerns over his appearance. After all, Parliament did not meet on Wednesdays, and he had plenty of time to have his valet brush away the fur before his appointment with Lord Blakemore.

He recalled Miss Hart's comment about only evil coming from people who did not like cats, but he would have to tell her of one exception. Poor Edgar could not be blamed if the beasts made him sneeze. Such an affliction did not mean that his cousin was evil. Not by any means.

At the thought of seeing Miss Hart again, warmth spread through his chest much like the effects of Crumpet's purring. Neither of the two other ladies he had attempted to court this Season had generated such feelings. But Winston would heed Edgar's cautions and make certain this young lady possessed sufficient family connections before launching a full pursuit.

No matter what Catherine did to her hair, even using a round, hot iron that scorched her stubborn locks, she could not force it to curl. She had never thought much about her coiffure until last evening's ball, where she observed that most young ladies wore masses of pretty ringlets swept up in back and adorned with flowers, ribbons or strands of jewels. Even a few saucy curls to frame her face would certainly be just the thing to keep Lord Winston's interest. Or so it seemed to her as she regarded her reflection in the dressing-table mirror.

Why could she not have plump cheeks like all of the fashionable young ladies? Or a well-rounded shape, like her own twelve-year-old sister? No, she was doomed forever to be a tall, thin reed, with hair as straight as a horse's tail. The most she could do was to pull her long tresses into a tidy bun, leaving a few wispy strands to hang free at the sides. Or to pull those back with the rest. She could not decide which looked better.

How silly she was. Lord Winston's interest in her had

been obvious from the first moment their eyes met. If she changed her appearance, he might dislike the new look. And today, she must do nothing to drive him away. In any event, he had enough curls for two people.

Moving on to her attire, she chose a pretty blue muslin morning gown. Lady Blakemore had provided a modest but adequate wardrobe so Catherine would have something appropriate to wear wherever she went. Shame pricked her conscience over accepting these lovely clothes, which she could well afford herself. But she must continue to play the part of the poor, genteel miss.

Standing in front of the tall mirror on her wardrobe for a final inspection, she declared herself ready for Lord Winston's visit and left her bedchamber on the third floor of Blakemore House.

When she first agreed to Mr. Radcliff's plan to work as the countess's companion, she had feared living in town would prevent her from getting her daily exercise. But this Mayfair mansion sat upon a large property with many acres to walk about in safety. Even on a rainy day, the long corridors that took her from her quarters to the rest of the house provided plenty of exercise. She arrived at the first-floor drawing room feeling quite invigorated.

"Miss du Coeur."

Catherine gasped upon hearing her real name, but it was Mr. Radcliff who addressed her in a quiet tone. Her friend was the only denizen of the bright, sunlit room, and he stood before a table in the corner admiring the earl's collection of small ivory sculptures of African animals.

"Good afternoon, Mr. Radcliff." She scurried across the large room so they could talk without fear of being heard by the footman just outside the door. The scent of freshly baked bread wafted from his clothes, an odd fragrance for a gentleman to wear. But to question his choice would be rude. "Do you have any news?"

"I? Why, no, my dear. Until I came to work this morning, I have been home with my wife and son. You are the one who has ventured out into the excitement of Society. What happened at the marquess's ball? Did you manage to dance with my cousin?"

Catherine's heart twisted at his injured tone. This poor gentleman had from the first expressed sorrow over Lord Winston's evil actions. How it must grieve him to be unable to expose the baron's treachery without seeming to covet the man's title.

"I did not have to manage at all." Catherine smiled at the memory. "Lady Blakemore accosted the baron and practically dragged him over to me for an introduction." Last evening, she had stared down at her hands and held her breath to generate a blush in her cheeks. But she need not mention such artifices, lest Mr. Radcliff think less of her. "He invited me to the supper dance, and we spent the rest of the evening together. In fact, he accepted Lady Blakemore's invitation to have tea with us after his appointment with Lord Blakemore."

"Ah, how fortuitous." He glanced past her toward the door. "Perhaps I had better disappear. I have told Winston we have barely spoken two words to each other and are not in the slightest way acquainted."

"Yes, that is best." That bothersome scratching within her soul began again, but she forced it away. "Before you go, do you have any words of advice for me?"

He gazed off toward the front windows. "Hmm. No, my dear, I believe you will know exactly what to do. Engage his emotions, make him love you. The next steps will come in due time."

The door swung open, and Lady Blakemore entered,

her gaze directed toward the front windows. Catherine hurried back across the room to greet her *and* to put some distance between herself and Mr. Radcliff. But when she glanced back, he was nowhere to be seen. An icy shiver swept up her back.

Chapter Four

"Ah. There you are, my dear." Lady Blakemore's expression was pleasant, but a hint of displeasure shaded her words.

"Forgive me, my lady." Catherine struggled to appear calm. How could Mr. Radcliff have vanished without a sound? He had been yards away from the servants' entrance and across the room from the door Lady Blakemore just entered. Perhaps a secret portal in that papered wall? The vertical fence posts among the rose vines might disguise a seam. Such an escape could prove useful to her one day. She struggled to dismiss the mystery and pay attention to her employer. "I thought I was to meet you here."

"Hmm. Well, no matter." Lady Blakemore studied Catherine up and down. "You look quite charming, my dear, but not too pretentious for a companion." She waved Catherine to a red tapestry settee near the alabaster hearth and sat in an adjacent chair. "Now, today, we will be *at home,* although not formally. Only a few friends will be calling to discuss plans for the upcoming festivities in August. While there will be countless formal state celebrations, many of us wish to have our own private parties to celebrate the war's end." She fluttered an exquisite blue silk fan before her face. "Mrs. Parton will be here soon, of course. Perhaps Lady Bennington…" Folding the fan, she tapped it thoughtfully against her opposite hand, listing other possible attendees for the afternoon.

And Lord Winston? Catherine could not help but wonder whether Lady Blakemore had entirely forgotten her invitation to the baron.

"So, of course that means we must cut short our time with Lord Winston. Should he fail to finish his appointment with Blakemore in time, we will have to inform him that his visit must wait." Was that a question in Lady Blakemore's eyes as she spoke?

"Yes, my lady." Catherine schooled her expression to display indifference, despite her disappointment. Yet why should she be disappointed? Hadn't Mr. Radcliff told her of Lord Winston's ambitions to accompany Lord Blakemore to France in late August? If the baron succeeded in attaching himself to the earl, she would be in his company for more than sufficient time to engage his interest and ply him for the truth about his plot against Papa.

On the one hand, she could hardly wait to get started. On the other, she wondered if she was up to the task, for her lies continued to grate upon her soul. At those times, she pictured poor Mama, Lucien and Isabella being confined to their home in Norfolk and living every moment in fear of bad news, even arrest. She imagined Papa hiding in some hovel or cave, unable to venture out even to obtain food. Such thoughts were sufficient to renew her determination to bring wicked, lying Lord Winston to justice.

"I admire your integrity, Winston." Lord Blakemore clapped him on the shoulder and guided him away from the oak desk across which they had discussed Winston's future. "Many a young whelp in his first year in Parliament would jump at the chance to play the spy." At a small grouping of furniture near the spacious office's tall windows, the earl gave a gracious wave of his hand. "Sit here, my boy, so you can view my wife's exquisite gardens." He chose a straight-backed chair for himself. "I had thought you the perfect candidate for espionage after the du Coeur affair. A great bit of luck, those letters falling into your hands the way they did." He absently lined up a book with the edge of the mahogany table beside him. "Tell me all the details of how it happened." Interest lit his round face.

Winston silenced the pride that tried to well up within him each time he related the event. After all, none of it had been his doing. "Very simply, in late January a young boy brought the packet of letters to my home in Surrey. A footman received them and placed them on my desk."

"Ah." Blakemore scratched his chin. "And who was this boy?"

"The footman said he was a short, stocky lad of about ten or so. He did not give a name."

"Hmm." The earl stared off toward the windows. "Lady Blakemore's roses have done exceedingly well this year, especially the reds." He seemed to have forgotten their conversation, at least for a moment. Then he focused again on Winston. "Perhaps we should question your footman a bit more. Find out what we can about that lad."

Winston's heart sank. He had no doubt the letters were authentic, but he had still been in mourning over Father's death and had not thought clearly how to handle the matter. "Harry had been with us only a few weeks, and the work did not suit him. He left in February to join the army, and I have no idea of his fate."

"Bad luck, that." Blakemore clicked his tongue and gave his head a little shake. "In any event, your quick thinking in delivering the letters to the Home Office was brilliant.

Why, you saved our country and the Prince Regent from great disgrace, not to mention saving old Louis's very life. Will you not reconsider espionage?"

"I thank you, sir, but no." Winston lifted a hand to cover an artificial cough while he considered how to make his excuses. He must take care not to sound overly proud of something that had come his way through no effort of his own. Nor must he sound judgmental of those who chose to spy. Father had often chided him for both pride and judging others too harshly. "Of course, I understand some men are called to employ subterfuge, even as the Scriptures tell us that both Moses and Joshua sent out spies to explore the land of Canaan. But the Almighty has not directed me to such a path."

Blakemore chuckled in his jolly, mellow way, but the wiliness in his eyes dispelled all impressions that he was anyone's fool. If that were not enough for Winston to trust him, he had Father's recommendation. *Look to Blakemore and Bennington for your examples, my son. They will not lead you astray.* In his four months in London, Winston had come to admire both earls. Now that Bennington was consumed with family matters regarding several of his eight offspring, Winston was grateful that Blakemore would consider stepping in as his mentor. Now if he could persuade him to take him to Paris as part of his diplomatic entourage, Winston would have achieved a cherished dream.

"I admire your determination to seek God's direction, for above all, we must receive our orders from above." Blakemore pointed upward, and his expression softened. "Kings and princes come and go, nations rise and fall, but only God is eternal."

"Indeed." Most Englishmen, Winston included, would say *England* was eternal as well, for she clearly had the blessing of the Almighty. Still, he was pleased to hear Blakemore speak of his faith, for it affirmed all that Father had said about him.

"Now." The earl sat forward in his chair. "Concerning your request, why do you wish to accompany my little band to France? What do you hope to gain?" With his lighthearted tone, the earl might well have been asking why Winston wanted to tag along on a picnic.

"To serve God by serving my king and country." And to obtain through his own efforts the earldom the old king promised to Father. But he would not bring up that matter. At least not until he knew Blakemore better, and Blakemore knew him.

"Very commendable." The earl slapped his hands on his chubby knees. "Just what I hoped to hear. And furthermore, I believe you, my boy. You are a credit to your father."

"Again, I thank you." Even as warm satisfaction filled Winston's chest, his mind sprinkled bits of icy doubt on the earl's last affirmation. While other gentlemen might praise him, Father had never quite given his full approval, nor had God. All the more reason to continue his quest for righteousness through serving his king or, in this case, the Prince Regent.

"Now, about another matter." One of the earl's bushy eyebrows rose while the other one dipped.

Winston sensed his peer was about to impart some sage advice or dire warning. He did not know whether to be honored or concerned. "Yes, sir?"

"Scripture states that whoso finds a wife finds a good thing and obtains favor of the Lord. It is my conviction that every gentleman who enters the diplomatic corps must be married. An agreeable wife provides stability, settles something in a man's heart, not to mention fulfills the du-

ties of hostess for those obligatory entertainments." Once
again, his expression grew wily. "Have you found a wife,
my boy?"

Winston cleared his throat, feeling the pinch of embarrassment. "I have not, but not for want of trying." The
only two ladies who had attracted his interest had chosen
others, two brothers, in fact.

"Ah, yes." The earl chuckled. "Well, never mind that.
Plenty of fish in the sea." Again one eyebrow lowered. "I
noticed that you sat with Lady Blakemore's companion
at Drayton's supper last night. Did you find Miss Hart's
company agreeable?"

Winston's cravat seemed to tighten around his neck. He
felt the need to loosen it, but clasped his hands together
to prevent such a self-conscious gesture. "Agreeable. Yes.
Entirely pleasant."

Blakemore leaned back with a frown. "I gather you have
some reservations about the young lady."

At this perfect opening for his questions, Winston gave
a slight shrug to suggest he was indifferent, though his
emotions were far from detached. The young lady had occupied his thoughts since last night and even more so since
this morning, when his discussion with Edgar had generated a certain protectiveness toward her. But it would not
do to confess such feelings to the earl. "In truth, I know
nothing of her family or her pedigree. Perhaps you can
enlighten me."

Blakemore blinked and gripped his round chin thoughtfully. "Why, I have no idea. Lady Blakemore would not
have hired her without the proper pedigree."

"Of course not." Winston hoped his question had not
cast aspersions on the countess. From Blakemore's good-
natured expression, he guessed it had not. Still, it would

help if he knew whether Miss Hart came from the gentry or the aristocracy.

"However, if she does not suit you, then do not give the matter another thought." Blakemore stood, and Winston had no choice but to do the same. Nothing had been settled by their discussion, but he dared not press the matter of accompanying the earl to France, lest he cause offense. Following him toward the door of the chamber, Winston had a clear view of the top of Blakemore's balding head, which barely reached his own shoulder. Yet so much character and power resided within the shorter man that Winston could not help but hold him in great esteem.

The earl stopped abruptly and faced Winston, wagging a paternal finger in his direction. "I would not have you marry in haste, my boy, but if you can find a suitable wife by mid-August when our party leaves for Paris, then all the better for your ability to serve king and country at my side."

Winston's heart raced. The earl had just as much as said he was accepted as part of the delegation to the French. At least, it sounded that way. "I thank you, sir. I shall certainly make every effort to do so."

"Now, you must excuse me. I have some correspondence that will not keep." Blakemore opened the office door and beckoned to his secretary. "Radcliff, see Winston down to the ladies, will you?"

"Yes, my lord." Edgar rose from his desk and hurried around it, bowing as he came. "This way, Lord Winston."

"Now, now, Radcliff." Blakemore chuckled in his inimitable way. "I know Winston is your cousin, and you are his heir. When we are in private company, you may call him Winston." He eyed Winston. "With your permission?"

"Of course." Winston punctuated his assertion with an

amiable pat to Edgar's shoulder. "My cousin is a friend who is closer than a brother."

"Indeed." Blakemore's eyebrows arched, then furrowed. "Well, then, carry on." He turned and disappeared into his office.

Edgar waved away Winston's apologetic grimace. "How did it go?"

"I think he said I am to accompany him, but it was rather indirect." He searched his mind for some way to interpret the earl's remarks. "He did say I should marry."

"Then let us begin the pursuit. This way to the drawing room." Edgar marched across the carpeted anteroom with the bearing of a footman. Always the perfect servant, even though he would have had the title after Father's death had Winston not been born. As always, Winston was humbled by his cousin's lack of self-importance. Somehow he must find a way to elevate his standing in Society.

As they descended the wide staircase to the first floor, passing giant portraits of Blakemore ancestors and other English nobility, the babble of feminine voices reached their ears.

"Ah. Lady Blakemore's guests." Edgar snickered. "A gaggle of giddy geese, if ever I heard one." He glanced at Winston as if seeking his agreement.

Winston shrugged, unsure of what to think. In this moment of uncertainty, Edgar was no help at all, especially when he nudged Winston forward. "Enjoy yourself, cousin." Then he scurried back up the broad stairway.

Neither did the blue-liveried footman at the drawing-room door offer any help, for his face was a blank page.

"I believe Lady Blakemore is expecting me." He tried to sound severe, but his voice cracked as if he were a twelve-year-old boy. Did every young aristocrat suffer such difficulties during his first year in London Society? Or was it merely the uncertainty of what lay beyond this door with all of those ladies?

The old footman's blank facade remained in place. "Yes, milord." He opened the door and announced, "Lord Winston."

Winston forced his feet over the threshold. The instant he entered, silence swept over the room, and a dozen or so mostly older ladies' faces turned in his direction, eyes sparkling with interest. A certain *young* lady, the only one he had hoped to encounter, directed her gaze toward the cold white hearth, clearly indifferent to his arrival.

Catherine could barely make out Lord Winston's reflection in the shiny silver vase beside her, but the view was sufficient to reveal he was looking her way with some degree of chagrin. Good. She would remain properly aloof until she had secured his interest.

"Gracious, Winston." Lady Blakemore moved toward him. "You gentlemen always claim that we ladies talk overlong, but you and Blakemore have prolonged your discussion into my meeting time." She lifted a gloved hand toward him. He took it and executed a perfect bow over it.

"My apologies, madam." Winston did not sound flustered, but the warm color of his cheeks indicated some high feeling. "Another time, then?"

"Oh, no," cried one of the ladies, Lady Grandly, if Catherine was not mistaken. "We must have a gentleman's opinion about our fetes, mustn't we, ladies?"

A chorus of indistinguishable but agreeable remarks filled the room. Catherine swallowed a laugh to see Lord Winston backing toward the door.

"I hardly think…" He held up his hands in an attempt to ward off two other ladies, to no avail. Each seized an arm and almost dragged him into the room.

Where had they learned their manners? Catherine's mother would be horrified to see such behavior. Perhaps members of London's *haute ton* had their own set of social rules. The two older ladies drew the baron to a long settee in the center of the room and across from Catherine. She slowly turned to face him so as not to seem as eager as the others for his presence.

Yet he stared at her with a helpless, hapless expression in his eyes. Could it be a plea for her help? She offered a brief consoling smile, but quickly sobered. A companion must never attempt to compete with eligible young Society ladies such as the Misses Waddington, each of whom took a seat at Lord Winston's side. One cast a cross glance at Catherine, and she stared down at her folded hands, forbidding her temper to rise. She was the daughter of Comte du Coeur, a French nobleman equal to an English earl, and she had precedence over these two spoiled daughters of a mere English baron. For now, she must play the part of a nonentity. Yet with the French nobility who had remained loyal to Louis all the rage among the English aristocracy these days, those silly girls would be appalled over their own rudeness to her if they learned who she was.

"Ladies, please." Lady Blakemore stood in the center of the room, her arms crossed. "Do release poor Winston to whatever business he must attend to."

"Indeed," dear old Mrs. Parton huffed. "You must not delay him from his work."

"But Parliament does not meet today." Lady Grandly gazed fondly at her two daughters, the girls sitting on either side of Lord Winston. "So his business cannot be too pressing."

A second baroness, plump and handsome in her old age, added, "We must convince Winston to attend the assembly at Almack's tonight, mustn't we, ladies?"

Again the room buzzed with agreement. Catherine stifled another laugh as Lord Winston's color deepened. How could such a wicked man blush? No doubt it was due to his fair coloring. She had always pictured Papa's accuser as being cool and calculating, utterly in command of himself and able to send a man to his death without a qualm. Perhaps even a ladies' man. Lord Winston seemed to possess none of those qualities.

"Tut-tut." Lady Blakemore, tall and regal, tapped her fan against her open palm. "Release the poor gentleman. I have an errand for him, so you must not imprison him any longer."

"At your service, madam." Lord Winston stood so abruptly that one of the Miss Waddingtons nearly fell into the spot he vacated.

Catherine had to bite her cheeks to keep from laughing. Apparently the baron was oblivious to his own charms. All the better for her plans.

Winston grasped Lady Blakemore's call to service like a lifeline. "How may I assist you, madam?"

The countess's jaw dropped slightly, and she batted her eyelids. "Ah. Well. It is not a matter that will interest these ladies. Would you be so good as to follow me out?" She stepped over and gripped his arm, propelling instead of leading him toward the door.

The footman inside the room opened the way for them, and the countess shoved him through the portal, leaving behind muted cries of disappointment.

Winston did not know whether to be flattered or irritated. Where were these ladies last night at the marquess's gala, when he could not find a supper partner until the last minute due to all the uniforms in the ballroom? Ah, the mysteries of women.

Once outside in the foyer, Lady Blakemore waved him
to an occasional chair beside a small table. "Sit here." She
disappeared back into the drawing room.

He sat on the brown tapestry-covered chair, not relaxing in the slightest. Had the countess merely meant to rescue him, she would have sent him on his way. But now he
had no choice but to wait for whatever she had planned.

Within thirty seconds, she reappeared, Miss Hart trail-
ing behind her. Winston's chest tightened. He did not care
for being manipulated, if that was what Lady Blakemore
was doing. But then, was he not contradicting himself?
Had he not brought Mrs. Parton's landau so he could take
the young lady for a drive if all went well?

"Winston, Miss Hart must run an errand for me. I saw
that you brought Julia's landau. Would you be so good as
to drive her?" The countess's face revealed no guile, but
her eyes did have a certain brightness about them.

"Madam, I should be honored to do your bidding." Most
errands were the work of footmen, but after she had rescued him from the bedlam of her drawing room, he would
not complain. "Miss Hart." He bowed to her and offered
his arm.

"Lord Winston." She curtsied and placed a hand on his
arm, but gave him no smile. Turning to the countess, she
said, "Before we go, my lady, perhaps you should tell me
what you would have me do."

"Oh." Lady Blakemore blinked. "Why, I… Hmm." She
tapped her chin with a long, tapered finger and stared off
for a moment. "Why, flowers, of course. You must go to
Mr. Lambert's flower shop on Duke Street and order several large bouquets of flowers."

Now Miss Hart blinked. "Flowers?"

"Why, yes, my dear. We must have flowers for the supper table this evening." More blinking, along with a tilt

of her head. "We always require fresh flowers when having guests."

"Forgive me, my lady." Miss Hart's lovely face crinkled with confusion. "I thought we were dining alone this evening. Who is your guest, if I may ask?"

"Why, Lord Winston, of course." The countess turned a beaming smile on him. "You seemed unenthusiastic about attending Almack's tonight, so I thought I should provide you with an excuse to decline. What better way to avoid the assembly than to have supper with us?"

He chuckled, then laughed aloud. "So you would have me fetch flowers for the sole purpose of entertaining *me?*"

"What a clever boy you are." She patted his cheek. "Now run along. And if you decide to take a turn around Hyde Park after going to Duke Street, I believe the rain will hold off for another few hours."

In spite of the warmth creeping up his neck due to her overly maternal gesture, he marveled at her ability to create such a scheme so quickly. With both Lord and Lady Blakemore pushing him toward Miss Hart, he had no choice but to go along with it. The drive in the park was his plan all along, and their approval seemed the confirmation he needed. If all went well, supper tonight would be an added benefit. If not, he could always beg off.

"Madam, I thank you." He placed a hand over Miss Hart's, which still rested on his arm. To his surprise, she did not seem to share their merriment, if her frown and lifted chin were any indication of her temperament. Perhaps this would not be the pleasant outing he had anticipated after all. This business of courting was thoroughly confusing to him. Was it his responsibility to cheer her? Or hers to amuse him?

Or would they merely tolerate each other while dancing to Lord and Lady Blakemore's tune?

Chapter Five

Catherine wanted desperately to give vent to the laughter bubbling up inside her. Could Lady Blakemore see her struggle? Lord Winston's sudden frown indicated he did not. Pretending to be aloof was proving to be more difficult than she had anticipated. With every deep breath taken to stifle her mirth over her employer's clever machinations, she reminded herself of her family's pain. And then there was the matter of going for a drive with this man who had destroyed their lives. Would he protect her on the rough streets of London, should the need arise? Of course, she could take care of herself with the proper weapons in hand, though she doubted any swords or pistols were available in Mrs. Parton's landau. But to what sort of man had her employer just entrusted her safety?

A footman was sent for Catherine's bonnet and parasol, another for Lord Winston's hat and cane. Once Catherine had donned her bonnet, Lady Blakemore eyed her critically.

"That will do very nicely. Now run along, my dears. I must return to my guests." The countess walked back toward the drawing room, the footman opened the door and her ladyship disappeared within.

"Shall we go, Miss Hart?" A hint of doubt colored Lord Winston's tone, but she refused to look at him as she took his arm again. His well-formed face and superior height were all too alluring, and she must not fall for his charms. Curiously, one of those charms was his apparent oblivion to his own handsomeness. She would have to find a way to use that.

"Yes, my lord." She forced a subservient tone into her voice.

To her surprise, he sighed as he led her to the stairway down to the ground floor. There he waved to his driver, who steered Mrs. Parton's horses out of the line of carriages circling the fountain in front of the mansion. Without a word, Lord Winston handed Catherine into the pristine white carriage with tooled leather upholstery. She chose the seat with her back to the driver.

"Miss Hart, I insist upon your taking the opposite place." The firmness in his voice sent an odd sensation skittering across her shoulder.

"Yes, my lord." She moved to the seat facing front, considered the right of those of a superior rank. By giving it to her, the baron showed extraordinary courtesy.

Once in place opposite her, he said, "To Mr. Lambert's on Duke Street, Toby."

"Yes, my lord." The driver echoed Catherine's very tone, and she hid a smile.

Lord Winston sighed again, this time with a hint of annoyance.

As they rode from the grounds, Catherine viewed the estate's many beautiful flower beds, noting that Lady Blakemore might easily have provided her own bouquets for tonight's supper. Catherine could only conclude that God was smiling down on her plot against Lord Winston. Otherwise, why would such a reputable couple work so hard to provide her with opportunities to be in the baron's company?

The sun peeked out from behind the clouds, then hid again, and a fine mist sprinkled over the carriage and its inhabitants. Although Catherine raised her parasol, the humidity quickly began to wilt her muslin gown. She reached up to touch her hair, but not a curl had appeared in the few strands she had left free from her bonnet. The baron, on the other hand, seemed to sprout curls from beneath his tall black hat even as she watched.

"Shall I put the top up, milord?" The moment the driver asked the question, the rain ceased, and the sun reemerged, shining its warmth upon the travelers.

"It seems that we may leave it down." Lord Winston eyed Catherine. "That is, if the lady has no objection."

"None, my lord." Brushing dampness from her skirt, she stared down at her lap and bit her lower lip to hide a smirk. She could hear his huff of annoyance.

"Miss Hart, it is not necessary for you to address me in that manner." His eyes blazed, and his lips thinned. "Furthermore, I think you know it. Last night we enjoyed an agreeable supper together, and unless I have offended you in some way, your subservient demeanor is nothing short of insulting."

Now Catherine permitted him to see her smirk. "Yes, my lord."

He tilted his head to the side and stared at her, disbelief registering in his intense green eyes. Then his jaw dropped, and a smile formed on those sculpted lips. "Ah. I see." He returned a smirk and relaxed against the back of his seat. "If that's the way you wish to play, I am game. *En garde,* my lady."

Her heart stilled. Had he guessed that she was the "young man" who had crossed swords with him only yesterday? But his eyes twinkled with mirth, and she knew she had him. They would not engage in swordplay, but rather wordplay. And she had every intention of winning.

Whatever her pedigree, the lady possessed an amusing wit. To his disadvantage, Winston had never learned to exchange clever quips. Father had been a righteous but grave gentleman, and Winston had always tried to emulate him. Yet since receiving his writ of summons from the House of Lords and making his pilgrimage to London, he had discovered that one could find humor in certain situations without committing sin. With Lord and Lady Blakemore being above reproach, perhaps he could trust their Miss Hart to help him learn how to laugh more often.

"Why, Lord Winston, I am shocked." Her sly grin suggested that shock was far from her thoughts. "Would you challenge a lady to a duel?"

"Only if it is a duel of wits, madam." He could see she would be a worthy opponent. If anything, he would be the student in this match.

As she appeared to consider his proposal, she idly grasped a wisp of hair that had escaped her bonnet and curled it around her forefinger to no avail. The moment she released the dark brown lock, it fell straight, emphasizing the graceful curve of her jawline. "Very well, then." She gave him a smug grin. "I accept your challenge."

Of course, they must keep their repartee above reproach, so he considered how to address that issue. "Perhaps we should devise some rules so as not to give one another any offense."

"Humph. That very suggestion is an offense." She waved her fan and stared toward the tall, elegant town houses of Hanover Square as they passed. "If you think yourself unable to maintain propriety, perhaps you should rescind your challenge."

Annoyance shot through him. Yet how could he respond? By suggesting that *she* might be the one to breach the bounds of propriety? Perhaps this game was not a wise idea. What did Proverbs advise about humor and jesting other than to say a merry heart did a man good, like medicine? But if nothing else, Miss Hart's hauteur suggested excellent breeding. Only a pure-hearted lady would bristle at any hint that she might do something improper.

The landau turned onto Oxford Street, and Miss Hart continued to watch the scenery, her chin lifted and a slightly wounded expression filling her lovely dark eyes. He stared out the other side of the carriage, taking in the scents of mowed grass and rain-washed gardens. And wondering how to repair the damage. Where did one go to learn the art of tasteful jesting?

A phaeton passed by, driven by a much older peer— Lord Morgan, if Winston remembered correctly—whose pretty young companion laughed raucously, no doubt at some great witticism from her protector. From the lecherous way the gentleman regarded the girl, Winston would hardly consider him a good source of information.

By the time they reached Duke Street, crowds of people from every class filled the narrow thoroughfare. The driver skillfully wove the landau in and out among carts, hackneys and pedestrians, reaching Lambert's Floristry without incident.

"Wait here, Toby," Winston ordered as he stepped down to the cobblestones. "Miss Hart." He reached out to her, and she placed a gloved hand in his to disembark, then breezed past him to wait at the door of the establishment.

Before Winston could reach her, the door swung open. "Ah, Miss Hart, welcome." The clerk, or perhaps the proprietor, welcomed her with a bow, then gave Winston a quizzing look.

"Good afternoon, Mr. Lambert." She gave the middle-aged man a charming smile that Winston suddenly coveted for himself. "Lady Blakemore sent me to choose some flowers for a last-minute supper she is hosting tonight. Do tell me that Lord Winston and I are not too late to find three or four arrangements of delphiniums or perhaps gladioli."

"Ah, Lord Winston, welcome." Mr. Lambert gave him a bow that was neither too low nor too shallow for his station. "Please permit me to assure you that even this late in the day, we still have a vast array of exquisite blooms in a variety of colors and can deliver them straightaway. Please come this way." He beckoned them to follow deep into the broad building containing every variety of summer flower and plant Winston had ever encountered and some he had not.

Rich, heady fragrances filled the rooms, some nearly overpowering. Winston watched as the proprietor advertised the qualities of the various flowers, with Miss Hart nodding or shaking her head. At last she seemed to settle on a large container of vibrant purple delphiniums.

"Yes, I believe these will be perfect. The fragrance is enough to freshen the room but not so overpowering as to spoil one's appetite. You may create—hmm, let me see." She tilted her head prettily, stared off thoughtfully, then refocused on the aproned vendor. "I believe four arrangements will be sufficient."

"Of course, Miss Hart. Would you permit me to include a spray or two of—"

"Wait."

Both Miss Hart and Mr. Lambert looked at Winston as if he were a squawking gander. In truth, he had no idea why he had interrupted the man, but now he must follow through with his challenge. "I cannot imagine that Lady Blakemore will prefer anything but roses." He gave Miss Hart what he hoped was a smug look. "Red roses."

Just as he hoped, her eyes lit with the same spark as when they had begun their verbal rivalry. Had he found the key to redeeming the game?

"Red roses? La, what an idea. Why, the fragrance of too many roses can overpower the aroma of even the most delicious roast beef." She arched her perfect brown eyebrows and sniffed for emphasis.

"Au contraire, mademoiselle." Winston crossed his arms over his chest and stared down his nose at her. Which was a bit difficult, considering her height. "The fragrance of roses can only enhance the flavors of a well-prepared supper." Not that he had ever noticed such a thing.

In the corner of his eye, he saw Mr. Lambert wring his hands as alarm spread over his slender face.

"Milord, Miss Hart, please. Perhaps alternating arrangements of roses and delphiniums would suit Lady Blakemore?"

"No." Winston shook his head. "Roses or nothing." Miss Hart's dark frown told him he had gone too far. He should have taken into account the power of his title, which would trump anything a lady's companion might say. But could he manage to redeem the situation once more?

"I beg your pardon." A well-favored and familiar gentleman dressed in a black suit approached from the direction of the front entrance. "Perhaps I may be of assistance in your decision."

"Mr. Grenville." Mr. Lambert appeared near to collapsing, and Winston felt a pinch of guilt over his charade. "If you give me a moment, I shall be pleased to help you myself."

"No hurry." Mr. Grenville tipped his hat to Miss Hart

and offered Winston a slight bow. "Good afternoon, sir. You will perhaps remember our meeting this Sunday past when you attended my brother Lord Greystone's wedding."

"Ah, yes." This gentleman's brothers had snatched away the only two ladies Winston had attempted to court this Season. Was this one about to take Miss Hart, as well? Still, he could not avoid introducing them. "Miss Hart, may I present Mr. Grenville, the vicar who conducted the viscount's wedding." He turned to the vicar. "Miss Hart is Lady Blakemore's companion."

The lady executed an elegant curtsy and held out her hand. "Mr. Grenville, I have heard nothing but the highest praise for you and your family from Lord and Lady Blakemore."

"I thank you, madam." He bowed over her hand. "I know you are a comfort to Lady Blakemore now that all of her children are married and living in different parts of the country."

"I do hope so." Miss Hart gave him a warm smile.

"By the by, Winston," the vicar said, "Greystone tells me you were quite the hero in the matter of the climbing boys. Not many peers would endanger their own lives by fighting criminals in defense of two small chimney sweeps."

"'Twas your brother's triumph," Winston said. "I was merely along for the ride." True, it had been a great adventure. But he was learning this day that entering a den of cowardly miscreants was actually much easier than discerning what might please a young lady.

"A hero. My, my." She shot a triumphant glance at Winston, as if she somehow sensed he would not continue their argument in front of the vicar. "Well, sir, we have completed our business." She spoke to the flower vendor. "The delphiniums, Mr. Lambert."

Mr. Lambert wrung his hands again and cast an anxious look at Winston. For his part, Winston had the urge to gently tweak Miss Hart's pretty little nose, as he had frequently done to his little sister when they had quarreled. He managed to squelch the temptation and instead gave the lady a bow of defeat. "The delphiniums. But do put at least a single white rose among them as a symbol of my surrender."

Mr. Grenville laughed. "Well, I see that my interference is not necessary." He clapped a hand on Mr. Lambert's shoulder. "I have come to fetch the bouquet my wife ordered. Do you have it ready?"

While the minister conducted business with the relieved flower vendor, Winston quietly exhaled *his* relief over learning the gentleman was married. He would be more than pleased to have a measure of whatever graces those Grenville brothers possessed, some intangible quality that gave them such charming airs, especially with the ladies. Was it something a gentleman could learn?

They took their leave of the vicar and left the building, but Winston tarried after handing Miss Hart into the landau. When Mr. Grenville emerged carrying a nosegay of daisies and other small flowers, he beckoned to him.

"Will you call upon me at your convenience, sir?"

"Indeed I will." The vicar beamed at the invitation. "It will be my pleasure."

With a time settled upon, they parted company, and Winston climbed into the carriage.

"In need of spiritual advice, are we?" Miss Hart gave him a pretty, innocent smile at odds with her impertinent question.

Winston could think of no clever response. Toby, on the other hand, harrumphed with disapproval of her insolence as he slapped the reins on the horses' haunches to urge them forward.

A dark look passed over her face, almost a scowl. Was she mortified by her question? Angry about being chided by a servant, even passively? Or had Winston somehow offended her…again? This time, he would not rest until they reached a truce. He tapped the driver's bench with his cane. "Hyde Park, Toby." To Miss Hart, he said, "We must do as Lady Blakemore instructed us."

She merely nodded. They drove in silence for several moments. At last she released a long sigh.

"I beg you, sir, you must not keep me in suspense any longer. Tell me about your gallant rescue of the climbing boys."

Catherine did not wish to hear the story, did not wish to know how this man could be a hero to little chimney sweeps and yet turn around and as much as murder Papa. Yet courtesy demanded that she ask him about the incident after the vicar mentioned it. Lord Winston would boast, of course, and expose his pride, which he had cleverly hidden from Mr. Grenville. But then, one always pasted one's best face on when talking with a clergyman. Even she had offered Mr. Brown, the pastor of her home parish, only her brightest smile and nods of agreement when he had counseled her and Mama about Papa's tragedy. While she knew some men entered the church for political reasons, Mr. Brown was all sincerity, and he had a gift for discernment, much like Mr. Grenville appeared to possess. Too much interaction with such spiritual guides would expose her lies. Therefore, she would avoid Mr. Grenville at all costs.

Now, having boldly demanded to hear about Lord Winston's heroism, she sat back, awaiting his response. Oddly, he tugged at his collar, and if she did not dislike him so thoroughly, she would find his reddening cheeks quite charming, in a boyish way.

"I fear, Miss Hart, that too much has been made of my part in the event. I merely accompanied Lord Greystone on the adventure. For some charitable reason I know nothing about, he had taken in the little chimney sweeps, and when their former master kidnapped them, Greystone was determined to have them back. After a Bow Street Runner located them in a disreputable tavern on the Thames, the three of us went there to rescue them. Greystone was the true hero, for he entered through an upstairs window and brought the lads out. While he and the Runner made their escape, I held off a few ruffians with my sword and pistol. They were cowards, the lot of them, for not a one attempted to engage me in a fight."

"Were you all that eager for a duel, then, master swordsman that you are?" The instant she said the words, Catherine cringed inwardly. He would no doubt wonder how she knew such a thing about him.

But he simply chuckled softly and shrugged. "Actually, I do like fencing, but I cannot be certain my instructor, Mr. Angelus, who owns the academy where I practice, would call me a *master* swordsman."

Against her will, she detected a hint of humility in his tone rather than the pride she had expected. Had all of his arrogance during their match yesterday been mere bravado? No matter. She would never relent in her belief that he was a villain, albeit a humble one. How the two qualities could reside together in a single man, she could not guess. One thing she did know: all this talk of swordsmanship must cease before she gave herself away.

"Still, you must admit your rescue of the little boys will be a grand tale to tell your own sons."

"Hmm. I had not thought of that." He grew pensive, as if envisioning such a scene.

The winsomeness on his handsome face pierced Catherine's heart. What did he dream of? Hope for? Did a titled gentleman of his wealth, who sat with the great nobles of England in the House of Lords, have any unfulfilled dreams? No, she must not think of such things, must not ask him of his ambitions as though they mattered to her. With no little effort, she thrust away every kind impulse toward him, silently hurling the epithets *liar* and *murderer* at him as the landau rolled into Hyde Park.

They continued their ride in silence, passing food vendors, grand carriages of every description and numerous well-dressed people on horseback. Catherine recognized several peers and elected members of Parliament who seemed to have taken advantage of their day off from lawmaking to enjoy the late-afternoon sunshine. Lord Winston received a few solemn nods, but no one called out greetings, although more than one lady eyed the two of them with open curiosity. With all the noises of carriage wheels and chattering people, Catherine felt no need to attempt further conversation with Lord Winston.

"Miss Hart." His mellow voice broke into Catherine's reverie. "May I offer you some refreshment? If I am not mistaken, strawberry and lemon ices are available across the way." He pointed his cane toward a line of trees.

She gazed in that direction. "That would be lovely."

He ordered his driver to the shaded area where several tradesmen had set up their carts to sell pastries, ices and even complete picnics. There he handed her down from the landau.

"Your choice, Miss Hart." He gestured broadly toward the numerous sellers calling out to passersby to come taste their wares.

"I thank you, sir." Catherine studied the row of eager vendors, choosing at last a lively old woman in a tattered apron selling strawberry ices and cream-covered currant tarts. While her escort selected his own food and drink and settled the bill, she strolled among the oak and willow trees toward the Serpentine River some thirty yards away. Having sat most of the day, she longed for the exercise of an invigorating walk, preferably here in the shade as soon as she finished her refreshments.

"What 'ave we here, Joe?" A scratchy male voice came from behind a wide oak. "A pretty lady with a heavy purse, and all alone, at that."

Another voice cackled, as if his friend had made a fine joke. "And all for the taking, wouldn't you say, Jigger?"

A violent shiver shot up Catherine's spine. These vile men meant to attack her, and she had no weapons to defend herself. A glance back at the carriage revealed she had wandered farther away than she had thought. There stood Lord Winston looking this way and that, apparently searching for her. Was he too far away to hear her cry out in the noisy park? Was every decent person too far to help her?

Before she could scream, one of the men grasped her around the waist from behind while the other covered her mouth with a filthy handkerchief that smelled of liquor and sweat. The other man wrested her fan and reticule from around her wrist, knocking her tart and ice to the ground and tearing her sleeve.

Then he began to tear at her gown.

Chapter Six

At the sight of Miss Hart being accosted by two villains, Winston's heart jolted with fear such as he had not felt since Father died. But while he could not save his sick, elderly parent, he could save this lady. Seizing his cane from the carriage, he called for Toby to bring his whip, and the two of them raced toward the melee.

As they quickly covered the distance, their hats flying off in the wind, Winston saw Miss Hart wriggling and twisting and cheered her courage. When the heel of her half boot connected sharply with her captor's shin, the man howled, which served to alert others in the park that a crime was in progress. To Winston's relief, a crowd began to gather. But to his horror, before he could reach Miss Hart, she was flung to the ground and landed hard. The impact sent her bonnet flying, and her long, dark hair fell loose from its pins and formed a silken shawl about her shoulders.

He reached the scene and slammed his cane against the skull of the man who had thrown her down. The attacker landed on his back and emitted a loud cry of agony. In one fluid movement, Winston slammed one Hessian boot down on the man's chest, unsheathed his sword from the cane and stuck the point into the villain's neck, drawing blood. Toby set upon the other man with his whip until he curled into a ball and screamed in pain.

The crowd grew larger, with ladies standing a safe distance away and several well-dressed gentlemen producing swords or pistols to complete the capture of the fiends.

"See to your lady, Winston." A middle-aged peer—Lord Alston?—stepped forward with another gentleman and took responsibility for Winston's conquest.

"My thanks to you, sir." He dashed to Miss Hart, not *his* lady at all, but the one for whose safety he was responsible. Yet he had failed to keep her safe. She had been horribly assaulted, and while her blue dress still preserved her modesty, its skirt was surely torn beyond repair.

"My dear Miss Hart." He knelt beside her, his heart racing. "Are you injured?"

"I...I—" Her eyes did not quite focus on him.

He longed to pull her into a comforting embrace. Of course, that would be utterly improper and, witnessed by these numerous members of the *haute ton,* would ruin her reputation. Not to mention the scandal it would cause for dear Lady Blakemore. And ruin Winston's chances for a career in diplomacy with Blakemore. But that hardly mattered in a moment like this.

"Shh." He set a hand on Miss Hart's upper arm, surprised by the firmness of it. Ladies rarely possessed such well-formed muscles, for their privilege was to be taken care of, not to work. He quickly set aside the observation for later consideration. "What a terrible fright for you. If you can stand, please permit me to assist you."

She reached out a trembling hand, waving it uncertainly, almost as if she could not see where to place it.

"I am here." He gripped her hand firmly. "Lean on me." Slowly, his other hand at her waist as properly as when they had danced together only the previous evening, he lifted her to her feet.

To his surprise, when her vision cleared, she did not gaze at him with gratitude, but glared at him as if it were all his fault.

She would *not* thank him. Would *not* call him a hero. Would *not* be grateful to him. Catherine shook off his hands and watched with satisfaction as disbelief and humiliation spread across his face. Only briefly did she feel the loss of contact with his strength.

"Kindly take me to Lady Blakemore," she hissed, then snatched up her bonnet, brushed past him and strode toward the carriage.

She could sense him striding along beside her, but refused to be comforted by his presence. When he had lifted her from the ground, she could not fail to be impressed by his powerful arms. Arms that had rescued poor little chimney sweeps. No. Arms that had carried lying letters to the Home Office condemning her innocent father.

The crowd parted before them, and she became aware of some important members of Society clucking out their sympathy for her and singing their praise for Lord Winston's bravery. She had not been presented to any of them, so she had no need to respond beyond a murmured, "I thank you." In truth, all she wanted to do was hide. As a companion, she had expected to escape the notice of Society while she brought Lord Winston to ruin. Yet here she was at the center of attention and likely the subject of many a gossip's *on-dits* for days to come. Perhaps the incident would even be published in the papers. To hide her chagrin, she shoved on her bonnet and endeavored to tuck her hair beneath it as she walked, a useless labor due to its length.

At the landau, Lord Winston wordlessly helped her step up and into her seat. He glanced beyond the conveyance and raised a hand to a gentleman on horseback. "I say, Melton, can you assist me?"

"Your obedient servant, sir." The young dandy in a bright green jacket and yellow riding breeches dismounted and approached.

"May I present Miss Hart, Lady Blakemore's companion?" To Catherine, he said, "This is Lord Melton, Lord Greystone's brother-in-law. You will be *safe* in his care." Irritation colored his tone. "Melton, would you be so kind as to see the lady home to Lord Blakemore's? My driver will be here for you momentarily. I must make certain those miscreants are taken to the authorities."

"Of course. Take my horse." The young blond peer handed the reins to Lord Winston and took his seat across from Catherine. "Are you well, Miss Hart? I saw the attack from across the park and hastened to your defense, but you are most fortunate that a superior defender was closer by." Before she could respond, he eyed Lord Winston. "Clever way to keep your sword handy, Winston. You must tell me where you got that cane."

"I have a spare I can give you." Lord Winston accepted his hat from another gentleman. As he brushed it off and settled it on his head, he glowered at Catherine briefly. "Madam, you are now in safe hands." Then he strode away.

Why had he felt the need to twice assure her of her safety in Lord Melton's care? Although she had never before met this young earl, Lady Blakemore had spoken of his recent reformation from a dissolute life. Perhaps Lord Winston's reassurances had more to do with his own sense of failure in protecting her. Did he then have a conscience, an awareness that he could do something wrong?

Catherine certainly felt the weight of her own misdeeds, and in any other circumstances, she would have immediately confessed her foolishness in wandering away from her escort. But she refused the nagging of her own conscience, refused to give Lord Winston credit for anything. For once she opened the door to kind thoughts about the baron, her quest to vindicate Papa would be forever thwarted.

Yet in the back of her mind, she could hear Lord Winston's words spoken with heartrending gentleness: *My dear Miss Hart...I am here. Lean on me.*

Oh, if only she were free to do that.

With the help of several other gentlemen, Winston made quick work of handing the attackers over to a magistrate's man who happened to be in the park. In fact, were the circumstances not so alarming, he could consider the incident quite fortuitous. A half dozen of his peers who had barely, if at all, acknowledged him on the floor of the House of Lords now warmly congratulated him on his chivalry and courage. Jolly, plump Lord Bascom had compared him to the knights of old from whom many in this aristocratic crowd had descended. Another argued that Winston would have been an asset to Wellington in the fight against Napoleon. Two or three well-dressed older ladies promised introductions to nieces or daughters upon their next encounter. He even heard demands that he must make an appearance at Almack's this very evening. It seemed that his actions in rescuing an endangered damsel trumped even a crimson army uniform.

But none of the praise breached the wall of confusion and doubt thrown up against his self-confidence by that very damsel's censure. Like Father, she seemed to think he fell short of what was expected of him. At least with Father, he had understood the expectations and knew that he came short of the righteousness of God, as Scripture taught. With Miss Hart, he could only guess and no doubt be wrong about the nature of his shortcomings.

In spite of wishing to distance himself from the young lady and her ill temper, he nevertheless rode back to Blakemore House to make certain she had not sustained serious injuries. He had little real concern about the matter. From the way she had stormed across the park back to the carriage, one would have thought she was charging into a battle, not emerging wounded from one. Still, he must apologize to Lord and Lady Blakemore for allowing such a terrible assault to occur while she was in his care. He would make no excuses for himself, despite her wandering off while he was occupied with the food vendor. Yet her lack of consideration grated upon his nerves. Clearly the young lady did not care for his company. After he made his apologies, he would make certain she would not be troubled by his presence again.

Try though he might, however, he could not dismiss her as a mere companion unworthy of a peer's notice. Miss Catherine Hart possessed some singular quality that he could not name, and it drew him to her as a bee to a flower. And it had nothing to do with that glorious dark brown hair set loose from its pins to flow around her shoulders like silk and glisten in the afternoon sunlight. Nor those dark brown eyes that could glow with warmth and kindness one moment and flash with anger the next. Nor those full, pretty lips that…that he would not think on any further. In truth, he had no idea why he found her so entirely intriguing.

At Blakemore House, he surrendered Melton's horse to a groom and was granted entrance to the vast mansion.

"You are expected, my lord." The silver-haired butler escorted him up the wide front staircase to the first-floor drawing room and preceded him to announce, "Lord Winston."

Heart pounding, Winston stepped inside, praying the ladies' meeting had long ago adjourned. To his relief, only five individuals populated the room.

"There's the hero now." Lord Blakemore scurried across the room, slapped Winston on the back and pumped his right hand. "Welcome, my boy. Good work. Good work."

"Oh, my dear Winston." Lady Blakemore rushed to meet him and grasped his other hand.

"Dear, brave cousin." Mrs. Parton followed closely behind the countess and, with the privilege of a relative, stood on tiptoes to plant a kiss upon his cheek, which was growing warmer by the second.

Beyond these three older friends, he saw Miss Hart sitting upon a settee in a fresh blue gown, her hair tucked into a tidy chignon, her hands folded primly in her lap. Her blush mirrored his own. Not two yards from her, Melton stood, or rather, *posed,* beside the hearth. Now that he had abandoned his ruinous life of gambling and drunkenness, he made a rather grand figure in his green-and-yellow riding ensemble, his blond hair perfectly groomed. Winston's heart lurched. Had he just put the object of his interest into the path of a charming young earl with a clever wit and a flair for colorful fashions?

"Come sit down, my boy." Blakemore escorted him to the settee opposite Miss Hart and took the place beside him. "Now, you must tell us everything. Melton has told us how the affair looked from his viewpoint across the park, and Miss Hart has confessed her lapse in judgment. What do you have to say for yourself?"

With all eyes upon him, Winston could not help but recall his days as a schoolboy at Eton. But unlike then, when he knew all the answers—and received more than one

beating from older boys for besting them at academics—
he could hardly form the words to relate today's incident.

"If not for my driver and several gentlemen who jumped
into the fray, I fear the matter could have gone quite badly."

"Oh, pish-posh. Don't be a bore." Melton laughed in
a rich, warm tone that probably pleased the ladies. "You
were quite the dashing hero, Winny."

Winston cringed at the byname. But then, perhaps he
should feel honored. Father had never permitted bynames.
Yet since being in London, Winston had noticed that close
friends often used them as a sign of affection. Although
he waved away Melton's praise, he did value his open
friendliness.

"It was all too alarming, I assure you." He turned to
Lady Blakemore with an apologetic grimace. "Madam,
I beg your forgiveness for not properly protecting your
lo—" he coughed to stop the word *lovely* "—your loyal
companion." Beside him, Blakemore chuckled, so he hastened on. "When I saw those fiends seize her, I had no
time to think, only to react."

"You should have seen him dash to her aid." Melton
grinned. "Hmm. Do you suppose that is where the word
dashing originated?" He stared off thoughtfully. "I must
investigate the matter. I do adore playing with words. One
discovers countless witticisms, often by accident."

Winston silenced a sigh of resignation. Like Shakespeare, Melton did excel at wordplay, something he had
utterly failed at this day, as he had everything else.

Catherine stared at the single white rose at the center of the tall arrangement of purple delphiniums gracing
the rectangular dining table. Lord Winston, despite his
subdued demeanor, must think himself terribly clever for
using the rose to signal his surrender at the flower shop.

To her it had been no surrender at all, merely his permitting her to win after he had made clear to both her and Mr. Lambert that his title gave him the final word in the matter. Yet now he sat opposite her and, unlike the night before at the marquess's supper, seemed unable to think of anything to say.

On the other hand, Lord Blakemore, at the head of the table, could not say enough about the baron's courage. Nor did the countess withhold her compliments, crediting his gallantry to his impressive lineage, which she proclaimed was a part of the bedrock of English aristocracy.

The couple had granted their guest a singular honor by hosting him in their smaller, more intimate dining room rather than the grand hall with its forty-foot table. Had Catherine been aware of their plans, she would have ordered only one bouquet and spared her employer the expense of the extra three. Yet when Mr. Lambert had delivered the flowers, Lady Blakemore had graciously dismissed Catherine's concerns. After all, she had requested several bouquets, had she not?

The countess then whispered to Catherine that the impromptu errand had been a ruse to send her off on a carriage ride with an eligible gentleman. She added that she had left the details up to Providence, so any decisions that missed the mark of perfection could easily be discounted. But she offered no explanation for why she found Catherine worthy of being courted by a peer. Or why she seemed determined to marry off someone who had been hired to keep her company. Was it possible that she and Lord Blakemore knew her true identity? She must seek Mr. Radcliff's counsel, for perhaps the earl had confided in his secretary about the matter.

"Miss Hart." Lord Winston's gentle voice cut into her musings like a sharp blade. "I am your prisoner until you forgive me for not preventing today's terrible calamity." His troubled tone exuded just the right degree of pathos. "I beg you to set me free." His eyes, glistening bright green in the candlelight, held the perfect degree of sadness to emphasize his plea.

How poetic. And how clever of him to effect such a humble attitude, for surely his intention was to force her into admitting her own error in his presence and in front of Lord and Lady Blakemore. While she'd had no trouble telling the earl and countess everything, she had not spoken more than two words to the baron since he arrived hours ago. Surrendering the point to him would gall her, but perhaps losing the battle would help her to win the war.

"I fear you mistake me, my lord." She noted with satisfaction that his eyes flared at the way she addressed him. "It is shame that prevents me from speaking. The entire incident was my fault alone for wandering away to see how the flowers newly planted by the Serpentine are faring in this summer heat."

"But, my dear—" Lord Blakemore began. Lady Blakemore cleared her throat, and the earl paused to plunge his spoon into his beef soup and eat a hearty bite. "Needs salt." He waved to a footman, who quickly produced a crystal saltcellar. The earl then made a great ceremony of measuring out a tiny spoonful and tasting his soup again, seeming to have forgotten his attempt to interrupt Catherine.

Lord Winston eyed the earl uncertainly before speaking to her. "I would have been pleased to escort you to the river, madam. In fact, you must permit me to take you there soon, perhaps even tomorrow." He glanced at Lady Blakemore, who smiled at her soup bowl.

Even as she felt a hint of victory, Catherine could not dismiss the threads of anxiety winding through her. Once again, she could not comprehend why her employer was so eager to see her in Lord Winston's company.

"I understand your hesitation, Miss Hart." The baron must have noticed the countess's smile, for his voice was firmer, denoting no doubt a return of his confidence. "But the best way to overcome the effects of a harrowing experience is to prove that it was an aberration. Hyde Park is a safe place to visit in proper company and even safer now that those villains are in Newgate Prison." He looked at Lord Blakemore for affirmation and received a cheerful nod. "To a man, their fellow miscreants will know that such crimes against their betters will not be tolerated."

Mischief stirred within her, and Catherine gave him a sober look. "Indeed, you are correct, my lord. They must return to their own part of the city and perpetrate all of their crimes upon their own kind."

Lord Blakemore, sipping his soup at that moment, spewed it across the tablecloth and fell into a fit of coughing and laughing at the same time. "By George, Miss Hart, you have a ready wit. Why on earth are you so quiet all the time?"

As he spoke these words, Lady Blakemore rose and hastened around the table to pound her husband on the back, laughing all the way. "Indeed, my dear, you do come up with the most amusing quips sometimes."

Lord Winston stared askance from one to the other and back at Catherine, clearly not comprehending her jest. For a moment, she almost felt sorry for him. Almost.

Winston could think of no rejoinder, for he had not the slightest idea why Miss Hart's assertion was so entirely amusing to the Blakemores. He cast a pleading look at his host, who laughed all the more.

"Sarcasm, my boy. Sarcasm." Blakemore swiped his

linen serviette over his lips and down the front of his white shirt and cravat, seeming not to care that they were ruined by dark brown soup stains.

Enough was enough. Winston would conquer this thing called humor or make a fool of himself trying. "Sarcasm. Yes. It abounds in Parliament between any two men who disagree with each other and hope to defeat their opponent with a scathing set down. But forgive me, pray, if I cannot grasp why you found Miss Hart's sarcastic comment worthy of such laughter." He looked across the table at the young lady, who was the picture of innocence. Or did he spy a glimmer of slyness in her dark eyes? Or was that simply the movement of the candle flames reflected there?

"I do not care for cruel or indelicate sarcasm any more than you do," Blakemore said. "But you must admit your comment invited such a gently done riposte. Permit me to explain why. First, one would not wish the villains to perpetrate *any* crimes, not even upon their own 'kind.' No Christian can countenance such behavior, no matter who the victim is. So the comment was utterly ridiculous." He chuckled. "But for a quiet little mouse like Miss Hart to say it, why, that made it all the more humorous." Ever paternal, the earl cast Winston a sympathetic smile. "Ah, poor lad. Your father was a fine Christian gentleman, but he never found humor in anything. Almost seemed to view laughing as a sin. I have often thought his sober disposition was the cause of his final illness." He clicked his tongue sympathetically. "Take my advice, boy, you will be a happier man if you learn how to laugh at life's absurdities." Now a wily look passed over his round face. "Miss Hart, would you consider taking Winston on as a student in humor?"

His own pulse quickening at the idea, Winston could not fail to notice a bit of chagrin, perhaps even alarm, crossing her lovely face. He must hand her a reprieve. "Sir, I hardly think Miss Hart would enjoy—"

"Not at all, Lord Winston." She offered what seemed like a forced smile. "Did you not challenge me earlier today to a duel of wits? While I cannot hold myself up as a proficient humorist, perhaps between the two of us we can find sufficient causes for laughter." Yet it was not humor he saw in her expression. More like a look of sharp steel. And though she stared into his eyes, he felt she was aiming straight at his heart.

Chapter Seven

"Surely you can understand my suspicions, Mr. Radcliff." Seated by a tall, sunlit window in Lady Blakemore's office, Catherine spoke quietly as she stitched a sampler, a task for her employer that gave her an excuse to be near her friend without generating suspicion. "If Lord and Lady Blakemore believe me to be an impoverished gentlewoman from an obscure family, why would they push me toward Lord Winston? Lady Blakemore has said she and the earl believe without reservation that the Almighty has ordained for kings and nobles to rule and manage the affairs of mankind." Barely avoiding the needle point, she dismissed the soft prick of conscience that questioned why she no longer thought of God as her heavenly Father, but rather as a distant deity. "If they do not know of my aristocratic birth, why would they seek to taint his *superior* bloodline?" She could not keep the mockery from her voice, though she had never been given to using such a disrespectful tone.

"I must admit I am as curious as you are, my dear." The gentleman focused on Lady Blakemore's household ledger, which he customarily examined for possible errors. "But I assure you that his lordship confides everything to me, and he has only the kindest of compliments for you."

He glanced at her, frowned and hastened to add, "Paternal compliments, of course."

"Of course." The doubt in his expression provoked suspicion in Catherine's mind. Lord Blakemore always appeared above reproach regarding moral issues, but why would he grant his countess's lowly companion such particular favor? Would it come at some future cost?

"Perhaps..." Mr. Radcliff stared toward the window with a frown. "No, never mind."

"What is it?" She could see further concern on his furrowed brow.

"There may be nothing to it," he said, "but if so, it should ease your mind...and mine."

His last two words were spoken in a whisper, and Catherine's heart warmed that he cared so much for her family.

"Please continue."

"You are acquainted with Lady Blakemore's friends, the Dowager Lady Greystone and Mrs. Parton."

"Yes, of course." While the dowager viscountess never spoke to Catherine, Mrs. Parton always treated her with kindness.

"You know that the companions of those two ladies recently married quite well—brothers, in fact—and I believe Lady Blakemore and Mrs. Parton's machinations were responsible for both of the matches." He spoke softly, as if thinking aloud. "Perhaps they are merely eccentric. Yes." He gave a decisive nod. "That's it. They are wealthy beyond counting, their own children are well married, and now they are bored. So they have decided to play matchmakers. Put simply, you and Lord Winston are their next project." He turned to Catherine, a triumphant grin on his slender face. Even his color heightened, revealing a great depth of feeling in the matter. "I am convinced of it. You and I may ease our minds, my dear. The mystery is solved." He turned back to his work, making notes in the ledger with a quill pen.

Catherine longed to accept his reasoning, but it still did not answer the question regarding her supposed place in Society. Why would they wish to attach a baron, whose title was hundreds of years old, to someone they believed to be a mere gentlewoman? Did they not wish to foster their friend's political and social advancement?

"What I am concerned about, my dear," Mr. Redcliff said, "is your apparent inability to focus on your purpose. In one moment your desire to vindicate your father is all you can speak of. Then next moment, your eyes reflect, dare I say, a weakness of some sort." He slid a kind but suspicious glance her way. "Have you formed a *tendre* for my cousin?"

She stiffened, and her lips puckered as if she had eaten a lemon. "Most certainly not," she huffed. "No," she added for emphasis, determined to erase the doubt from her voice…*and* her heart. "Why, I have known him for only four days and been in his company just two times. Well, three, counting our little meeting at the fencing academy."

"Hmm." Staring down at his work again, he chuckled. "One could not blame you if you did admire him, Miss Hart. He is a rather handsome fellow and has impeccable manners, though he's a bit awkward in social situations, poor lad."

Recalling Lord Winston's confusion over her silly re-mark at supper the other evening, Catherine could only agree with her friend's assertion. A gentle wisp of sympa-thy for the baron brushed past her, but she mentally waved it away, as one would a fly, before it could settle upon her soul. He deserved no sympathy, none at all, no matter how lacking his social graces.

"There is nothing awkward about his swordsmanship,"

she said, "or his willingness to run a blade of lies through the heart of a good man like Papa."

"My dear." Mr. Radcliff placed his quill into its stand and swiveled around to face her. "If you are to win my cousin over so you can discover exactly how he ruined your father, you must set aside your anger and ply him with kindness."

Catherine longed to ask him why he himself could not simply confront Lord Winston about his campaign against Papa. Perhaps that would put him in some sort of danger. No one must know that he had helped Papa escape imprisonment. And of course, if Mr. Radcliff exposed the baron's evil lies, it would deprive Catherine of the satisfaction her own revenge would bring. The bothersome fly of guilt buzzed through her mind again. With growing ease, she brushed it aside and hardened her heart against Lord Winston.

"Can you manage to do that, Miss Hart? Can you manage to be kind to my cousin so that you may achieve your objective?"

Mr. Radcliff reached over and gave her hand a reassuring squeeze just as the door opened and Lady Blakemore strode into the room. The countess's eyes widened, and fear shot through Catherine. Would her employer misunderstand the scene and reprimand or even dismiss her?

Instead, the lady smiled and said cheerily, "There you are, Miss Hart. Lord Winston has arrived to take you to Hyde Park."

Winston despised the way his hands and knees shook as he anticipated Miss Hart's entrance. The last time he had waited in a drawing room for a young lady, she had already surrendered her heart to another gentleman—a soldier, of course—and he had no wish to be disappointed again. At least in this case, he had not come to court Miss Hart, for she had made clear her dislike for him, had even taunted him at supper in this very house only a few nights ago. If not for Blakemore's ridiculous order that Miss Hart must instruct him in the mysteries of humor, neither she nor he would be in this uncomfortable situation.

Still, in an odd way, he was not entirely averse to the idea of spending the afternoon with her. Something deep within him felt challenged to overcome her dislike, perhaps even convince her to consider him a friend. If humor was the key to softening her feelings for him, perhaps this endeavor would not be in vain. After rescuing her from the brigands in Hyde Park, he somehow felt responsible for her despite the anger she had displayed. No doubt she had been frightened and embarrassed by the incident, as any sensitive lady would be, and had merely lashed out at him because he was there.

In addition to a changeable temperament, she also possessed an elusive and compelling quality that drew him to her, a sweet vulnerability that made him want to defend her whatever the cost. Just this morning, when Edgar reminded him of her inferior birth, Winston found himself protesting the idea, even though he had no clue whether or not it was true. If nothing else, her deportment and grace bespoke elevated origins.

On the other hand, to be fair to both himself and Miss Hart, he must find a way to actually uncover her family connections. He might have been ordered by Blakemore to spend time with her, but he would hold the reins of his emotions securely. As Father had taught him, developing strong feelings for a lady too quickly could result in a lifetime of sorrow.

The drawing-room door swung inward, and Lady Blakemore entered, with Miss Hart following close behind. Winston's heart jumped into his throat. Great mercy, the young lady was beautiful. He clenched his jaw to keep from gaping at her exquisite face and her tall, elegant figure dressed in a pretty walking gown of green-sprigged muslin. No matter what color she wore, no matter whether it was day or night, no matter her temperament of the moment, her ivory complexion seemed to glow with health and beauty. Such a striking vision!

"Good afternoon, Winston." Lady Blakemore crossed to him and held out her hand. "How good of you to agree to entertain our Miss Hart."

With difficulty, he directed his eyes away from the young lady and focused on the countess as he bowed over her hand. "Lady Blakemore, you look well."

"I must return the compliment. Either London is doing wonders for you, or you are anticipating your outing." She gave him a sly smile.

He cleared his throat. "Undoubtedly both, madam. I am honored to sit in Parliament, and I have certainly looked forward to this afternoon." He paid his addresses to the younger lady, noting that, although her eyes appeared guarded, she gave him a slight smile along with her curtsy. "I thank you for permitting me to take your companion from your side. I assure you I shall return her safely." He gave them both a rueful grimace. "This time." To his surprise, Miss Hart appeared to smother a laugh, for she placed a gloved hand over her full pink lips. Why did she find his reassurance amusing?

"Of course you will, dear boy." The countess stepped back to let them pass. "Enjoy yourselves. I shall be occupied for several hours, so you have no need to hurry back."

They took their leave of the lady and descended the staircase. As they walked out the front door, Winston could not help but wish she had given him a time limit, for he had no idea how long a proper outing might be. He would have to look to Miss Hart for the answer. If nothing else, he knew without doubt no lady wished to be the subject of gossips. More than one peer and MP had asked him about the pretty young lady involved in last Wednesday's incident, but he had refused to name her.

"Why, Lord Winston, you have a new carriage." She smiled her approval of his shiny, well-appointed black landau. "It is quite lovely. You must put your family crest upon both of the doors so everyone will know whose it is."

"I thank you, Miss Hart. I shall order them straightaway." An excellent idea he should have thought of himself. He handed her into the place of honor and took his own seat behind the driver, brushing one hand over the well-padded, dark red leather upholstery and, at the same time, trying to quiet the pride of ownership the elegant conveyance stirred within him.

He had hastily purchased the landau from Birch's only yesterday so he would no longer have to depend upon Mrs. Parton's kindness. While such an acquisition usually took weeks, he learned that an elderly gentleman had ordered it, then died before making payment. Father would have been proud of the bargain he struck with the carriage maker, although he would have found the red upholstery entirely too bold. Father had always preferred plain black carriages bearing no ornamentation whatsoever. Yet some of the ancient vehicles in storage at their estate in Surrey were quite ornate and, though now dusty and faded, had once been painted in vibrant colors and sported gold, red and green shields. Winston could think of no reason at all why this carriage should not bear the family crest on its two doors.

The driveway gravel crunched beneath the wheels as they wended their way to the entrance of the mansion's grounds. Clouds clustered above them, yet the air held not a hint of rain, a sign that the day would no doubt be fair.

Miss Hart was quiet, but her demeanor was cheerful enough. Perhaps he had mistaken her opinion of him. Would a lady suggest something beneficial, such as his use of the family crest, to a gentleman she disliked? He had no idea.

He supposed it was his responsibility to begin their conversation. The only comment he could think of concerned the pleasant fragrance of Lady Blakemore's roses that permeated the landscape. However, he did not wish to revive their discussion—disagreement—they'd had at the flower shop. Best to begin a new page in their acquaintance.

"Do you like to read, Miss Hart?"

She tilted her head in a pretty pose, not unlike any other young lady might do, but much more charmingly than anyone he had yet to meet. A slender strand of dark brown hair came loose from her brown straw bonnet and arched across her fair cheek, reminding him of the way it had all flowed down around her shoulders the other day. He clenched his fists to keep from reaching out to brush aside the strand. Lord help him. Did every gentleman have to fight such impulses?

"Yes." Her cheeks turned pink, and as if she could read his thoughts, she tucked the strand back under the edge of her bonnet. "Why do you ask?"

Ask what? Now his own cheeks warmed. "Why, I suppose to start a conversation. Do you prefer another subject?" What had he asked her? Where was his mind? In Parliament, he never lost track of a word that was spoken or who had said it.

"No, no. Reading is fine."

Thank you, Lord. He released a quiet sigh, certain she

noticed his chagrin, if her mild smirk was any indication. "Well, then, whose work do you read?"

"I have recently read and enjoyed a book entitled *Sense and Sensibility* by 'A Lady.' Do you know the work?"

"Regrettably, no. However, if it is a lady's book, I have no doubt my mother and sister have read it."

"A pity you have not." She made a great ceremony of raising her white parasol as a shield against the sunlight, then lifted her fan to cool her face. "One can learn so much about human frailties and strengths by reading a well-written novel." She stared off toward the town houses they were passing along Grosvenor Street, but did not appear to focus on them. Nor did she say anything more.

He would not point out his own town house on the east side of Grosvenor Square, for that could be perceived as an inappropriate invitation for her to visit him. He did wonder whether she would like his cat, whether Crumpet would like her. But the last thing he needed was to say something else wrong, something else that disappointed her.

Why had he brought up the subject of reading? And why was he trying so hard to please her when she appeared to care little for his company? Once they made a turn around Hyde Park and had some refreshment, he would take her back to Lady Blakemore and be done with it.

Catherine measured the seconds, the minutes before speaking. From Lord Winston's furrowed brow, she could see he was discomfited. While her natural inclination was always to speak soothing words to any other person in distress, she had to force herself not to console him.

Why did she have such kind thoughts about this wicked man? The answer came to her straightaway. Because he was devious and had duped everyone into believing in his nonexistent integrity. Well, two could play the game. She could be devious, too. She even had a Scripture verse from Matthew's Gospel to silence her concerns. *"Behold, I send you forth as sheep in the midst of wolves: be ye therefore wise as serpents, and harmless as doves."* She would play the wise serpent in this charade, but she would be anything but harmless once she had cajoled the baron into making a confession. Only briefly did she admit the verse did not truly apply in this situation.

After several minutes of pretending to admire the tree-lined streets and houses with window boxes filled with bright red or purple geraniums, she offered him a smile. "Where are my manners? You asked if I like to read. Now it is my turn. Do you like to read?"

He brightened so quickly that she would have laughed had her stomach not been knotted with guilt.

"I do, but these days I have little time to read for pleasure. However, upon your recommendation, I shall certainly look for your *Sense and Sensibility*."

She measured out a slight smile and an agreeable nod, after which followed an awkward pause that she refused to fill.

At last he cleared his throat. "Perhaps to be in compliance with Blakemore's instructions, we should begin our lessons. You have been charged with teaching me about humor." The eagerness in his expression lent a youthful look to his handsome face.

Her feminine sensibilities responded with a wildly racing pulse she could not rein in. Oh, why could this man not resemble an ogre? How much easier to hate him if he were hideous to behold or had loutish manners. But he *appeared* to be perfect in every way. "Ah, yes," she breathed out, hoping he would not notice her discomfort. Or if he noticed, would not realize he was the cause of her reaction to his very masculine presence. "But perhaps we can combine reading and humor."

Interest lit those eyes, more green than gray in the sunlight, so piercing yet so unseeing of who she truly was. "How so?"

"First permit me to ask you, do you read Shakespeare?"

"Of course." He grimaced, apparently realizing how harsh his retort had been. "I do not intend to sound arrogant, merely to indicate that every English gentleman with any schooling at all has read Shakespeare." A thoughtful frown crossed his brow, and Catherine could not deny he was every bit as handsome when not smiling. "However, my father encouraged me to read the history plays rather than the tragedies and comedies." He emitted a rueful chuckle. "As you may have already surmised, I was reared in a rather sober house."

Once again sympathy welled up inside of Catherine. Her home had been a merry haven. That is, until this man had destroyed their joy and safety.

"Well, then." She managed to sound a bit tutorial, much like her childhood governess. "My first assignment for you is to read the comedy *Much Ado About Nothing*. The repartee between Beatrice and Benedick is a perfect example of the humor to be found in a duel of wits."

"Hmm. How interesting." His expression grew grave. "I will do as you ask, but please be advised that I have two objections to that particular play."

"Indeed?" Catherine searched her memory for any flaws, but could think of none. "Pray tell, what objections?"

"The jests between Beatrice and Benedick are sarcastic and cruel, striking at the very heart of their opponent. I would never speak thus to a lady and would think very little of a lady who spoke thus to me." He paused as though considering his next words. "Then in the matter of the love match between Claudio and Hero, the count is entirely too quick to believe evil about his beloved. Should I ever love a lady, as he claimed to love Hero, I shall trust her with every secret of my soul, even with my very life."

For a moment, Catherine could not think, could not speak, could not even breathe. Was this not the very thing she hoped to gain? His absolute trust? But while Shakespeare's Hero was the very picture of innocence, Catherine had only vengeful intentions toward this gentleman.

"Ah, here we are." Lord Winston's mood brightened again as the carriage rolled between the posts of Grosvenor Gate and into Hyde Park. "If you are thirsty, shall we try those strawberry ices again? I seem to recall that last time yours was spilled before you could finish it."

"Yes, I thank you." She gave him a weak nod, although she could not anticipate any pleasure in the cold refreshments, not when icy prickles of guilt were cutting deep into her soul.

Her only thirst was for revenge, but guilt struggled against vengeance within her, and only one could have preeminence. How she longed to leap from this carriage and run all the way back to the sanctuary of her home in Norfolk, there to reclaim the life that had been stolen from her family. Instead, she must spend the afternoon with the very man who stole it. How could she manage to keep up her charade?

Chapter Eight

Now that their conversation had improved, at least somewhat, Winston decided he had been wrong about Miss Hart. She had no special dislike for him, but was merely anxious about entering the park so soon after being attacked. She said nothing, but the distress on her lovely countenance clearly announced her struggle. He considered whether to take her home now or ride on as planned. She would benefit from getting back on the horse, so to speak, but he had no right to force her. Still, unless she became agitated, their excursion would continue.

To his satisfaction, Miss Hart stayed close by his side as he purchased their refreshments from the same vendor. Today the old woman had only lemonade, and her clotted cream had gone sour, so they must endure plain tarts.

"Never mind about the cream." Miss Hart regarded the tart as if it were a feast. "I am certain it will be tasty." She glanced back toward the landau. "If you are going to leave your driver in the sun, Lord Winston, you must purchase refreshments for him, as well." Her dark eyes gently chided him.

Annoyance shot through him, but he bit back a protest that he always took care of his servants. After all, Toby always knew he was welcome to find shade for himself and the horses.

"Your thoughtfulness puts me to shame, Miss Hart." Winston dug another coin from his waistcoat and gave it to the grateful vendor. "Take something to my driver, will you?"

"Aye, milord." The old woman hobbled away to obey.

"There. Happy now?" He gave Miss Hart what he hoped was a teasing smirk.

"Mmm-hmm," she said around a mouthful of tart, adding a nod for emphasis.

After they consumed their repast, he offered her his arm. "Shall we view the river?"

To his surprise, she nodded again without hesitation, and he came close to cheering. She was managing her fears remarkably well. He retrieved his cane and her parasol from the landau, then, arm in arm, they strolled beneath the trees.

"The foliage is uncommonly lush, is it not?" What a foolish thing to say. He had never before spent a summer in London, so how would he know how uncommon the lushness was?

"Due, no doubt, to this dreadful heat." She waved her fan furiously, loosening that same strand of hair from her bonnet and draping it across her cheek in the most enchanting way.

Once again he felt the urge to brush it aside. Instead, he pointed the tempted hand toward the well-tended marigold beds, where yellow, gold and orange blooms formed circular patterns. "How clever of the gardeners to plant the flowers in such artful designs." Another foolish observation. Every flower garden he had ever seen was planted thusly.

"Indeed. And see how those children and their dog are

cavorting in the river to escape the heat." Her fan moved so rapidly, he thought she might injure her wrist. Was she frightened for the children's safety? Or her own after last Wednesday's attack?

"Have no fear, dear lady." He nodded toward the crimson-coated soldier standing nearby. "The sergeant is keeping a watchful eye on them."

"Ah, yes, and so is their governess beside him." She peeked out at Winston from beneath her parasol in the most charming way. "I wonder whether his woolen jacket or her black dress makes the wearer hotter."

Her winsome gaze was sufficient to cause warmth to creep up Winston's neck. "Hmm. I cannot guess. Black does absorb the heat, perhaps as much as wool." Were her remarks meant to be hints? "Miss Hart, are you suffering from the weather? We can leave at any time you—" Her impish grin stopped him. So she was deliberately being contrary. Very well. Two could play the game. "Or we could join the children in the water."

Gasping, she stiffened, and alarm sparked in her eyes. "You would not dare."

"What?" He gaped at her briefly before catching her meaning. "Great mercy, Miss Hart, do you think I would throw you in the river? I was merely recalling my happy boyhood hours spent swimming in the lake at my family's estate."

"Oh." She relaxed against his arm and sighed softly. "Of course."

"I would never harm you. You must believe me."

Her troubled gaze melted his insides into porridge. Who had harmed her that she could not bring herself to trust him?

And how did a gentleman keep from losing his heart

straightaway to such a lovely lady? That was one of many lessons Father had neglected to teach him.

As they continued to stroll among the trees, Catherine forced herself to smile. "Of course," she repeated. "You are a gentleman, and you would never harm a lady." She slowly turned her smile into a smirk, a ploy she found very useful, for it never failed to discomfit Lord Winston. "After all, Society frowns upon such behavior, and gentlemen prefer to own spotless reputations, do they not?"

As she hoped, confusion filled his countenance. Then understanding lit those green eyes, and against her will, her heart dipped.

"Ah." He stopped beside the gnarled trunk of a linden tree and crossed his arms. "Now you mock me. Is this my first lesson in humor?"

She gave him a careless shrug. "But you are not laughing, so perhaps not."

"Forgive me if I do not find it amusing. Mockery is the twin of sarcasm, and I have already made known to you my opinion of such set downs. Which, I must repeat, abound among my fellow lords during every debate in Parliament. I will never understand why gentlemen cannot speak plainly and honestly with their peers. Let good sense reign in every matter rather than having a gentleman attempt to defeat an opponent through attacks upon his character." He began walking again, and she fell into step beside him on a well-trodden pathway.

How could he speak of character? Of honesty? Was he truly blind to his own evil actions? With no small amount of difficulty, Catherine mastered her temper and her tone to keep from ruining everything. "Perhaps such attacks are justified if that opponent does not own the spotless reputation I mentioned a moment ago."

He pursed his lips and stared off toward the road, where numerous carriages conveyed well-dressed members of the *ton* on their afternoon drives. Some of them studied Catherine and Winston briefly, but to her relief, none stopped or called out. "Even then, when the disreputable lord takes his seat in Parliament, honor should be imputed to him, for God himself has placed him there, as the thirteenth chapter of Romans instructs us. It is the responsibility of the lord's peers to encourage the betterment of his character."

"Indeed." Again she tried to quench the flames of anger roaring up within her. "What an admirable sentiment." And how despicable that he should mention the Almighty and Holy Scriptures, for it made his crimes even worse.

Yet when he gave her a gentle smile, the flames of her anger died away. How easily she could love the gentleman he pretended to be. *Oh, traitorous heart, he is your enemy!*

"But not in the least amusing," he said. "And we have been instructed to discuss humor."

"Yes, of course."

They strolled quietly for a while, her arm resting upon his. Catherine decided she would let her escort bear the responsibility for their conversation. Yet as her discomfort grew, he seemed to relax more and more with every step they took in silence, whether in the shade of the willow trees or along the open pathway.

At length, the baron stopped. "Miss Hart, I must confess I have no idea how long a proper outing should be. You may have noticed, as I have, that we have drawn a small amount of scrutiny from passing carriages. I should not wish to generate gossip, especially after last Wednesday's—" he winced, a charming, apologetic gesture "—incident. Shall we return? Or I can hail Toby from here."

"Not at all. I have missed my long walks in—" She clamped her mouth shut. She had almost mentioned Norwich, the town near her home where she, Mama and Isabella often shopped. "—the park near my home."

"Would I be overstepping if I were to ask where—"

"Oh, look. A kite."

Catherine broke away from him and scurried between carriages to cross the roadway toward the grassy center of the park. There the two children from the river raced over the wide lawn, attempting to catch the wind with a red diamond-shaped kite. Close behind the little boy and taller girl were the governess and sergeant. A hot gust of wind suddenly lifted the kite and yanked it away from the boy, and both the squealing children and their guardians raced to catch it. Catherine ran after it as well, but it was Lord Winston who leaped into the air in a graceful bound and caught the tail, just barely, and pulled the toy back down to earth.

Laughing with delight, the children arrived to reclaim the runaway, while their adults slowed to a walk and arrived somewhat breathless.

"Here you are, my boy." Lord Winston gave the child a kind smile. "What a fine kite you have, but I do think it requires a longer tail."

"I say," the small lad chirped, "what a brilliant rescue." He appeared to be no more than seven years old, but his bearing was surprisingly mature. "I must reward you, sir." He beckoned to the girl. "This is my sister, Lady Anne, and I am Lord Westerly." From the manner of his introduction and no correction from his governess, Catherine surmised that the young lord was an earl or perhaps a viscount whose father was an earl. The boy watched his sister curtsy, then turned back to the baron and Catherine. "You may present yourself."

The baron had the grace not to laugh. Instead, he bowed in all seriousness. "No need for a reward, sir. I am honored to assist you. This is my friend, Miss Hart, and I am Lord Winston."

The boy reached out to Catherine and gave his own proper bow over her hand. "Mademoiselle du Coeur."

She gasped. "Why, I…" Who was this child? How did he know her real name?

"Non, non, mon petit." The governess, a fair young French lady of perhaps five and twenty years, moved up beside her charge. "Not *Coeur.* Not *Heart.*" She traced the figure of a heart in the air with both hands. *"Mademoiselle's* name is *Hart,* like a deer. Is that not so, *mademoiselle?"*

Catherine nodded as her stomach settled back into place.

"Ah." The boy did not appear embarrassed by his error, even when Lady Anne giggled beside him. He looked up at the baron, his blue eyes exuding sweet innocence. "And is Miss Hart your dear, Lord Winston?"

The baron coughed and swallowed hard, and his eyes started to water. But Catherine could not determine whether he was embarrassed or holding in a laugh. She was having difficulty with the latter, from both relief and delight. What a charming child! Never mind that she would not be dear to Lord Winston once he learned of her true identity. Nor did she wish to be.

"Mais non, mon petit." The governess spoke in a musical voice that held not a hint of scolding. "Again we have the confusion. A hart is a deer." She made gestures with her hands like a deer bounding over a field. *"Monsieur,* eh, my lord, I am most grateful to you for rescuing Lord Westerly's kite. I am his governess, Mademoiselle Renaud."

"Your servant, madam." As he lifted his hat to her, his mass of blond curls was tousled by the wind, once again emphasizing his youthful appearance.

Little Lord Westerly eyed his governess. *"Les chevaux de monsieur sont très frisés."*

Mademoiselle Renaud blinked and frowned in confusion. The sergeant coughed. A gurgling sound very like strangled laughter escaped the baron. Catherine's knees almost buckled from holding in her laughter.

"Ah." The governess's expression lightened. *"Je comprends.* I understand. You wish to say the gentleman has very curly hair, not horses. *Cheveux, mon petit. Cheveux."* Mademoiselle Renaud caressed her charge's cheek with a gloved hand. *"Cheveux,* hair. *Cheveux,* horses. *Oui?"* She eyed Lord Winston. "And we must not make such personal comments about people, *oui?"*

"Oui, mademoiselle." Clearly in charge of the expedition, the little lord bowed again to the baron. "You will excuse us, sir?" He reached out to shake his hand. *"Hors d'oeuvres."*

Apparently that was too much for Mademoiselle Renaud, for she gripped the young earl's shoulder. *"Non! Au revoir. Au revoir."* With blazing eyes and flaming cheeks, she bent down to stare into the boy's eyes. "You must not make these mistakes." To the baron, she said, "You will forgive, *s'il vous plaît?"*

"Of course. I had my troubles with French myself when I was his age." He bent down and whispered none too softly, "And I prefer *hors d'oeuvres* myself."

The boy and his sister giggled, the governess sighed and the sergeant chuckled.

After their adieus, Lord Winston seemed in a hurry to make his departure, for he took Catherine's elbow and urged her at a fairly rapid pace in the direction of the waiting landau. Alert to his duty, Toby began to drive the horses, and they met many yards from the children and their guardians.

"That…that was…" Wiping away tears with his linen handkerchief, the baron leaned against the side of the carriage and fell into a fit of laughter, pressing one hand against his chest as if he feared it would explode.

"Indeed, it was." Catherine released her pent-up laughter until her stomach ached. What a harmless and wonderful and innocent situation. How long had it been since she had enjoyed such a hearty laugh?

The question sobered her. She could count exactly how long. Six months had passed since Mr. Radcliff arrived at her home and warned Papa that Lord Winston had produced letters accusing him of a plot to assassinate King Louis. All laughter ceased in the du Coeur household on that day, and at the memory, her present laughter ceased, as well. Still, she struggled to catch her breath and regain her dignity.

Lord Winston's guffaws slowed to a chortle. At last he exhaled a final chuckle. "There, now. *That* was highly amusing." He gave Catherine a triumphant grin. "Miss Hart, we have found the secret. The best humor originates accidentally from human frailties or childish innocence. No one is injured. No one is shamed."

Catherine could not disagree with his assertion. At home, all the laughter had been harmless and loving, with no member of the family suffering injury or shame. Yet even now, she felt the bite of remorse for permitting herself those few moments to thoroughly enjoy the company of the very man who had brought both injury and shame to her loved ones.

Winston found their drive back to Blakemore House to be entirely pleasant. Their merry interlude with the children lifted his spirits considerably, yet it seemed to have tired Miss Hart, for she made no attempt at further conversation. Nor did he feel the need to press her, even when her faraway gaze grew troubled. Her earlier merriment suggested that she had overcome her fear of being attacked again in the park, yet perhaps she had not. Or did she have some deep grief that she must bear alone? He did not know her well enough to inquire about the cause of her distress, but perchance if...*when* they became friends, he could find a way to comfort her in these moments of moodiness.

"Back so soon?" Lady Blakemore met them in the front entryway. A tall, dark green satin bonnet covered her red hair, increasing her stately height by at least sixteen inches. "Did you enjoy yourselves? Actually, Miss Hart, our encounter is fortuitous. I am on my way to Julia's, and I know she will want to see you, so come along, my dear. Winston, do you require tea, or may I dismiss you without offense?"

He had thought having tea with both ladies would be a pleasant way to end the afternoon, but manners dictated another plan. "Madam, I fully understand. Another time, then?" He bowed to Miss Hart, then to the countess and, after proper adieus all around, took his leave.

Halfway to his Grosvenor Square town house, he realized he had made no headway whatsoever in learning about the young lady's family connections. But at what point in the conversation could he have inquired about her bloodlines without causing serious offense? Even his attempt to question where her family lived had been interrupted by the incident with the kite.

He exhaled a long sigh, causing his belly to ache deliciously from all the laughter in the park. He would not trade this afternoon's enjoyment for all the genealogical information in the world. How true was the proverb "A merry heart doeth good, like a medicine." He had not felt so entirely well since before Father's final illness.

Once home, he found Edgar alone and lounging in his drawing room. The other morning, after his cousin had reacted strangely to his comment about marriage, Winston had begun to wonder if Edgar and Emily were unhappy. Another question he could not ask, at least not directly.

"Is cousin Emily well?" Winston thumbed through the pile of correspondence he'd retrieved from the entryway table. Since his intervention in Miss Hart's attack, he had received an unending tide of invitations from members of the *haute ton,* most of them people he either did not know or had no wish to know. He must ask Blakemore which invitations to accept, for he had no time to waste on acquaintances who could not help his diplomatic career.

"I suppose." Edgar sipped a brandy. "I have not been home for weeks. Blakemore barely gives me time to breathe."

"But you write." Mild annoyance threaded through Winston. He wanted Edgar to feel at home here, but it seemed a little early for brandy. And, as he was the earl's secretary, his referring to the gentleman without his title echoed with disrespect.

"Of course. Correspondence is my primary occupation for his lordship, as you can see." Edgar held up an ink-stained hand, staring at it with disgust.

"No, I meant you write to Emily."

"Why ever would I write to her after a long day of tending to business for the earl?" His dismissive attitude toward Emily's welfare answered Winston's question. Best to drop the subject.

Edgar rose from the settee and ambled to the sideboard to refill his glass. Then he returned to his seat and rested his feet on the occasional table in front of him. "Prime brew, cousin. Excellent stuff."

"If you say so." Winston had never cared for brandy,

but kept a supply for guests who expected that form of hospitality. Of course, he rarely had guests. And when he thought about it, he realized Edgar had been the one to suggest the purchase. "You will excuse me?" Thirsty himself, he started toward the door to summon a footman to bring tea.

"Going?" Edgar jumped to his feet. "But you haven't told me about your afternoon with the lovely little chit."

Winston expelled a harsh sigh. "Do not call her that. I despise hearing that term used in regard to any decent young lady." But especially Miss Hart, whom he henceforth would have difficulty not thinking of as Miss Heart.

"Ah, Winny, are we falling in love? Before you know anything about her family? Or did you discover it all today?"

It was one thing for Melton to give him a byname, another entirely for his cousin to do so. "Pray do not call me Winny. I am not a horse." He added those last words without thinking and, even as he spoke, felt a measure of pride over his first pun. He pursed his lips to keep from laughing. Too bad Miss Hart was not here to appreciate his attempt. Or help him improve it.

"What?" Edgar stared at him, mouth agape, until understanding dawned on his face. "Ah, I see. Winny, whinny. My, my, I have never known you to be witty, *my lord.*" He offered a subservient bow, not even trying to hide his smirk. "I see the young lady has improved your sense of humor. Now you *must* tell me about your afternoon."

The drawing-room door swung inward, and Llewellyn, Winston's butler, stepped inside. "Begging your pardon, my lord, the Dowager Lady Winston has arrived and asks whether you will receive her."

The news slammed into Winston's chest, leaving him

breathless, speechless, while Edgar's derisive snort echoed softly around him.

How did Mother dare to come to London when he had given strict orders for her to stay at home in Surrey?

Chapter Nine

Weariness from her afternoon with Lord Winston bore down upon Catherine. How difficult it had been to remain cool toward him on the drive home from the park, to dismiss his fine manners, his handsome face and, dare she say, his *winsome* attempts to discern what constituted humor. She especially struggled not to place too much value upon their laughter over little Lord Westerly's French mistakes. While at home a shared laugh always brought her family members closer together, she must refuse to let Winston into any part of her good graces.

Yet when he presented such a charming facade, knowing the truth about his evil ways went only so far in forestalling a favorable sentiment toward him. She had never reacted to any gentleman as she did to Lord Winston's very masculine presence, so perhaps her inexperience made her vulnerable. In spite of Mr. Radcliff's assertion, she was not developing a *tendre* for the baron. Indeed, she was not. So, she must put Lord Winston out of her thoughts and concentrate on being Lady Blakemore's companion.

As tired as she was, she looked forward to this visit with Mrs. Parton. The lady was generous and kind and always included Catherine in her hospitality. Although neither

Lady Blakemore nor her friend knew of Catherine's true standing and the social privileges it should afford her, they had no objections to her offering comments in conversation so long as other members of Society were not present. Missing her intimate talks with Mama and Isabella, Catherine treasured the ladies' company. Yet it grieved her to think of the blow dear Mrs. Parton would be dealt when her kinsman's evil was exposed. How could such a good lady be related to Lord Winston?

The late-afternoon sunlight illuminated the large drawing room where they sat having tea. Catherine noticed an exquisite porcelain figurine of a pretty fishmonger girl that was an exact duplicate of one that graced the mantelpiece at home. Papa had managed to bring it to England, along with a few other treasures, when he escaped the Reign of Terror. How she longed to ask Mrs. Parton where she obtained the figure, but such a question would be far beyond the boundaries of proper conduct for a companion.

"Did you enjoy your afternoon in Hyde Park?" Mrs. Parton looked at Catherine expectantly.

A moment passed before she realized she had not been paying attention.

"Why, I do believe you are daydreaming, Miss Hart." Lady Blakemore's eyes twinkled. "I wonder why."

As if her faux pas were not sufficient to embarrass her, her cheeks grew warm, a sure indication that a blush had appeared. "I—I..."

Both ladies laughed in a kindly way.

"Never mind, my dear." Seated to her left, Lady Blakemore set down her teacup and patted Catherine's hand. "We understand. I am certain you and Lord Winston had an enjoyable outing."

"Yes, my lady." Much too enjoyable. "We had no rain, despite the clouds." They continued to watch her, so she searched her mind for more to say. "Although it was a bit warm." As if to emphasize her words, her hand took on a life of its own by lifting her fan and waving it furiously.

"Ah." Mrs. Parton dipped a small pastry into her teacup, then tapped it on the side of the delicate china cup. "Precisely what I had hoped for. A report on the weather." She laughed merrily before consuming her refreshment.

Lady Blakemore spared her any further need to speak by beginning a new conversation about the entertainments the ladies had discussed earlier in the day. And at this moment, Catherine was far too tired to risk asking them why they found a lowly companion worthy of Lord Winston.

"I thought Eleanor was banished forever to your country estate." Edgar's question grated on Winston's nerves. When had his cousin become so contrary? "Have you softened toward her?"

"You know very well that it was Father who insisted she stay in Surrey." And had refused to tell Winston why she was not permitted to return to London. When Winston had received his writ of summons to Parliament, he had not had time to sort out the issue and had told Mother that Father's dictates must remain in effect.

"Hmm." Edgar frowned and chewed his lip. "I never understood why. Poor Eleanor." He glanced at Llewellyn and moved closer to Winston to whisper, "You do not suppose… No, of course not." His slender face creased with genuine concern.

"What? You must tell me. I insist."

Edgar sighed deeply, sadly. "How many years has she been in exile? Eighteen?"

"Seventeen." Winston had been six years old and delighted to have Mother return early from the London Season. She, however, had been plunged into deep depression.

"Do not misunderstand me, I beg you." Edgar's eyes reinforced his plea. "How old is Sophia?"

For the second time in five minutes, Winston could not speak or breathe. His sweet young sister, so lively and so dear to him, had turned seventeen last November. What was Edgar suggesting? What did Edgar know? He questioned his cousin with one raised eyebrow.

He shrugged. "There was an incident with Lord—" He slapped a hand over his lips. "But then, it could have meant nothing." He nodded his head decisively. "It was nothing. I am certain of it."

Winston refused to ask for more information. Father's reasons for banishing Mother had been buried with him, and until Winston had assumed the title, he had never tried to guess what those reasons might have been. Now he could not dismiss the cord of concern and suspicion winding through his thoughts.

Too far away to hear their whispered conversation, Llewellyn coughed softly into his gloved hand. Winston nodded to him. "Ask Lady Winston to come in."

Before the old butler could do his bidding, Mother rushed into the room and crossed to Winston. When she saw Edgar, her eyes flashed briefly. Then she tore off her black bonnet and flung herself into Winston's arms.

"Oh, my darling boy. I have missed you so." She was tall enough to reach up and kiss his cheek without too much effort, and the fragrance of lilacs wafted from her dark blond hair, reminding him of home.

"Mother." Against all good sense and his new, frightening suspicions, his heart gladdened, and he returned her embrace. "What a surprise. Is Sophia with you?"

Mother stepped back, still holding his arms, and nodded. "But she thinks you are angry with us, so she is waiting downstairs in the entry hall. I told her she was being a silly goose." She smiled, and her gray eyes sparkled, reflecting the color of her silk gown. "Do send for her, my darling, or her heart will break."

Before Winston could respond, Edgar moved closer and gave Mother an ingratiating smile. "If I am not mistaken, Eleanor, only a week and a year have passed since the late Lord Winston left us, and yet you have put off full mourning."

Her eyes flashed again, and she looked down her nose at him. "I have." To Winston, she said, "Mr. Stone found nothing wrong with my wearing half mourning. If you do not approve, I shall return to wearing only black."

The vicar who held the living at Winston's home church was a sensible and spiritual gentleman whose opinions Father had always trusted. "If Mr. Stone approves, I concur." Yet he could not help but wonder whether, now that she could wear somewhat more becoming clothes, she would go in search of that mysterious lord Edgar had mentioned.

What was he thinking? How could he doubt his own mother's character?

"About Sophia?" Mother broke into his thoughts. "Will you send for her?"

Joy burst into his chest at the thought of seeing his sister, who was the true picture of innocence and purity. "I shall fetch her myself." He strode across the room and dashed down the front staircase. "Sophia!" In six short months, his pretty but awkward little sister had become a beauty. Her curly blond hair was pinned up in a lady's coiffure, and her soft pink gown brought roses to her cheeks. She stood in the center of the entryway holding Crumpet and murmuring nonsense into his furry ears. When Winston called her name, she released the cat and ran to him.

"James!" She laughed and cried at the same time. "I mean *Winston,* though I shall never get used to calling you by your titular name." Like Mother, she flung herself into his arms, and he held her in a tight embrace. Had she not been in mourning for Father all this time, he might have summoned her to London last March for her first Season. Now that the anniversary of their loss had passed, his sister was more than welcome to join him.

Suddenly the weight of his responsibilities toward his sister bore down upon him. In Father's absence, he was responsible for this precious child, and if Mother had any moral failings, he must make certain she could no longer influence Sophia. Just as when they were children and he had taken her by the hand and led her safely through the forests and woodlands surrounding their home, he would lead her safely through the dangers of London Society.

"Shall we go up?" He took her hand and guided her toward the stairs. Although she did not skip, as she had in childhood, her gait was light as they ascended to the drawing room.

"Mother!" Sophia ran to her with arms extended for an embrace, as if they had not seen each other fewer than ten minutes before.

As they embraced like long-lost friends, Mother gazed over Sophia's shoulder at Winston, her eyes shining with tears. She must have doubted he would receive them, and not without cause. Yet to be fair to her, he must somehow find out why Father had banished her, no matter how distasteful the truth might be. However, he would not ask Edgar, who now sat in a corner sulking, his nose stuck in the latest copy of *The Gentlemen's Magazine*.

Something must have happened between him and Mother while Winston fetched Sophia, but he would not ask about it. The antipathy between the two was palpable, so any story either might relate to him would be filled with prejudice toward the other. And of course he could not speak to Blakemore about any possible taint upon Mother's character. He lifted a silent prayer for the friendship of some trustworthy soul in whom he could confide.

Llewellyn stood by the door, his posture straight, his face blank, yet with an expectant demeanor only an experienced butler could exhibit. Annoyed, and yet alerted to his own failing, whatever it might be, Winston searched his mind. Sometimes the Welshman treated him as if he were still a schoolboy. And often when his butler was present, it seemed as if Father were still in the room, making certain Winston did everything correctly. Their relationship did not seem quite right to him, but he had no idea how to repair it.

Arm in arm with Sophia, Mother crossed the room to his side. "My dear, you must carry on with your plans for the evening and not concern yourself about us. Our journey was long, and so we require only a small repast in our rooms. I am certain Llewellyn will relay the message to your cook." She spoke so casually, Winston could not be offended by her taking control. After all, she had managed their country estate very well, despite Father's frequent contradictions to her orders.

"If that will please you, Mother. And of course you may have your choice of rooms." Rewarded by her pretty smile, so like Sophia's, he nodded to Llewellyn.

"Yes, my lord." The butler returned a properly shallow bow and departed. After more kisses and embraces, the ladies followed him out.

Edgar sauntered over to Winston, worry written across his pale features. "Well, now you have a dilemma. How will you see to dear Sophia's debut? The Season is well spent for such celebrations." His brow furrowed thoughtfully. "Though I have no doubt that is the reason Eleanor brought her along with her."

Did he mean to suggest Mother had another purpose for coming to London? It was another question he would not ask his cousin. "I have the same concern about my sister's debut. I doubt such an affair can be accomplished hastily." Winston exhaled a long breath as he considered possible solutions. "Perhaps Mrs. Parton can advise us. She has launched two daughters, not to mention her former companion, and has seen them all successfully wed." Another thought slowed his racing mind. "But of course, Sophia is very young. Does a young lady make her debut before her guardians have decided she is ready for marriage?"

"Why do you ask me about such things?" Edgar eyed him with mild annoyance. "I have no daughters, only a son who has failed to impress his tutors."

Pity for young Marcus welled up within Winston's heart. Thin and frail like his father, he was nonetheless expected to excel in ways that Edgar never had. Instead of responding, Winston decided to search for a footman, for he still had not had his tea. At the door, he met Llewellyn.

"My lord, Mr. Grenville is here to see you. Are you in?"

"Mr. Grenville. Ah, yes." Winston had forgotten about this appointment. Fortunately, he was home to greet the minister. In fact, this seemed like an answer to his prayer for a confidant. He silently said a prayer of thanks, as Father had always taught him to do.

Edgar, however, muttered an uncharacteristic oath. "Do send him away, Winston. I cannot endure a clergyman tonight, not while I eat."

Winston eyed his cousin. "You are staying for supper?"

Edgar winced as if struck, and his posture slumped. "Forgive me, but do I not have an open invitation to sup with you?" The pain in his voice cut into Winston like a knife.

"Forgive *me,* cousin. Yes, of course you are always welcome here. But I must speak with Mr. Grenville."

"So be it." Edgar waved his hand impatiently and strode toward the side door. "I shall be in your office when you are finished." Before Winston could respond—or send him to a different room—he made his escape.

Only a snippet of worry scratched at the back of his mind over the confidential papers tucked in his unlocked desk drawer, letters Lord Blakemore had entrusted to him just yesterday as they departed Westminster after the House of Lords had adjourned.

Nonsense. Edgar was completely trustworthy. Winston would have to examine this silly disquiet about him at a later time.

Chapter Ten

Catherine read the first scene of *Much Ado About Nothing* for the third time, making notes on a small sheet of paper to use in her arguments with Lord Winston. She was not yet persuaded by his denunciation of Shakespeare's popular comedy, which she had recently viewed at the Royal Olympic Theatre and found quite amusing.

Lady Blakemore had released her for the evening while she and Lord Blakemore attended an important function, leaving Catherine free to read a book from the earl's vast library. The countess suggested the latest writings of Hannah More or the poetry of Sir Philip Sidney for the improvement of her mind. Instead, Catherine selected a volume of the Bard's works in the hope that she could win a duel of wits with Lord Winston upon their next meeting. Surely the verbal jousting between Beatrice and Benedick served a deeper purpose than that of simple insults intended to generate laughter from the audience. Shakespeare's insights into human behavior were renowned, and Catherine had no doubt he was revealing some useful piece of wisdom in this play.

With each reading, however, she grew more dismayed and more in concurrence with Lord Winston. She could not agree with Beatrice's declaration that "I had rather hear my dog bark at a crow than a man swear he loves me." Unlike this disdainful maiden, Catherine did long to be loved one day by someone as handsome and charming as Lord Winston—but without his lies. Nor could Benedick be called a good choice for a husband, for he proclaimed all ladies to be faithless.

Yet even as she tried to contradict his assertion, Catherine's conscience would give her no peace. Was she not attempting to beguile Lord Winston into loving her so that she could expose his lies? She had always tried to be utterly truthful and above reproach, yet now she was one of those very females whom Benedick scorned as untrustworthy.

But Lord Winston's offense was even greater than that of Benedick, who had apparently broken Beatrice's heart prior to the play's opening scene. Catherine would gladly suffer a broken heart rather than see Papa punished for a crime he had not committed. Lord Winston deserved her deception *and* her revenge.

Weary of her inner conflict, she closed the leather-bound volume and returned it to the bookshelf. Better to spend the evening in her chambers practicing her swordsmanship than to waste time planning to fence with Lord Winston using mere words.

Winston chided himself for imagining his cousin might open his desk drawer. Even if he did, his search would no doubt be harmless and his discovery of the documents accidental. Edgar was Blakemore's secretary and saw many such important papers and could certainly be trusted with state secrets. Perhaps he had even written those confidential letters for the earl. Winston dismissed the matter without another thought.

To the waiting butler, he said, "Send in Mr. Grenville and bring tea."

"Of course, my lord." As he strode from the room, Llewellyn lifted his chin and sniffed, clearly offended.

Despite his insolence, Winston could not fault him. As Father's butler for more than twenty years, Llewellyn knew to bring tea for guests without being told. Winston would have to show him due consideration in the future.

He met Mr. Grenville at the door and shook his hand. "Welcome, sir. I have been looking forward to your visit." He waved him toward two chairs near the back corner of the room, where they could talk without being overheard by the footman now in attendance.

"As have I," his guest said as they walked across the room. The tall, well-formed gentleman looked very much like his brother, Lord Greystone, except that his hair was lighter brown. He wore a dark blue jacket and gray trousers, not the usual somber black attire worn by men of God. The minister had no more than eight and twenty years on him, yet his blue eyes exuded a mature intensity that suggested he could search the very depths of a man's soul. Winston valued that same quality in his vicar at home. Perhaps that was why he felt so drawn to Mr. Grenville.

After they discussed the usual pleasantries about the weather and the newly won war against Napoleon, the minister accepted a cup of tea from Llewellyn and focused his gaze on Winston. "Would I be correct in assuming you invited me to call so that we could discuss the young lady who accompanied you the other day?" His tone held only interest, no insinuations, as Edgar's had.

Relaxing at last with his cup of tea, Winston stirred in his usual three lumps of sugar. "An hour ago you would have been correct in that assumption." He prayed it was not a mistake to confide in this gentleman. If he was as upstanding as his brothers, surely he could be trusted. With that thought—and a sip of hot tea—a warm peace flooded his spirit, and his concerns seemed to wash away. "However, just before you came, my mother arrived unexpectedly, and at the moment, she is my main concern."

He proceeded to explain how Father had decided years ago that Mother could no longer come to London and how he'd not yet had time to investigate the reasons. With some hesitation, he also told the minister about Edgar's implied accusations, although he did not name his cousin. Even as he spoke the words, deep emotion welled up inside him, and he choked out, "It is no small thing to doubt my mother's—" Virtue. Morality. His sister's paternity.

Mr. Grenville reached out and gripped his shoulder. "I can well imagine that it causes you great pain."

"Yes." Winston expected immediate advice, but none was forthcoming. Yet Mr. Grenville's presence in itself gave him comfort, not to mention a desire to purge his soul of many troubling issues. He would begin with one that had distressed him for some time. "In addition to that concern, I find my responsibilities weighing heavy upon my shoulders. I have been Lord Winston for just over a year and have been in London since late January. Yet I can find no firm footing on this road. How did your elder brother learn to manage his duties to both king and family? Did your father guide him?"

"My brother was elevated to his title at the age of six, upon our father's death." A sad smile graced Grenville's lips. "Our mother taught Greystone—in fact, taught the three of us our responsibilities. She was assisted by Lord Blakemore and the late Mr. Parton."

"Ah, yes. Of course." Winston should have remembered that. "I fear my father's lengthy final illness left him little energy to teach me many of the required lessons." Regret was quickly displaced by a realization. "Blakemore does excel in mentoring younger peers. I am fortunate to have his direction and his interest in my political ambitions."

"I would say so." Mr. Grenville nodded agreeably, then grew silent again, a silence that nonetheless invited confidence.

"One thing Father did advise was that I should marry as soon as I found a suitable lady." Winston frowned and shook his head over the enormity of such a decision. "Blakemore says a diplomat must have a wife."

"I fully understand. It is the same for a minister of God." Mr. Grenville's expression grew tender. "I am blessed with a godly wife and an infant daughter, so I understand the value of a happy marriage." He focused again on Winston. "When I saw you at the flower shop on Wednesday, you appeared to be enjoying the lovely Miss Hart's company." Again, no insinuation tainted his tone. "Do I sense a hesitation on your part in regard to her?"

"I have known her but a few days, yet I find her company agreeable." More than agreeable. "Yet I cannot help but wonder why she is employed as a mere companion. I know nothing about her family, which must be entirely unimpeachable if I am to pursue her. Marriage to the wrong lady could destroy my career."

"Ah, yes." While Mr. Grenville seemed to understand, a question remained in his eyes.

"Tell me what you are thinking."

"Only that my brother would have missed his greatest happiness if he had permitted Lord Melton's reputation to prevent his marriage to Melton's sister." He took a moment to sip his tea. "Sometimes the Lord surprises us. Why not ask Lady Blakemore who the young lady is? If her pedigree is unsuitable, do not see her again. If you find her family acceptable—" he leaned forward "—begin your pursuit."

Winston chuckled. "You, sir, are a romantic."

"Guilty as charged," he said with a laugh. "I cannot deny the truth. After watching my two brothers agonize over their choices, I would wish for less drama for every gentleman seeking a wife." He sobered. "Do you desire my counsel regarding your mother, as well?"

"I do." Winston held his breath, fearing the worst.

"First, if Lady Winston bears any guilt in the matter you mentioned, remember that we have *all* sinned and come short of the glory of God." Mr. Grenville recited one of Father's favorite passages of Scripture in a conversational manner, not at all like Father's somber, warning tone that often crushed Winston's spirit, even when he had done nothing wrong. "Yet through Christ, our heavenly Father has forgiven us, as Scripture tells us. And of course that means we must forgive one another." He gave Winston a reassuring smile. "Perhaps Lady Winston is faultless in regard to the rumors you have heard. You must confront her in love and discover the truth about why the late Lord Winston required her to remain in Surrey all these years."

This was exactly the advice he had feared. How could he manage such an encounter? Did he even want to know the answer? "Pray I will have the courage to do it." He could imagine the pain in Mother's eyes if he misspoke and she was entirely innocent. "And pray that my words will not wound her."

"Gladly."

To Winston's surprise, Mr. Grenville slipped down to his knees by his chair in the posture of prayer. He found himself following suit while the minister voiced his petitions.

When they had reclaimed their seats, Winston persuaded his guest to have another cup of tea. They chatted about inconsequential matters, the sort of things that nonetheless increased their friendship and understanding. At last, claiming the late hour, the minister stood to take his leave.

"And I shall ask Mrs. Grenville to call upon Lady Winston early next week. That is, if it will please you."

"Indeed it will." Winston had not thought of the advantages of having Mother with him. With a lady in the house, he could also invite Miss Hart to call. The thought stirred a feeling of hope and anticipation. And in preparation for his own next encounter with the young lady, he would send a footman to purchase a copy of *Sense and Sensibility* first thing Monday morning.

As they walked from the drawing room to the staircase, Winston glanced back down the hall, where Edgar appeared to be exiting the same room through the side door. He could only wonder whether his cousin had come looking for him or had been listening to the conversation with the minister the entire time. And if so, why?

Catherine had always enjoyed the services in the village church near her home, but today she could barely keep from squirming like a child in Lord Blakemore's box pew in St. George's Church. Vicar Hodgson, robed in ecclesiastical splendor, stood in his exquisitely carved and canopied pulpit high above the congregation. He preached on the text "Vengeance is mine; I will repay, saith the Lord." Halfway into his sermon, Catherine relaxed, for his examples made clear that his message was meant not for her, but for those who wished to see Napoleon executed rather than exiled to the island of Elba.

She permitted her gaze to wander from Mr. Hodgson to the brightly lit church's beautiful furnishings: the glowing candelabra, the stained-glass windows, the double-decked reading desk to the left of the altar and the enormous Holy Bible thereon. She especially admired the painting above the altar. Surrounded by a finely carved mahogany frame, it depicted the Last Supper in brilliant colors and detail. In the center, Christ glowed with holiness, while his disciples gazed at him with adoration. On the left, the artist had added the shadowy figure of Judas making his escape through a side door to complete his evil deed.

Thoughts of Judas brought Lord Winston to mind. Just as Catherine could never understand how a disciple who had walked with Jesus could betray him, she could not comprehend why the baron would falsely accuse a gentleman he did not even know.

"'Therefore if thine enemy hunger, feed him,'" the vicar read from the smaller Bible in front of him. "'If he thirst, give him drink: for in so doing thou shalt heap coals of fire on his head. Be not overcome of evil, but overcome evil with good.'"

Lord Winston is my enemy, but this does not apply to me. No, her enemy was more like the dragon slain by the patron saint of this church and all of England, and she was St. George, wielding the avenging sword. Yet the more she tried to convince herself, the more her stomach ached from her inner battle. The only thought that could soothe her was the memory of Mama's terror when Papa had been forced to flee.

The service ended, and the congregation began to file out of their pews and toward the rear of the church, accompanied by a thunderous Handel composition played on the fifteen-hundred-pipe organ in the western gallery. At the door, Mr. Hodgson greeted his parishioners, the Geneva bands of his clerical collar rippling in the wind. He modestly deflected compliments about his sermon and kindly spoke to even the humblest of congregants. Of late, Catherine had taken to hiding behind Lady Blakemore or one of the white columns of the portico to escape his notice. Unfortunately, her height equaled her employer's, and the vicar always found her out.

"Miss Hart, I hope you are well." He extended his hand, and she had no choice but to curtsy and reach out to shake it. Of modest height and graying at the temples, the minister extended kindness even to a companion.

"I am, sir." To her relief, he released her and turned to the person behind her.

"Lord Winston, I am pleased to see you attending St. George's."

Catherine whipped around to see the baron shake hands with the vicar. To her knowledge, he had never before attended this church. Why was he here?

"It is my pleasure, vicar. I have been advised by my mother that St. George's is the parish church for all of Mayfair, so it should have been my choice all along."

Mr. Hodgson chuckled. "We are blessed to add you to our congregation."

"I thank you, sir," the baron said. "And I thank you for a very fine message. If all Christians would obey the Lord's admonitions regarding revenge, what a better place this world would be." He turned to two well-dressed ladies behind him. "Mother, may I present Mr. Hodgson. Vicar, my mother and my sister."

The vicar bowed to them. "Lady Winston. Miss Beaumont."

While they exchanged pleasantries, Catherine studied the baron's family. Of medium height and elegant carriage, the baroness did not look old enough to have a son in Parliament. Her unlined face was framed by blond curls pushed forward by a black satin bonnet. Miss Beaumont, dressed in yellow and her eyes wide with liveliness, caused a stirring of jealousy, not for her beauty but for her innocence. Six months ago, Catherine had enjoyed that same cheerful disposition before her world was shattered by this girl's brother. Their presence complicated her plans, for her revenge would harm them as well as the baron.

Trembling inside, she struggled to appear calm as she moved toward the Blakemores, who had descended the several steps of the church. Perhaps as surprised as she at the baron's appearance, the earl and countess stood watching the scene with interest.

At last Lord Winston donned his hat, and he and his family stepped out from under the portico into the sunshine. Catching sight of her, he smiled. "Miss Hart." He glanced beyond her and bowed. "Lady Blakemore. Blakemore."

"Good to see you here, my boy." The earl shook Lord Winston's hand as if they had not seen each other in a month.

Introductions were made all around. Lord Blakemore offered his condolences on the baroness's loss and stated that the late Lord Winston had been a fine gentleman. The countess and baroness announced their long-ago acquaintance, which they were eager to renew.

"You must come visit me," Lady Winston said to the countess. Her eyes darted to her son. "That is, with your permission, Winston."

He drew back a little at her question and frowned. "But of course, Mother. Lady Blakemore is always welcome in my…our home." He gave Catherine a slight bow, and his gaze softened. "And Miss Hart, as well."

"Oh, Miss Hart." Miss Beaumont practically skipped to Catherine's side. "Did you make your debut this year? You must tell me all about it. Winston has not yet told me whether he will sponsor my debut, but if he does, we shall need all the advice we can gather. Mother has not been to London since before I was born, so she has no idea what the latest customs are. You will help us, will you not?"

For the first time in her life, Catherine experienced utter mortification. Although she was fully worthy of having a debut among the *haute ton,* she had never aspired to such a spectacle. Had never wanted Papa and Mama to announce to the world that they were offering her up like some show horse to be auctioned off to the wealthiest titled bidder. And now, with Lord Winston and the Blakemores staring at Miss Beaumont askance, with pretty, uninformed Lady Winston gazing at her daughter with a delighted smile, Catherine could find no words with which to explain that she was a mere companion. But worse than her own embarrassment, this sweet young girl would be devastated by her faux pas in front of the earl and countess.

Chapter Eleven

Winston's heart ached for dear Sophia, but he could find no words to repair the damage her error had caused. Even he knew that one did not call attention to a companion, or any employee, or suggest that she should be elevated to aristocratic privileges. The poor child's face fell, and she stared around the circle, eyes wide with fright, as if searching for someone to explain her faux pas.

"I—I..." Miss Hart, bless her, gave Sophia an uncertain smile, elevating the lady considerably in Winston's regard. She clearly wished to console his sister, but seemed to have the same trouble as he did in not knowing what to say.

Lady Blakemore's laughter rang out, perhaps a trifle too loudly for the front of a church where other parishioners milled about. "Why, my dear girl, not every young miss is as lively and outgoing as you are." She reached out to pat Sophia's cheek, prompting from the girl a small, hopeful smile and forestalling the tears on the brink of falling. "Our Miss Hart is quite shy, you see, and she could not be persuaded even to attend a ball with us until last week, so one doubts she could ever endure the rigors of a debut."

Miss Hart nodded soberly, and Winston wanted to thank her profusely for her sweet humility. And he would forever be grateful for the countess's generosity. In this small company, it would have been her duty to correct Sophia. He had seen more than one older lady deliver a cruel set down to some green young girl and crush her spirits.

"Oh. I see." Sophia was now all kindness and benevolence. She clasped both of Miss Hart's hands. "Why, as pretty as you are, Miss Hart, I am sure you would be all the rage." Her brightest smile now returned. "I have never been afflicted with shyness, but—" She blinked and once again searched the group to see if she had made another blunder. "I mean to say..."

Annoyed with his own social ineptitude, Winston could no longer remain silent. "No, dearest, no one would ever accuse you of being shy." To his delight, she rolled her eyes, while everyone else chuckled in a kindly way. "But we love you all the more for your—what did Lady Blakemore say? Your liveliness."

"And with that all settled," Blakemore said, "I propose that you all join my wife and me for a midday repast. You and your family are free, are you not, Winston?"

Nothing could have pleased him more, but he would not gush out his feelings like dear little Sophia. Instead, he gave Mother a slight bow. "Your decision, madam."

She beamed her delight. "Of course we are free, sir."

With all the enthusiasm of a party of picnickers, they scrambled into their carriages, and orders were given to the drivers. While they rolled through the streets of Mayfair toward the mansion, Winston considered Lady Blakemore's warm welcome to Mother when they were renewing their acquaintance. As generous as the countess was, he doubted even she would be so kind to a lady whose character bore some stain, even from years ago. On the other hand, Edgar had sent an urgent message early this morning advising Winston not to permit Mother to renew her acquaintance with Lord Morgan or even to socialize in the same circles with the known rake. He had not explained any further. Whom could Winston believe?

Since meeting Miss Hart last week, he had been concerned about her family's standing in Society. Now he was beginning to worry about how his own measured up.

Seated in the carriage across from Lord and Lady Blakemore, Catherine wished it were proper to give her employer a daughterly embrace, but words would have to do. "My lady, how kind of you to rescue Miss Beaumont from embarrassment." And Catherine, as well. But she doubted a companion should expect such a defense. "Nothing else anyone might have said could have so graciously smoothed over the situation."

"Tut-tut, Miss Hart." The countess waved her hand dismissively. "One never wishes to see anyone embarrassed, especially young ladies new to London."

"Of course, she will have to be told the truth about my position." Catherine's face warmed as she spoke, and she pulled up her fan to cool herself. It would not be her responsibility to inform Miss Beaumont. "Should she misspeak to the wrong person, she will be mortified beyond repair. I mean to say, she should know that I am your companion, not your protégée."

"Tut-tut," the countess repeated. "I cannot imagine why. I do not recall announcing to anyone that you are my employee. Let them think what they will. We do not owe anyone an explanation." She turned to Lord Blakemore. "I do believe Mr. Hodgson's sermon may be listed among his best, do you not agree, my dear?"

"Indeed, my dear."

The couple fell into a discussion of the particulars of the vicar's message, effectively dismissing the subject of

Catherine's place. As disarming as their acceptance of her was, she could not grow careless and presume upon their kindness. Nor did she have any idea of how to behave from now on.

As grateful as she was to the countess, she could not be pleased with Lord Blakemore's invitation to Lord Winston and his family. Now she would be in their company for hours, and with each passing minute, she could imagine herself loving Lady Winston and Miss Beaumont more and more, even as she loved her own mother and sister. How could she befriend them and then grieve them by destroying Winston?

Yet why should her own family suffer while they all blissfully celebrated debuts and balls and countless "at homes," the latter of which did nothing more than spread gossip couched in the innocuous French phrase *on-dits?* Well, there would be plenty of gossip once she exposed the baron's lies about Papa.

Perhaps she should wait until the end of the Season, after his family returned to their country estate. After all, she had yet to secure his affection, and that was essential to her plans. If only she could speak to Mr. Radcliff, she would ask him if she should be friendlier to the baron now rather than remaining aloof the better part of their time together. But that gentleman apparently attended a different church, for she had never observed him worshipping at St. George's. Even if he did, she would not have been able to secure an audience alone with him without drawing attention.

With her back to the driver, she could see Lord Winston's carriage following behind, and when they made a turn into the half-circle drive to the mansion, Lady Winston and Miss Beaumont became visible to her. Catherine waved, and they returned the same.

Just as when Catherine had ridden in his landau, the baron had given the place of honor to his mother and sister so they could have a better view of the oncoming scenery. Too bad he had not shown the same measure of kindness toward Papa, a gentleman whose social standing exceeded his own.

The carriages rolled up under the white-columned portico at the front of the mansion, and the entire party alighted. At the front door, Catherine paused to watch Lord Winston hand his mother and sister down. He must have felt her eyes upon him, for he turned toward her and smiled in his winsome way. Her traitorous lips returned the smile, and her traitorous heart skipped a beat. How would she ever be able to maintain her aloofness over the next few hours when her own emotions betrayed her just as surely as Lord Winston had betrayed Papa?

"Why, James, your hand is shaking." Sophia followed his gaze toward Miss Hart. "Have Mama and I arrived in London too late to make a match for you?"

"My hand is not shaking. What you feel is my new landau bouncing upon its excellent springs." Winston made certain his sister's feet were firmly on the ground before he tweaked her nose. "And I have not made a match, imp. A smile is not a proposal." He had forgotten how she often could read his thoughts. Somehow he must redirect her thinking. "And it is Winston to you, miss. How will you ever succeed in London Society when you call people by the wrong name? Everyone knows that the moment a gentleman attains his title, his former mode of address is no longer used, not even by family." At least, Father had always required everyone, even Mother, to use his title rather than his Christian name.

"Oh, dear." Her eyes widened, and her teasing grin disappeared. "You must help me, James...Winston, or I shall bungle everything."

"I shall do what I can." He gave her a grave look, and she wilted a little more. Yet after all of his own social missteps, he could only attempt to advise her. "The first lesson is that you must not be so impetuous. In our home village, everyone loves you for your merry and agreeable disposition. But in London, young ladies new to Society are expected to be more reserved. You must think before you speak."

"Oh, I shall, Ja—Winston. I shall." Her sober nod and threatening tears deeply moved him.

When they were children, he had always given her a reassuring embrace to soothe away her tears. Now, with the others watching, he could give her only an encouraging smile. "Everyone will love you here, too, Sophia. At least, anyone worth knowing." He was not certain that was true, but he could not continue to torment her with doubts. Offering his arm, he led her toward the large front door of Blakemore House and was gratified to see Miss Hart watching him, approval written across her lovely countenance.

As Catherine watched Lord Winston's gentle manners toward his sister, she could not ignore the warmth flooding her heart. Try though she might to dismiss her feelings, she *was* developing a *tendre* for him. Mr. Radcliff would say she was forgetting her purpose for being here, that she was being disloyal to Papa. Yet how could she not admire such a kind gentleman? He treated Miss Beaumont with the same brotherly affection that Lucien showed toward Catherine and Isabella. As dangerous as it might be to her own heart, she would be friendly to him today and endeavor to secure his deepest regard. Perhaps Miss Beaumont would be her ally in the scheme.

Well into their luncheon of cold meats, cheeses and a variety of fruits, Lord Blakemore sat back in his chair at the head of the table and gave Lord Winston a sober look. "Well, my boy, has Miss Hart succeeded in teaching you the value of wholesome laughter?"

Seated between the two gentlemen, Catherine eyed the baron and smirked.

He returned a wide grin. "She did, sir, with the help of a small boy. Miss Hart, would you care to relate the story?"

"Oh, no. I fear I would not be able to speak for laughing."

He reported the entire episode in the park with all the proper pauses and inflections of a seasoned storyteller. Everyone at the table laughed until their eyes watered.

"Why, James," Lady Winston said, "I had no idea you had such a fine wit."

James? So, that was his Christian name. Glad to have that bit of information for further use, Catherine noticed Miss Beaumont's widened eyes.

"But, Mama, you must not call him James. He has informed me that everyone must call him Winston now."

"What utter nonsense." Lady Winston gave her son a mischievous grin over her teacup. "I shall address you as I always have."

Still chuckling from the story, Lord Blakemore laughed aloud again. "I wish you good luck in getting your mother to change her habits, my boy. Mine called me Gerald until the day she died, God bless her. When she spoke of Blakemore, it was always in reference to my father, even after I had sat in Parliament for nearly twenty-five years."

Lord Winston's face reddened slightly, but he did not lose his smile. Instead, he leaned forward and stared at his sister across the table. "Very well, then, imp. Since Mother will not support me in this, you may also call me James." He glanced at Catherine, and her heart jumped into her throat. Never had he looked so charming or so kind. "I shall grant the privilege only to very special friends."

She could only assume that he meant this as an invitation to her, but she clamped down on her eagerness to accept *and* the giddy feelings filling her chest. "La, what will happen next? Shall we all now have leave to address every duke and lord and lady by their given names? Why, the entire English aristocracy, even England herself, will crumble away under the weight of such laxity."

While the others renewed their laughter, Lord Winston shrugged off her rebuff with good humor. "Ah, well, we must not have that."

"Now that England is safely secured," Lord Blakemore said, "how shall we entertain ourselves this afternoon? A carriage ride in Hyde Park? Perhaps we shall encounter little Lord Westerly, and he can give us more French lessons."

"Oh, no, my dear," Lady Blakemore said. "Every tradesman on his day off will be there trying to sell us something. How they do take advantage of Society when we all should be relaxing on the Lord's day."

Disappointment clouded the faces of Lady Winston and Miss Beaumont. The mother quickly regained her composure *and* her smile, but the daughter came near to pouting. Catherine could easily see Isabella reacting in the same manner. These ladies seemed particularly eager to be out in Society, yet if anyone else noticed their plight, no one mentioned it.

"Ah, yes, my dear," the earl said. "I had forgotten how annoying the tradesmen can be on Sundays." He eyed Miss Beaumont. "Young lady, what would you advise for our afternoon entertainment?"

Her pout vanished instantly under his scrutiny. "Oh, there are so many things I should like to do. Perhaps someone could teach me how to play charades. Father never permitted us— Oh!" Staring at her mother, she clamped a hand over her lips and blanched.

"Never mind, child." Lord Blakemore's gaze became paternal, as it often did when he spoke to Catherine. His kindness reinforced her opinion that he would never do anything improper, despite Mr. Radcliff's concerns. "As I have told your brother, the late Lord Winston was a gentleman of the highest honor but sadly lacking in humor. If your mother agrees, I believe an afternoon of charades would be just the thing."

Against her will, Catherine traded a look with Lord Winston and was delighted to find that his eyes twinkled with the same eagerness she felt for the game.

Winston had never enjoyed himself quite so much as he did in this company. Lady Blakemore's inclusion of Mother went far in lessening his concerns about her character. Somehow he would find a way to discover why Father had forbidden her to return to London all those years ago. But that could wait. Today was filled with too many pleasant surprises, and he would not permit any clouds to darken his enjoyment of another afternoon in Miss Hart's company.

With Lady Blakemore now treating her more as a ward or protégée than a companion, he could only surmise that she came from a reputable family. And although the young lady had declined to address him in a more familiar way, he could see from her many friendly smiles that she found his company at least somewhat agreeable. In fact, her humorous rejection of his veiled, and no doubt improper, invitation served as a warning to him not to be as impulsive as Sophia. He had already learned through the examples of others that Society frowned upon anyone failing to give due honor to another person's rank.

After they adjourned from the dining table, Blakemore led the way to the drawing room, with everyone voicing their enthusiasm for the upcoming activity. Like Sophia, Winston had never played charades or any other game. He felt confident, however, that under Miss Hart's tutelage, he could master any such harmless entertainment.

He managed to sit beside her on a settee in the furniture grouping near the hearth—not that he had much competition for that particular spot. Mother and Sophia sat opposite, as they had at dinner, only now Sophia kept grinning and blinking, clearly teasing him. He sent her a menacing glower, which only made her laugh. He could only surmise that his attempts to appear as severe as Father among his peers would be scuttled by his mother and sister.

Once everyone had found a place, Lady Blakemore stood in the center of them all to announce the rules for the game. "First, you must decide upon a word, such as *ball* or *bonnet* or *glove*."

"How like a lady to begin with those suggestions, my dear." Blakemore gave his countess a fond smile. "Now, a gentleman would say *horse* or *hound* or *boot*. Would you not agree, Winston?"

"Um, well—" Winston had no idea how to answer. Without thinking, he questioned Miss Hart with a raised eyebrow. She gave him a noncommittal shrug. As she turned her attention back to the countess, the fragrance of roses wafted from her dark brown hair toward him. His next breath was an entirely agreeable experience.

"My dear." Lady Blakemore glared humorously at her husband. "You have asked me to teach the game to our guests. I beg you, permit me to do so."

Their good-natured teasing refocused Winston's attention. He glanced at Mother, whose pleasant expression held a hint of sadness. Was she thinking of Father? Missing him? Winston had never observed any form of teasing between his parents, nor any affection, at least not on Father's part. His manner toward Mother had been cool and formal. Had it been the vast difference in their ages that had prevented either of them from being happy in their marriage? Or had it been something else?

In that moment, he knew he wanted a marriage exactly like the Blakemores', one in which happiness and good humor abounded. But if a man found fault with his wife, something so dreadful that he could not trust her to go out into Society, how could they be happy together?

He was weary of worrying over Mother's failings. Somehow he must find out what had happened all those years ago so he could avoid marrying someone with the same fault. But he had no idea where to begin.

His gaze turned unwittingly to Miss Hart, and something shifted within his emotions. Was his future already sealed?

Chapter Twelve

Everyone else was enjoying the bantering between the earl and countess, so Catherine could not account for Lord Winston's sudden sobering. Perhaps he had mistaken her shrug as another rebuff. She should have smiled instead of turning away, but it was not too late to make up for it. She tilted her head and sent him a pleasant look. His solemn expression barely lightened, yet his gaze remained on her, as if he were searching for something. She broadened her smile, and at last he returned one that seemed to bespeak more than simply good manners. Was he already falling in love with her? Good. All the better for her plans.

"Yes, yes, my dear." The earl waved a hand at his wife. "Do go on with your instructions, or I shall fall asleep for my Sunday-afternoon nap."

"Gracious me." The countess beckoned to the butler, who stood by the door. "Do bring coffee for his lordship, Chetterly," she chirped in a high, mocking voice. "We must have his participation."

Lady Winston and Miss Beaumont snickered, and Catherine gave herself leave to echo their gaiety. Even the baron chuckled. Poor Chetterly, newly raised from footman to a senior staff position, bustled about serving coffee and tea as if he were serving the Prince Regent.

"Now, where was I?" Lady Blakemore placed a finger against her cheek in a thoughtful pose. "Ah, yes. You must think of a word that you wish the rest of us to guess. Then you must give us clues. Of course, the best clues are given in the form of a poem, but if you have no talent for poetry, you can devise some other method of hinting."

While his mother and sister expressed their delight over the challenge, Lord Winston groaned. "I have already lost the match. When I attempted to write poetry at Eton, my professors wept over the clumsy results."

"Come, come, my boy," Lord Blakemore said. "This is not Eton but a friendly gathering of amateurs. None of us is Shakespeare."

Catherine had played charades at home just last Christmas. The game was a family favorite, and she often won. Should she help Lord Winston or try to best him? Offering to help him might flatter his ego, but her competitive nature would not approve such a plan.

"I agree, Lord Winston." She gave him her sweetest smile. "And remember that the best humor comes by accident. Perhaps your clumsy poetry will give us the most enjoyment."

As she hoped, he sat back and gave her a long glare. "Am I to assume, Miss Hart, that you are challenging me?"

"Do not assume at all, *my lord*." She grinned when he winced comically at her choice of address. "You may take it as a fact."

As the room rang with even more laughter, the earl beckoned to his butler, who seemed unable to keep up with the various beverage choices. "Paper, pens and ink, Chetterly. And bring out a card table so we each have a writing surface."

The beleaguered butler at last strode to the door and summoned footmen to help him. They brought the required supplies, and soon all was in order.

Catherine moved to the collapsible mahogany card table, the sides of which had been raised to accommodate four players. She had taken off her gloves before dining and now saw her mistake. After five days, the bruised lump on her right hand where Lord Winston had struck her during their fencing match was still a little sore and quite visible. She tugged at her sleeve to cover it, then picked up the quill pen with her left hand.

Across from her at the table, the baron watched with concern. "Have you had another encounter with the countess's cat, Miss Hart?"

"What?" Lady Blakemore approached the table and took the injured appendage in hand to inspect it. "I have no cat. My dear, whatever happened? This looks more like the result of a blow. Did you strike your hand?"

"You have no cat?" Lord Winston's eyes narrowed. "Then how were you injured?"

"Well, you see…" Catherine swallowed hard. She was not accustomed to lying, in fact, despised lies. "You and I had just met at the ball when you inquired about my injured hand. I was embarrassed by my clumsiness while simply walking through a door earlier in the day, so I asked if you liked cats and let you assume…" No need to force a blush this time. She could feel the heat rising in her cheeks. But she refused to feel guilty for her dissembling. Was this any worse than Lady Blakemore's clever deflection of Miss Beaumont's error in front of the church?

On either side of Catherine, Miss Beaumont and Lady Winston studied the bruise and cooed their sympathy.

"Poor dear." Lady Blakemore gently set Catherine's hand back on the table. "How fortunate that you are ambidextrous and can write with your left hand as well as your right."

"And eat with it, too." Plump Lord Blakemore, who always enjoyed a hearty meal, chimed in from his desk across the room. "Now, may we get on with our charades? I need silence if I am to compose an interesting rhyme."

With everyone back at their tasks, Catherine took a few moments to gather her wits. She could feel Lord Winston's stare boring into the top of her head as she bent over her page. If he determined that she was the "youth" who had fenced with him only last week, that he himself was the one who had wounded her, what would he do? Feel guilty for hurting her or expose her? Oh, if only Mr. Radcliff were here to advise her.

"I am all astonishment, Miss Hart," he whispered. She looked up sharply to see his gray-green eyes exuding kindness and sympathy. "All this time, you have borne your pain without complaint. How fortunate that you are ambidextrous. One rarely meets a person who possesses such a talent. You never cease to surprise me."

The relief flooding through Catherine's entire body brought tears to her eyes and made her knees go weak. Had she been standing, she surely would have fallen to the floor.

Winston tried to resume his awkward attempts at poetry but could not concentrate. He thought of the many times over these past few days of their acquaintance when he had taken Miss Hart's hand or she had rested it upon his arm, and all without a word of complaint from her. Poor lady! He should have inquired about it. Another failure on his part, so he could easily forgive her for misleading him regarding the nature of her injury. After all, they had just met and neither of them had had any idea they would become friends. Indeed, he'd had some mild hopes of it, should her pedigree prove acceptable, yet now their friendship had exceeded every expectation.

How curious that within the space of a week, he should encounter two of the rare people who could use both hands with equal skill. Over these past days, he had not thought much about the youth he had fenced with at Monsieur Angelus's academy, for all of his contemplations had been taken up with the young lady now seated across from him. Nor had he thought to inquire of the fencing master about the boy's identity. When he returned for practice this next week, he must find out who he was. Perhaps he could befriend him, for the lad seemed unconnected to anyone there that day.

"Have you completed your poem, Lord Winston?" Miss Hart bent forward to examine his page, which contained very few words.

Nevertheless, he quickly covered it. "Now, now. No cheating."

Beside him, Sophia giggled and also leaned over to try to read his poor attempts. "Shall I help you, James?"

He shielded the page with his shoulder. "Ha. What help would you be, infant? I want to win the game."

"Ha, yourself." Smirking, she tucked a loose curl behind her ear, looking at once like a child and a lady. "You are a novice, the same as I."

Winston caught the bemused look in Miss Hart's face as she watched their playful argument. "Do you have a bothersome younger sister, Miss Hart? Perhaps a brother who bedevils you when you are trying to concentrate on creating a literary masterpiece?"

Her lips parted, as if she would answer, but then she clamped her mouth shut. After a moment, she said, "I believe your constant chattering is bothersome enough to hamper my creativity." Staring decisively down at her page, she began to write again.

Although she was the one who had broken their silence, he chuckled at her spirited response, even as he noticed how she had avoided answering his question. Did she have something to hide? Or was he merely suspicious because of his doubts about Mother? In both cases, he would have to tread carefully as he sought the answers, or he would risk losing the regard of the mother he dutifully loved and the mysterious lady who was rapidly capturing more and more of his heart.

Catherine willed her hand to stop shaking as she continued to write her verses, scratching out entire lines as better ones came to mind. Impulsively, she had chosen *lies* as her word to be guessed, and now all of the hints she devised came dangerously close to revealing her mission to expose the baron as a liar.

When he'd asked whether she had a sister or brother, she'd been caught off guard and almost said yes. That would have led to more questions, and all would be lost. Her quick response proved that dissembling was growing much too easy for her. Yet the spiritual convictions she had possessed since childhood seemed to fade in the light of Lord Winston's crime against Papa. How she wished she could talk with Mr. Radcliff. He would help her reason it out.

"Are we ready?" Lord Blakemore stood from his desk and beckoned them all back to the grouping of chairs and settees.

Far from finished, Catherine had no choice but to join the others. This exercise would require more misleading statements, but at least it was a game, not a gentleman's very life.

The earl first called upon his countess, and she took her place before the large white marble hearth with all the elegance and grace of an actress portraying Queen Gertrude in *Hamlet*.

"Ahem," she began in a high-pitched voice, and everyone laughed. Lady Blakemore had never before revealed this playful side.

Catherine loved her all the more for it. Would the countess despise her once the truth was out?

"'If I should bay at the moon some bright midnight in June,'" the lady read from her page, "'would you bring me a bone so I will not be alone?'"

"Oh, come now, Grace," Lord Blakemore scolded merrily. "You have always bested me at charades, but that is far too easy." He glanced around the group. "Surely you all know the answer. Winston?"

The baron gave the countess an apologetic shrug. "Madam, I do believe you have borrowed from your husband's list and have chosen *hound*."

"Of course she did, James." Lady Winston, so pretty despite her black mourning gown, nodded approvingly at Lady Blakemore. "As hostess, she has generously given you and Sophia an easy example so you can learn to play the game."

"Ah. I see." Lord Winston's face brightened with appreciation. "I thank you, Lady Blakemore. I can see I labored too strenuously in my attempt to be clever." He crumpled his page and crammed it into his pocket.

"Really, sir." Catherine sniffed her disdain. "Giving up already?"

"I bow to your superior wit, Miss Hart." He dipped his head accordingly. "Oh, wait. You have not yet regaled us with your verse. Perhaps it will leave something to be de-

sired, and I shall win the challenge after all." He retrieved
the paper ball from his pocket.

Lord Blakemore had not ceased his chuckling, but
somehow managed to say, "Ladies must go first, Winston. 'Tis your turn, Miss Hart."

Her stomach churning, Catherine took her place. Why
had she been so foolish as to engage in this competition?
The answer was clear. The joys of her childhood had not
entirely left her. She loved parlor games, loved the company of good friends with whom she could be merry. But
all merriment had ceased the day Lord Winston destroyed
Papa. Now she would bolster her courage by taunting him,
and he would not even comprehend her meaning. Although
the poem was incomplete, she had no doubt she could
come up with a clever finish. With a flourish, she lifted
her page before her and read what she had written.

"'One day I sat at ease, doing what I pleased. I saw a
happy lord, and being somewhat bored, I thought to make
him sad, make others think him bad. Proceeding to devise a vicious web of lies, I—'" Catherine faltered. She
had not meant to say *lies*. Now the rhyme was ruined because she had no sensible answer to it. A verse she had
once used at home came to mind, and she quickly substi-
tuted it. "'I slandered his good wife's name, his jealousy
did inflame. And now in death they sleep, while all their
loved ones weep.'"

"Ha! This one is too easy, as well." Lord Blakemore
looked around the room. "But I shall let someone else answer. Miss Beaumont?"

"Not I, sir." She shook her head, and her thick blond
curls bounced. "I have no idea at all."

"Hmm." Lord Winston frowned thoughtfully, but his
lips twitched, as if he were trying not to laugh. "Such a
mystery, Miss Hart. At first I thought you were referring

to Don John in *Much Ado About Nothing,* since you and I discussed that play just yesterday. But of course that play is a comedy and the lovers do not die. Therefore it must be Iago, for his lies cause Othello to murder Desdemona and commit suicide." He gave her a triumphant smirk.

"Alas, you have found me out, sir." She gave a dramatic sigh and emphasized it with a hand to her forehead. With a curtsy to them all, she took her seat. "Now do tell us yours."

"Yes, but you see, that is just the thing." He once again crammed the ruined page into his pocket. "I could not find such clever rhymes. Like Benedick, I was not born under a rhyming planet."

"Ho, ho, my boy," the earl cried. "Doesn't that quote come from the scene in which Benedick struggles to write a love poem to Beatrice? Precisely what were you trying to say? And to whom? Perhaps I can complete the rhyme for you."

Lord Winston's face reddened as the others joined in teasing him.

Catherine merely smiled. In spite of her many missteps, the baron was falling in love with her. Now all she had to do was trick him into admitting the truth about his evil schemes against Papa.

Chapter Thirteen

Catherine had not expected Lord Winston to come calling every day, but when he did not visit early in the week, or even on Wednesday when Parliament did not assemble, she began to doubt his interest. Nor had she been able to speak with Mr. Radcliff, for Lord Blakemore kept his secretary very busy these days. How could her plans go forward if the gentleman in question had not fallen in love with her after all?

On Thursday, Lady Blakemore summoned Catherine. "Fetch your bonnet, my dear. We shall visit Lady Winston."

"Yes, my lady." Catherine's heart lifted as she hastened to obey.

Perhaps the baron would be at home, as well. Even if he was not, his mother and sister would surely report that she had been there. That should garner some attention from him. Catherine's only concern about the visit was for the dowager baroness and her daughter. She could not deliberately cause either of them pain, any more than she could hurt her own loved ones.

The carriage rolled up in front of Lord Winston's Grosvenor Square town house, and Catherine's pulse began to race. She could only attribute it to her longing, no, her *interest,* in seeing the baron.

These past nights as she had struggled to find sleep, she could see his winsome smile, his gray-green eyes bright with interest in *her,* his anxious attempts to learn how to laugh. Her heart warmed as she recalled the delightful way he teased his sister, just as she teased back and forth with Lucien and Isabella. And she admired his nose, of all things, narrow at the bridge, and in profile an attractive triangular shape that seemed to point him toward a promising future.

But sleep would not come until she reminded herself that his ambitions for his own career had destroyed the prospects of her brother and sister. When a gentleman like Papa was ruined, his entire family suffered ruin with him. With Napoleon defeated, Papa might have gone to Paris with King Louis to become a part of the new French government. Or if he preferred to stay in England with Mama's people, he could continue his good work in managing her Norfolk estate, where everyone who lived nearby loved him. Lord Winston had also destroyed all of those possibilities.

While the brownish-gray brick exterior of the baron's town house looked much the same as the others in Grosvenor Square, its austere interior lacked the interesting furnishings that would make it homier or a place where one would wish to entertain. But then, Catherine supposed he was far too busy ruining other people's lives to attend to such matters.

"Lady Blakemore, Miss Hart, I do hope you will forgive my son's inattention to his home." Lady Winston seemed to be reading Catherine's mind after she joined them in the large drawing room. "The late Lord Winston did not care for what he called 'fripperies' when it came to furnishing this house. And of course, it has not been lived in for six years. James has been here only since January, so he has not had time to make improvements, only repairs." She laughed in her musical way. "And of course, the poor dear would have no idea how to decorate."

"Gracious, no, Mama." Miss Beaumont flounced into a brown leather chair beside its mate, where Catherine sat. "He would doubtless turn it into a somber replica of the House of Lords. Or a stable."

Catherine laughed with the others, but she also felt a surprising twinge of sympathy for the baron. She had been employed by the Blakemores long enough to know that entertaining the right people was an important part of any gentleman's political career. Lord Winston needed a wife to take charge of this house and make it more presentable. If it were hers to decorate, she would know exactly what to do. She would begin right here in this plainly furnished drawing room, re-covering these sturdy chairs in a floral brocade and exchanging those dark brown velvet drapes over the tall front windows with something bright and airy.

What was she thinking? This would never be her home. Furthermore, she scolded herself, Lady Winston could no doubt manage quite nicely when it came to making improvements for her son.

As all the usual niceties were spoken among them, Catherine noticed the formal way in which the baroness spoke of her late husband. Nor did any sadness dim her bright blue eyes as she mentioned him. One would almost think she was speaking of some ancient English lord or king rather than the father of her children. How different from the warmth Catherine had noticed between her parents and between Lord and Lady Blakemore.

Lady Winston had put off the black mourning gown she wore on Sunday in favor of a gray silk dress with black piping around the long sleeves and high neckline. Even in gray, her complexion glowed with a warmer, healthier tone, and Catherine imagined she would look quite lovely in brighter colors.

The butler brought an unadorned black china tea set, and the baroness supervised while Miss Beaumont served, making sure each of their guests had a beverage to her liking.

"I have not yet decided whether Sophia should make her debut this Season." Lady Winston addressed Lady Blakemore, but she also included Catherine with a glance. "What would you advise?"

Catherine had hoped the topic would not come up, for she still felt uncertain about her own place in Lady Blakemore's regard. But after their shared merriment with these ladies last Sunday afternoon, how could she claim that shyness prevented her from being launched into Society? She should have thought of that when she so heartily took part in the games and teasing. How difficult it was to remember all the lies and misinformation and how they might affect upcoming situations.

For once, Miss Beaumont did not interject her own thoughts in answer to her mother's question. Instead, she sat forward in her chair and looked anxiously between Catherine and Lady Blakemore as if her entire success in Society depended upon their responses. That desperation suggested to Catherine that the girl was too young, but she would never say so.

"My dear," the countess said to the young lady, "Her Majesty will not have another Drawing Room this Season, and it is important for young ladies to be presented to her before they make their debuts. Otherwise, no one of importance will consider them officially *out*."

A pout formed on Miss Beaumont's plump lips, but she

quickly and admirably forced a smile. "Yes, of course. I have often thought what an honor it will be to meet the queen when my turn comes."

Lady Winston's eyes misted, and she gazed off across the room. "Indeed, it is an honor. When I was presented at court twenty-five years ago, His Majesty had not yet become ill, so he attended the ceremony, as well." Her voice broke slightly on her last words.

"Ah, yes." Lady Blakemore seemed caught up in the same sort of wistful memory, for she too grew pensive.

Catherine could not speak for the lump in her throat. When King George had been in his right mind, he had been a fine monarch and more than welcoming to émigrés like Papa during the French Reign of Terror. Now that his son, the Prince Regent, ruled in his place, it seemed to give wicked men like Lord Winston license to do as they pleased.

"What is this?" The baron appeared at the door and strode across the room. "Four ladies in my drawing room, and not a sound of chattering to be heard." His gaze landed upon Catherine and intensified, as if he had found a lost treasure.

While the other ladies laughed at his comment, her heart seemed to jump into her throat. She struggled to subdue her giddy emotions, for she must not forget that this man was her enemy. Forcing other thoughts to the forefront of her mind, she was pleased with his timely entrance. Now she need not worry that the subject of debuts would be renewed. And from the way he looked at her, she could see that her other worries had been ill-founded. The baron was smitten, and she would find a way to use his regard to her advantage.

Even as she thought it, a sad chord reverberated within her. How she wished she could be free to return that regard. How she wished that he actually *was* the good man that he seemed to be instead of a wicked, scheming liar.

The instant he saw Miss Hart, Winston's pulse began to race. At first, she appeared pleased to see him as well, but then she frowned and looked away. If she did care for him, no doubt she had been taught to hide her feelings until he declared himself. Despite his growing feelings for her, he was certainly not prepared to do that, not after knowing her for just over a week. Still, not seeing her for these past few days had been difficult while he worked on his secret projects, which he hoped would delight her. Now that they were completed, he had left the Lords' Chamber early today planning to put on a fresh suit and visit her at Blakemore House. But here she was in his own drawing room. What a pleasant surprise—no, an absolute delight— to find her here.

He bowed over Lady Blakemore's hand first, then her fair companion's.

"How is your wound, Miss Hart?" He would not neglect to inquire about it until it was entirely healed.

"I thank you, sir, it is well. I am able to wield this spoon without difficulty." She retrieved her hand from his grasp and lifted the implement from her teacup, giving him her most charming smirk. "And my pen."

"Ah, very good. I look forward to another of your delightful poems." He hoped his tone held exactly the right degree of gentle sarcasm. If the young lady's laughter was any indication, he had succeeded. Greeting Mother and Sophia, he then chose a chair beside Miss Hart. "I see that all of you have had your tea."

"Another cup, Llewellyn." Mother signaled the butler with a wave.

These past few days, Winston had noticed how readily the old man took orders from her, far more quickly than he did for Winston. After Father's death, Llewellyn had been a rock for them all in managing many important details. Winston had hoped he would prove helpful in restoring this town house. But the butler seemed to passively begrudge him his service. Since Mother's arrival, his attitude had improved, but only for her. The situation confounded Winston.

"My darling James." Mother interrupted his thoughts. "What has brought you home so early in the day? Should you not be in the Lords' Chamber reviewing some important law that Commons wants to pass?"

All of the ladies focused their attention on him, and he tugged at his suddenly tight cravat. Just as her question suggested, he had deserted his post. Father had never missed a single hour of a single session during his long tenure as Lord Winston—that is, until his final illness. The urge to acquit himself proved too strong, for he would not wish for Miss Hart to find him negligent in his duties.

"You have found me out, madam. I stole away in the midst of yet another round of arguments against Wilberforce's proposed law to protect younger climbing boys. When the vote comes up, I am for it, of course, but I do not believe we have much hope for its passing."

"Such a shame," Lady Blakemore said. "At Blakemore House, I absolutely refuse to let the smaller boys climb into those narrow spaces, no matter how much the chimney requires cleaning. That is what those circular brooms are for."

Winston had not meant to start a discussion on the topic, but the countess and Mother began to bemoan the general ill-treatment of small children of the lower classes, with each giving examples of some tragedy or another.

While they chattered away, Winston focused on the young lady who sat primly by his side.

"Miss Hart," he said softly, "I have two surprises for you, and I hoped we might take a carriage ride this afternoon so that I can reveal them."

"Surprises?" She tilted her head in her charming way. "What—"

"Oh, yes, do take us out, James." Sophia clapped her hands and bounced in her chair. "I have been wondering if you intended to make Mama and me prisoners in this gloomy house. Oh!" She slapped a hand over her lips. "I mean, oh, it is a very nice house, but—"

The other ladies appeared to struggle against laughing, and Winston could only be grateful for their generosity. Once again, Lady Blakemore declined to give his impulsive sister a set down.

"I have no idea what you mean, imp." He could not resist teasing her. "Why would anyone call this house gloomy when you are here?"

His sister rewarded him with a giggle.

"A carriage ride will be lovely." Miss Hart gave him a beguiling smile. "As will surprises," she whispered.

"Shall we all go?" Mother spoke lightly, but her eyes implored him with the same fervor as Sophia's.

At once he knew his fault. He had neglected the poor dears in favor of his secret projects, and now he must make amends. "If Lady Blakemore is willing, I should be honored to escort all of you to Green Park, where we can partake of the refreshment sold by the famous milkmaids."

"I would be delighted." With the countess's approval, the expedition was launched.

While Winston quickly changed clothes and ordered his new landau brought around from the mews, the ladies saw to their bonnets, spencers, parasols and gloves. They filed out through the front door and were met by a brilliant sun that seemed to add its approval of their plans. As he had arranged, Winston signaled the footman not to open the carriage door.

"Why, Lord Winston." Miss Hart hurried to the landau and reached out to touch the new decoration. "You have added your family crest. How beautiful. This *is* a lovely surprise." She traced the red griffin and green laurel wreath resting on the shiny black shield. "'*Confortare, Integritatem et Victoria,*'" She read his family motto emblazoned in gold across the top. "Courage, integrity and victory."

Her sidelong glance and approving smile caused a minor disturbance in the vicinity of his heart. He quickly cleared his throat.

"I would not have thought of it without your suggestion." The crest would do for now, but he would wait until they were alone to give her his other surprise.

"Exactly like the crests on the old Winston carriages," Mother said, while Sophia proclaimed the work exquisite.

"Winston, it is no small thing to proudly display such an historic emblem," Lady Blakemore said. "Your crest goes far back in English history, and no taint has ever been attached to your family's name."

He bowed in her direction, more to hide the foolish pride that must show on his face than to thank her. Yet he had done nothing admirable to deserve such praise other than to be born. "I thank you all. Now, shall we go?" He spied the Blakemore carriage and had a thought to prolong his time with Miss Hart. "Lady Blakemore, since we may be out for some time, may I suggest that you dismiss your driver? I shall see you and Miss Hart safely home."

To his delight, the countess gave her consent to the idea. The ladies looked to him to designate their places, and of course he invited the countess and Mother to take the seat of honor facing front. Without being told, Sophia wedged in between the two ladies, leaving Miss Hart to sit beside Winston. Her charming blush, accompanied by a slight smile, revealed that she did not object to the arrangement.

Toby clucked to the horses and slapped the reins on their haunches, and the excursion began. Straightaway, Winston's heart lightened. Perhaps this would be just as enjoyable as entertaining Miss Hart alone, for now he felt almost at a loss for words regarding his other surprise.

The trip to Green Park would take at least a half hour due to the many turns and heavy traffic so characteristic of midafternoon. They passed several other lords who, like Winston, should have been in their seats in the Lords' Chamber but were taking advantage of the sunny day.

"I say, Winston," a gentleman called out from a passing barouche. "May I have a moment?" He ordered his driver to stop.

Winston had no choice but to tell Toby to pull to the side of broad Regent Street so they would not block traffic. But when he saw who had hailed him, his stomach turned. This was the man about whom Edgar had warned him. He glanced at Mother, but her openly curious expression showed neither alarm nor recognition.

"Morgan." Tipping his hat, he stood up in the carriage, only now spying a disreputable-looking young woman beside the viscount. Instantly, he regretted stopping. "How may I be of service?"

The gray-haired rake laughed. "Why, can you not guess, sir? Must I beg for an introduction to these charming young ladies crowding your carriage? I have plenty of room in mine if you would like to share."

"Indeed he may *not* be introduced!" Lady Blakemore

barked with uncharacteristic hauteur. "Away, Toby!" She waved her hand impatiently at Winston's driver.

Toby cast a questioning glance at Winston, who nodded first to him and then to Morgan.

"Good afternoon, sir." Winston replaced his hat and sat down, trying as he did to shield Miss Hart from Morgan's view as Lady Blakemore was shielding Sophia.

As their carriages rolled in opposite directions, Morgan merely laughed and said none too softly that old crones should not be ruling England.

"Gracious, can you imagine the nerve?" The countess fanned herself furiously. "A rake like that daring to ask for introductions to decent Christian ladies."

Mother and Sophia looked at her with identical and supremely innocent expressions.

"Oh, my." Mother gripped Sophia's hand. "We are so grateful for your intervention, Lady Blakemore." She looked at Winston. "Of course, I know you would not have introduced us, James."

"No, of course not." Winston studied her beautiful, beloved face and could detect no guilt, no deception there. What had Edgar meant in his note warning him not to permit Mother to become *re*acquainted with Morgan?

Chapter Fourteen

"This milk is supremely delicious." Miss Beaumont dabbed her lips with a serviette. "I should like more, but two cups have entirely filled me."

Catherine managed to drink only one cup of the rich, creamy beverage, but it was so tasty that she must remember one day to bring Lucien and Isabella here to partake of the treat. That day seemed closer now that she was more certain of Lord Winston's regard.

He stood slightly apart from the ladies and leaned against an oak tree enjoying his drink. When he noticed Catherine looking his way, he smiled and lifted his cup in a salute. A thin white mustache coated his upper lip, enhancing his youthful appearance, and Catherine's heart skipped. If he were closer, she would be tempted to dab it away. In any other circumstances, she would willingly surrender to the warm affection trying to grow within her, especially when he looked at her in that charming manner. Nor could she discount the way he had gallantly postured his broad shoulders to protect her from that horrid Lord Morgan's improper stare. Such a simple gesture, but one that had made her feel valued and protected. Always, always, she must remind herself of his crime against Papa.

The baron had mentioned another surprise, yet seemed to have forgotten it. Curiosity almost got the better of her. What would they all think if she imitated Miss Beaumont and skipped over to his side to beg him to reveal his next scheme? Of course, she would not, and yet the impulse tormented her. Mr. Radcliff would advise patience, so she calmed herself with the knowledge that soon she would achieve her purpose.

"You must visit us, Lady Winston." With a glance at Catherine, Lady Blakemore seemed to include her in the "us" of her invitation, a more frequent and puzzling mode of reference. Was the countess merely continuing to cover Miss Beaumont's erroneous assumption regarding Catherine's position? That hardly seemed likely, for rank and position were of supreme importance to both Lord and Lady Blakemore. Every time she found the courage to ask about it, however, someone or something interrupted her.

"I would be delighted beyond words." Lady Winston's radiant countenance reinforced her assertion. "I have been away from Society for a very long time, and I fear everyone I knew has forgotten me. With your friendship, perhaps that can be overcome."

"But, my dear, why did you not accompany your late husband for the Season all those years before he took ill?" Lady Blakemore asked the question Catherine had thought too improper to pose.

"Shall we go?" Lord Winston strode across the space from the tree to the landau, his milky mustache gone and his blond eyebrows bent in a dark frown. "I'll warrant that you ladies have had enough of this heat."

Had he meant to interrupt and keep his mother from answering? How very odd. Even Lady Blakemore gaped at him briefly, yet offered no rebuke.

Despite that awkward moment, the drive home was

pleasant enough, with Miss Beaumont entertaining them all with an unending stream of questions. How often did they see the Prince Regent? Did he attend all the balls? What was that thick redbrick building over there? Did they call their homes "town houses" because that was where everyone lived when they were in town? Catherine could not fault the girl for her enthusiasm, for she herself had once been excited about the prospect of coming to London. Yet when she had come, the gravity of her mission weighed too heavily upon her for her to enjoy much of anything.

"James, do take Sophia and me to your house before going to Lady Blakemore's." The baroness gave her son a sublime smile that seemed to say more than her words.

"But, Mama, I want to see Blakemore House." Once again Miss Beaumont's boldness proved she was unprepared to be out in Society, at least to Catherine's way of thinking. But if the other ladies agreed, they did not say so.

"Not today, my dear. We must not overdo." Lady Winston's gently spoken words nonetheless held sufficient authority that her daughter did not argue *or* pout.

Catherine hoped she would remember that exact tone to use with her own children, should she be so blessed to have some one day.

"Take us home, Toby." Winston could have kissed Mother for her clever manipulation of the situation. Sweet Sophia never knew when to stop chattering, and he was eager to reveal his other secret to Miss Hart without his sister's interference.

Once his family had been delivered to the town house, proper adieus had been said and the remainder of the party was on its way to Blakemore House, he could not keep from sighing rather more loudly than he had intended.

"Now, now, Winston." Lady Blakemore laughed. "Your

sister is delightful. Do not begrudge her that youthful enthusiasm."

"You are too kind, madam."

This was the perfect opportunity to ask Miss Hart again whether she had a younger sister or brother. If so, perhaps she would commiserate with him, which would advance their friendship. And of course, he would learn something more about her. Yet in light of his next surprise for her, he would postpone such questions, for it might reveal much about her family.

In the hope that Lady Blakemore would invite him in, he reached beneath his leather seat as stealthily as he could, retrieved a package and hid it in the inside pocket of his jacket. Neither lady appeared to notice, for they did not question him.

"Of course, you must come in for tea." Lady Blakemore did not disappoint him or give him the opportunity to decline. Once he handed them down from the carriage, she looped an arm around his and urged him toward the front door.

He glanced over his shoulder at Miss Hart, whose bright eyes and smile seemed to indicate she had not yet tired of his company, either. Last week, when he had taken her for their first and very eventful drive, he had been concerned about Society's view of the length of their outing. Today, Lady Blakemore's insistence on his staying was sufficient approval to cast aside his worries.

Before they even took their seats in the drawing room, Lady Blakemore announced that she required a lie down if she was to manage attending a party with Lord Blakemore that evening. Catherine bit back a protest that no such party was written on the countess's schedule. If her employer wanted to play matchmaker, that would work right into Catherine's plans.

"Do not think you must leave, Winston." Lady Blakemore gave his shoulder a maternal pat as she passed him. "The footman is here by the door, so all will be proper for you and Miss Hart to enjoy a nice chat." Without giving him a chance to respond, she swept out of the room with more energy than one would expect from a lady requiring a lie down.

Lord Winston's well-formed face creased with concern. "I do hope Lady Blakemore is well."

"Perhaps she merely wants to avoid overdoing." Catherine sat down and waved him to a chair several yards away.

After a moment of hesitation, he chose a closer one. Catherine's foolish heart skipped a beat as the scent of his bay-rum cologne reached her. Its heady fragrance had teased her the entire afternoon, and now there was no breeze to alleviate its pleasing effects. If she were free to love him, if he were truly the gentleman he presented to the world, his always-pleasant scent would be an important factor in winning her favor.

"I must admit I'm happy to have a moment of your time." He reached into his black suit jacket and retrieved the brown paper package he had placed there during their carriage ride. How charming he had looked as he tried to keep her from noticing his actions. Surely this was the surprise he had mentioned. Once again her heart skipped.

"I have taken your suggestion and purchased this book." He removed the twine and paper to reveal a brown leather copy of *Sense and Sensibility.*

"Oh, my." Catherine jolted at the revelation. She had not expected him to remember the book or to care in the slightest that she had advised him to read novels. "This is indeed a surprise, Lord Winston."

A rather foolish grin spread over his face, like a child who had pleased his tutor. No, rather like a gentleman who had pleased his lady. And indeed, she *was* pleased.

"I sent for it this past Monday and have been reading it ever since." He shrugged in a charming way. "I even read it while in my seat in the Lords' Chamber when the opposition grew tiresome in their rants."

"You did not." Catherine leaned back in her chair and laughed heartily at his confession. "Not in front of your fellow lords."

"Oh, but I did." Now he smirked. "And you would be surprised at how many peers noticed and told me that they had read this book and others written by the same author." Another shrug. "Of course, they are convinced that only a gentleman of great intelligence and education could have written them."

"Tsk." Catherine shook her head in annoyance. "Do you agree with them?"

"Not at all. I find that ladies are not only witty and insightful but entirely much better company all around." He sat back, a slight smile on his finely sculpted lips. One would have to be blind not to notice the esteem in his gentle gaze.

Catherine swallowed hard, trying without success not to welcome his kind regard. She could not help but enjoy his admiration, but she must not return it. "W-well, then, what did you think of the story?"

If he noticed her stammer, he was too much the gentleman to say so. "Brilliant. Entirely enjoyable. And, as you said last Wednesday, filled with insights into human nature."

For a moment she could not speak. No gentleman, not even Papa, had ever valued her thoughts or recommendations to this degree. "Please, go on."

"Very well." He sat forward and opened the book. "Where shall I begin?"

Only then did Catherine notice slips of paper sticking out from the pages. He had actually bookmarked it. Once again, her traitorous heart beat faster.

"Hmm." She scrambled to think of a question that would reward his good opinion of her intellect. "Where indeed? If we are examining human nature, then we must discuss the characters. Which one do you find the most interesting?"

"I had not thought to mark any one of them over the others. Rather, they are altogether a finely woven garment." A shadow crossed his eyes. "However, I would say that Marianne, with all of her impulsiveness, troubles me. I see my dear, innocent Sophia in her and worry that my sister will likewise fall for some man's flattering attentions. As for Willoughby, he is an utter scoundrel. Should any man treat Sophia thusly, I would thoroughly thrash him."

"But you will never permit that to happen." She pictured him, sword in hand, its exposed tip pointed at some hapless suitor's chest. "You will protect her just as you shielded me from Lord Morgan's view this afternoon." Her heart warmed at the memory, and she could not manage to cool it, not while sudden hot tears of gratitude spilled down her cheeks.

"My dear Miss Hart." He set the book on an occasional table, moved to the chair beside her, took her hand and brushed his thumb across her damp face. "It was my privilege and honor to shield you." His green eyes shone with an ardor she had never imagined she would receive even in her most sublime girlhood dreams. Then his gaze moved to her lips.

Her heart raced madly. Would he kiss her? Most irrationally, she wished he would.

The footman cleared his throat, the sound of it holding a slightly menacing hum.

Lord Winston blinked, grinned sheepishly and sat back in his chair. "There is another matter in the book that disturbed me." He spoke lightly, as if they had not just been rescued from a terrible impropriety.

As guilty as he in the matter, Catherine inhaled deeply to recover herself. "And that is?" The words came out on a breathy sigh, and heat rushed to her cheeks.

This time, Lord Winston had the grace to ignore her discomfiture. "I cannot think well of Edward Ferrars because of his secret engagement. He was living a lie, which no gentleman should ever do if he expects to be highly regarded. I simply cannot tolerate a liar."

As if cold water had been dashed in her face, Catherine's mind and emotions cleared, and her giddy, girlish sensibilities yielded to good sense. "Neither can I tolerate a liar." She stood and strode away from him by several paces, then spun back to face him. "No matter how he justifies himself, such a man deserves no sympathy or happiness." If she sounded as strident to him as she did to herself, he would simply have to cope with it.

Ever the gentleman, he jumped to his feet. "Clearly you no longer speak of our book, Miss Hart. I am grieved to think that anyone has lied to you and caused you harm." He lifted one hand in an invitation for her to return to her chair. "I would gladly hear your story."

She could only turn away and clench her jaw. If she confronted him now, unprepared and with heightened emotions, she might ruin every possibility that Papa's reputation could be restored.

Lord Winston sighed softly. "Perhaps you could confide in Mr. Grenville. He is a true man of God. I must warn you, though, that for your own sake, he will advise forgiveness, whatever the circumstances."

Without responding, Catherine forced herself to move back across the room and reclaim her chair.

"Dear lady, I fear I have tired you. We can return to our discussion of *Sense and Sensibility* at another time." This time, the tenderness in his gaze failed to breach the stone wall now surrounding her heart, even when he gave her a teasing grin that enhanced his boyish appeal. "But I must tell you that Sophia has been begging to read the book, so we may have to include her in the conversation." He gave her hand a gentle squeeze. "Do promise me you will speak with Mr. Grenville."

"Perhaps that would be wise." It was also the last thing she would consider doing.

All the way home, Winston tried to reason out what had happened in his conversation with Miss Hart. Once again he had failed to win her trust. Once again she refused to confide in him. What could have happened to fill her with such anger? Or had she been so mortified over their almost kiss that she now would feel uncomfortable in his presence? He certainly felt a large measure of shame for it.

Thank the Lord for the footman. He was an older man, bewigged and liveried, who doubtless felt a fatherly concern for the young lady. Winston would have to make certain every servant in his own house watched over Sophia with the same care.

Arriving at home to find two grand carriages in front of his town house, he exhaled a sigh of frustration as he stepped down from his own. The unfortunate end to his visit with Miss Hart made him consider whether he had chosen the wrong way to spend the afternoon. One of the conveyances belonged to Blakemore, who would laugh away any such concerns. But the other much grander landau bore the crest of Lord Bennington, another very important earl whose favor Winston had long sought. That gentleman would surely be displeased over having to wait for him to return home.

Llewellyn met him at the door and took his hat, gloves and cane. "Lords Bennington and Blakemore are in the drawing room with Lady Winston, my lord."

His cold tone echoed with a rebuke that raked over Winston's nerves. He would have to resolve things with the butler soon. For now he settled for returning ice for ice and gave the man no answer as he strode to the drawing room to meet his guests. He first saw Bennington, whose cross, almost surly countenance reminded him of Father.

Then Blakemore bustled toward him. "Ah, there you are, my boy." The earl shook his hand as if welcoming him into his own abode. "Your charming mother has been entertaining us while we waited. Where have you been? We have news, great news, my boy."

Chapter Fifteen

"Did you have a pleasant visit with Winston, my dear?" Lady Blakemore sailed back into the drawing room not thirty seconds after the baron departed. Had she been waiting outside to pounce upon Catherine the instant he left?

Still seated where he left her, her face continuing to burn with anger over his hypocritical pronouncement about not tolerating liars, she nonetheless managed to give the countess a wavering smile. "Why, yes. Quite pleasant."

"He is an engaging young gentleman, do you not agree?" The countess took the chair he had recently vacated. "With such a promising future."

"How fortunate for him."

"Hmm." Lady Blakemore eyed her quizzically, and then her eyes narrowed. "My dear, I do believe it is time for you to have a lady's maid of your own instead of borrowing mine all the time."

Catherine gasped. "My own lady's maid? But madam, I am only your companion." Never mind that she had a lady's maid at home in Norfolk. Poor Abigail would be deeply hurt if anyone else attended her. She had, in fact, begged to accompany Catherine to London. Of course, that would have ruined all of Catherine's plans, for the girl chattered as much as Miss Beaumont and would surely have betrayed her identity. "I could never manage such an expenditure."

"That will be my responsibility." Lady Blakemore stood and started toward the door. "If you are to continue accompanying me out in Society, you must look your best." She paused at the door. "I do not mean to say your appearance has disappointed me, only that you would do well to have some finer clothes and a few more adornments. And your lovely hair should be coiffed by someone with skill. I shall begin the search early tomorrow morning. You will have the final say on whom we hire, of course."

Not waiting for a reply, she walked out the door, leaving Catherine to wonder why the countess would be so extravagant on her account.

"Oh, James, I am so proud of you." Mother crossed the drawing room to embrace Winston. "You continue to honor your family name." She laughed. Giggled, actually. "Though that name will soon be changed."

Cringing at her girlish glee, he gently removed himself from her grasp. Had she forgotten all her manners? One would think Sophia was speaking, not a mature lady. Yet when he offered an apologetic grimace to the two earls, neither indicated they had noticed anything amiss.

"Now, Lady Winston." Standing beside Winston, Blakemore playfully waggled a finger at Mother. "Do permit me to give the boy our news."

"Of course, sir—" Winston began.

"Indeed not." Bennington strode over to them, his firm gait belying his many years. "I am responsible for this, and I demand the right to tell him." Although he was of medium height, he was almost a head taller than Blakemore, and he bent over him in a domineering pose.

"Well!" Blakemore puffed up to his full short stature. "I have been his mentor and sponsor, and—" He stopped and stared at Winston, his eyes narrowing. "You have no idea what we are going on about, do you?"

"Well, I—" Winston felt as he had under Father's frequent questioning, as if he could do nothing right. But what did these gentlemen expect of him?

"Did you not read those letters I gave you last Saturday?" His tone held all the loftiness of a scolding tutor, although his eyes exuded nothing but merriment.

"Letters?" Winston now cringed at his own failure. In his eagerness to read the novel so that he could discuss it with Miss Hart, he had completely forgotten Blakemore's charge that he should read the letters entrusted to him. Neither had Edgar hinted at their contents, although Winston had no doubt his cousin knew what they said. In fact, since Mother's arrival, Edgar had ceased to visit the town house. "You must forgive me, sir. I put them in a safe place and forgot to read them."

"Forgot?" Blakemore shouted, but his indignation seemed artificial.

"Forgot?" Bennington's growling tone caused the hair on Winston's neck to stand on end.

"Oh, do be quiet, you two old bears." Mother grasped Winston's arm and dragged him toward the nearest settee and sat beside him. "My darling son, these good gentlemen have sponsored a petition to the Prince Regent requesting that you be granted the title your father was unable to claim due to his failing health."

"Indeed we have." Blakemore scurried after them and sat in a facing chair. "The letters I gave you were copies of ours recommending that His Royal Highness elevate you to an earldom."

Clearly not wishing to be left out, Bennington planted

his fists at his waist. "*I* recommended the title Lord Dearbourn."

"Dearbourn?" Winston searched his mind for some connection to the name, but found none.

"'Tis a title from the last century that fell into abeyance," Bennington said. "No taint is attached to it, only glory. The last Lord Dearbourn perished in 1743 at the Battle of Dettingen fighting beside George II…*and* my father." He lifted his chin, and his chest puffed out with pride as though he himself had joined the fray. "Of course, if you prefer another name—"

"Oh, James, I adore the name Dearbourn." Mother fairly bounced on the settee, just as Sophia would. "Do say you will choose it."

Winston sat back and looked around at the others, all of whom stared back at him expectantly. As eager as he was to please them, he could not come up with a single sensible response. "I beg you, do give me some time to consider—"

"Ah, so you do not care for the name." Blakemore cast a triumphant glance at Bennington. "*I* suggested Lord Hartley."

"But who has ever heard of a Lord Hartley?" Bennington pulled out his gold-and-black enamel snuffbox and proceeded to partake of its contents.

While the older gentlemen bickered back and forth, Mother leaned over and whispered, "You will make the wisest decision, my son. I am confident of it."

"I thank you, Mother dear." Suddenly ashamed of the way he had regarded her, he placed a kiss on her unlined cheek and was rewarded with a blush and a smile. "Did you know about this? Is this why you came to London?"

Her lovely face grew pinker. "Yes, I confess it. But Sophia knows nothing about it."

An odd, giddy sensation tickled his insides at the prospect of delivering this remarkable news to his sister. "We shall surprise her at supper tonight." He noticed that the two earls had ceased their quarrel, which clearly held not a whit of enmity. "Gentlemen, I beg you to tell me how this has all come about." In truth, he had planned to wait to petition for the advancement until he felt more worthy. But if they regarded him so highly, how could he refuse the honor?

"We wrote the letters," Bennington said, "and the Prince Regent, remembering your father's service to His Majesty, was more than pleased to order the college of arms to have the patent drawn up."

"Now that His Royal Highness has signed it," Blakemore added, "the official investiture will take place at a levee at St. James's Palace. When you make your first appearance under your new title in the House of Lords, Bennington and I will stand with you, of course, and—"

"And," Bennington hastened to put in, "your only cost will be the levee itself and the new fees for recording the honor in the House of Lords, and of course, you will require new robes."

"And a coronet." Blakemore shot a cross look at the older earl. "And *of course,* Lady Blakemore will insist upon giving a ball in your honor."

"Ah, there you have trumped me, Blakemore." Bennington bowed to his rival. "Lady Bennington no longer entertains."

While the others discussed the elderly countess's health and other matters, Winston battled a flurry of conflicting thoughts. He truly had not expected this elevation, and the news left him stunned. What would Miss Hart think of it? Would she regard his new title as reason enough to confide in him, to trust him as these older, wiser peers did? On the other hand, he must consider whether or not to continue his pursuit of the young lady. An earl must have a wife of the proper pedigree. If Miss Hart was a gentlewoman instead of an aristocrat, some in Society might continue to snub her, even if she became his countess.

Yet if he refused to pursue her simply because of her rank, a lady who was growing dearer to his heart day by day, was he any better than Willoughby, the scoundrel of *Sense and Sensibility,* who chose to wed a wealthy lady for her money instead of the poor lady he loved? Winston could even excuse Willoughby for marrying to secure a substantial living, while he himself had more wealth than any gentleman could spend in a lifetime—wealth enough to bring Society to his door even if he married a gentlewoman.

If only Father were here to advise him so that he did not fail to do the right thing.

"Lord Winston must be very proud of his coming advancement." Catherine had spent the hours before supper in her bedchamber practicing with her sword, and the exercise had done much to control her anger at the baron. Now at the supper table with Lord and Lady Blakemore, she managed to eat her roast duck without being afflicted with indigestion. Not that the fowl lacked flavor, for the earl's cook excelled in his art. But since coming to London, especially since meeting Lord Winston, Catherine's stomach often felt tied in knots.

"I would not say he is proud." Lord Blakemore gazed off thoughtfully. "Humbled is more like it." He frowned briefly, shrugged and plunged his fork into his food. "Not at all like his father."

"Indeed not." Lady Blakemore's tone held a modicum of indignation.

Neither explained further, and Catherine could hardly ask them to. Yet somehow she could not believe their account of the baron's humility, not even with the evidence of her own eyes and experience and heart in agreement. For only a prideful man like the present Lord Winston could deliberately forge letters to destroy a good Christian gentleman like Papa, and she would not rest until she saw him pay for it, no matter what position he attained.

With no little difficulty, she silenced the quiet voice that whispered deep within her, *Lord Winston is an upright gentleman worthy of your highest regard.*

"Oh, James, you look so grand in your father's regalia." Mother fluffed the three-tiered white ermine cape while Winston's valet, Dudley, applied a brush to the red velvet robe.

Still overwhelmed by the good earls' revelation, Winston studied the exquisite garment reflected in the long mirror in his bedchamber. "I thank you for bringing it to London, Mother. When Father ordered this new robe, I doubt he knew he would never wear it."

"No, I do not think so." She shook her head, but did not seem overly sad. "When he accepted His Majesty's offer of advancement, he did not expect to become ill. And of course he would think it foolish of you not to spare yourself the cost of several hundred pounds to purchase another one when this will do quite well."

"Indeed, my lord." Dudley had not ceased to grin since hearing of Winston's upcoming elevation. "No one will ever know that it has been packed away and carefully preserved these past six years. It will do quite nicely for your investiture."

The valet spoke freely, as Winston had always encouraged him to do when they were alone, but Mother's eyes widened briefly as he spoke.

"I thank you, Dudley. What would I ever do without you?" This was their usual signal that the valet could consider himself dismissed.

"Do permit me to tend the robe, my lord." Ever jealous of his duties, he untied the white satin ribbons at the neck and removed it from Winston's shoulders. After carefully draping it over the mahogany valet stand and giving it a final swipe with the brush, he bowed out of the room.

Once he left, Mother walked around the room studying drapes, paintings and furniture. "Goodness, James, this is such a dreary room. You must redecorate."

"Sophia would agree with you." He gestured to a chair and sat beside her. "But if it was good enough for Father, I cannot see the necessity."

"Good enough. Humph." Her hand flew to cover her lips, and she inhaled sharply, as if surprised by her own reaction to his words. Then she bit her lip. "If you wish to economize, I shall not disapprove."

"Nor approve." He gave her a teasing smile that seemed to please her. "I cannot understand why Father did not assign you the task of decorating this entire town house. Is that not the office of a peer's wife? When I marry, I shall certainly permit my countess to make any changes she deems necessary. Within reason, of course." To his shock, Mother's eyes misted over, and she seemed unable to speak. He gently touched her arm. "What is it, dearest?"

She shook her head and pulled a lace handkerchief from her sleeve. "Oh, nothing." She wrung her hands for a moment. "No, it is not *nothing*. I did wish to make this house more appealing, but Lord Winston would not permit it."

Lord Winston? Now that he thought of it, he had never heard Mother speak of Father in any other way, and certainly she had never used a fond byname for him. Nor had Father ever addressed her as anything less than Lady Winston, not even on the last day of his life.

He took her hand and lifted it to his lips. "Dear one, you may take the house in hand straightaway. Do as you wish." He offered a smile, but it seemed to increase her silent tears. "Of course, you may have to contend with Sophia for all of your decisions. Or should I say Lady Sophia?"

Mother rewarded his attempt to cheer her with a teary laugh. "Oh, how she did go on and on when you made your announcement. I was concerned that she might faint from joy."

"Hmm. I was a bit worried myself." Winston took her handkerchief and dabbed at her tears. "Mother, you know I adore my sister, but we must persuade her to not be so impulsive, dare I say *imprudent,* when she is talking with anyone outside of our family. I do not worry about myself, for as you saw this evening, I have influential friends. But even an earl's sister will not be welcomed into Society's drawing rooms if she does not know how to guard her tongue."

To his chagrin, Mother began to sob. "Oh, my darling, how can she help it? She is my daughter, and I have ever struggled to control my own behavior. Why, had I been half as wise as a goose, Lord Winston never would have banished me to the country."

Winston's hair, curls and all, seemed to stand straight on end. He lifted a silent prayer of thanks for this opening and prayed for guidance. "That seems dreadfully harsh, dearest." He spoke lightly and sat back in his chair to feign mild curiosity. "Whatever could you have said to warrant such treatment?"

But his insides twisted with fear over what her answer might be.

Chapter Sixteen

Mother struggled to control her tears. Once composed, she said, "When we married, I knew he was a severe man, but he seemed to enjoy my merry ways. But in time, I could see I made him uncomfortable. He would not attend parties and in time forbade me to attend them. I could not even visit friends or have my own *at home* so that other ladies could visit me. This dark, dreary town house became my prison."

Her voice had progressively risen in pitch, and she stopped again to gather herself. "One day when you were six years old and still at home in Surrey with your nursemaid, he refused to permit me to attend a ball in the company of your kinswoman Mrs. Parton. I—I told him he was a cold, cruel old man. He had enjoyed his youth and was cheating me out of mine." She sniffed crossly. "Though I earnestly doubt he ever enjoyed his youth, because I do not believe he knew how to enjoy anything." Looking away, she bit her lip. "Oh, there I go again."

Her gaze settled once again on Winston. "He refused to forgive me for the insult and straightaway ordered me back to Surrey. Even when I told him we would have another child by Christmas and I needed to be with him, he refused all my entreaties." Another sob escaped her. "And all I wanted was to attend one last ball."

Winston could think of nothing wise or comforting to say in response to her confession, so he gently pulled her into an embrace. As he did, a calm melancholy settled over his shoulders and flowed into his innermost being. Mother might have spoken unwisely, but she had not been a faithless wife after all. A better man than his father would have remembered the disparity in their ages and would have forgiven her youthful affront, would have delighted in her energetic gaiety instead of shutting her away from the world all those years. What a terribly long time for her to pay for a childish rant. Such treatment was nothing short of spiteful.

Mother was right. Despite his upright behavior, despite his constant reciting of Bible passages, Father had been a cold, cruel man to her. Even in his last days, when she faithfully sat at his bedside and tended his needs, he had granted her no kind word or glance, at least none that Winston had observed. Nor had he himself ever received such approval. Unlike the loving, forgiving heavenly Father of whom Mr. Grenville had spoken several days ago, the late Lord Winston was ever the stern patriarch utterly lacking in compassion, even toward those whom he should have loved. Try though he might, Winston had never pleased him, nor ever would he have been able to, no matter how courageous or noble his actions.

The thought startled him, for he had never before questioned anything Father said or did. He swallowed hard and ran a hand over the worn leather arm of his chair. He should get down on his knees and beg Mother's forgiveness for doubting her character. But she had no idea about his suspicions, so the apology would only cause her pain, as Father had.

How could he have ever thought ill of her? Never in his life had he observed anything in her but purity and kindness and a steadfast devotion to Father during their long, unhappy marriage.

Edgar. He had put the suspicions in Winston's mind. But why? And to what purpose?

Mother sat back and retrieved her handkerchief from him to wipe away the last of her tears. "Now you understand why I will never address you as Winston, for that name does not bring me joy, even though I must bear it myself. But do not think I shall call you by whatever name you choose for your new title." She laughed in her girlish way, gladdening his heart. "You will always be my dearest James."

He clasped both of her hands and brought them up to his lips. "Are you not the clever one, dearest, keeping the secret about my advancement all this time? You see, you are not so impulsive after all." Her sweet smile rewarded him more than he could have imagined.

Later, as he lay abed considering Mother's unwitting revelation of her true character, a new sense of freedom bathed his soul. In fact, he felt entirely more sanguine about women in general. Since beginning his quest, instead of seeking a wife whom he could love for her own charms, he had sought to please his implacable dead father by choosing someone from the right family. Yet he continued to be drawn to Miss Hart, whose family remained a mystery. While he could not be certain the lady returned the favor, he would continue his pursuit, for his heart demanded it. And on the morrow, he would let nothing stand in his way of asking Lady Blakemore more about her lovely companion.

His last thought before surrendering to sleep was a

prayer of thanks that the lady he married would never be subjected to Father's scorn and censure.

"Mr. Radcliff." Catherine whispered as loudly as she dared as her friend passed by the door of Lady Blakemore's suite, his head held high and a grin on his thin, pale face.

He stopped and gave her a sideways glance, then looked up and down the broad hallway. Apparently satisfied no one had observed them, he hurried into the room and shut the door. "Zounds, my dear, where have you been? I feared perhaps Winston had stolen your heart and swayed you from your course." His sly grin—almost a smirk—did not reinforce the concern in his words, and an uneasy sensation filled her chest.

"I—I thought you had deserted me." She studied his pale eyes, wondering at the change in him. Her plans to confide in him about her torturous conflict over the baron now seemed ill-advised.

Before doubts could settle too deeply into her thoughts, however, he patted her hand and gave her a paternal smile. "There, there, dear girl, all is well. Superb, in fact. You have heard about your enemy's advancement, of course."

"Yes, but why is this superb?" She could think of no reason that this gentleman would wish for a scoundrel to gain a higher rank.

He chuckled. "All the farther for him to fall, of course. The Prince Regent will regret elevating him, and he will have no friends, no influence." His smirk returned briefly, but then he grew solicitous again. "Has he declared his affection for you yet?"

"Goodness, no." Catherine had never been the object of any gentleman's affection and often doubted that she could ensnare the baron's devotion. Not when her temper threatened to expose her every other moment she spent in his company. "Would you not say it is much too soon?"

"But you must secure his heart, my dear." Mr. Radcliff leaned close to her, and she had difficulty not taking a backward step to avoid the scent of his strong bergamot cologne. "All of our plans depend upon your success." A slight hiss accompanied his words, sending an unpleasant shiver down her back.

This would not do. Everything about this interview grated upon her nerves. "Mr. Radcliff, why have you not spoken to Lord Blakemore about Lord Winston's lies? He is responsible for the baron's elevation, and you could have stopped him." She spoke somewhat more harshly than she had intended and immediately regretted it.

His eyes widened briefly, then grew red while his shoulders slumped into a pose of dejection. "Oh, if only you knew, Miss Hart. How could I, an aristocrat forced to earn my living as a lowly secretary, speak against my own cousin without seeming to covet his position?" He sniffed softly. "The good earl is a jolly old fellow, but he is also a fool."

Although *fool* sounded a bit too much, Catherine could not entirely disagree. As fond as she was of the earl and countess, they did seem a bit naive at times. Perhaps their hearts were so pure and good that they could not imagine evil dwelling in their friend Lord Winston.

"I must go." Mr. Radcliff put his hand on the door latch. "Do all that you can to win my cousin's affections, my dear. As I said, all our plans depend upon it." He scurried out the door, leaving Catherine to wonder how on earth she could accomplish her assignment.

The answer came straightaway. She would be nothing but agreeable in Lord Winston's company, no matter what thoughts stirred her anger.

* * *

"Without qualification, Miss Hart comes from an excellent family." Lady Blakemore spoke quietly to Winston, although they were alone in her large drawing room.

The tension in his chest disappeared. "Then you do not object to telling me who they are." He had awakened with the confidence that such a refined, engaging lady must come from good stock, but knowing for certain now put to rest the last of his concerns.

"We do not speak of her connections because of the French war. Although Napoleon has been defeated, he still has many supporters in France and even some here in England. Until the Bourbon throne is secured, it would not be wise." The countess glanced over her shoulder. "We have not even told *her* that we know who her family is, so you must promise not to discuss this with her."

"What? Why?" He felt foolish for questioning this good lady. Perhaps he should have spoken to the earl. Was Miss Hart a French noblewoman whose family had escaped the Reign of Terror? A princess? Someone far above him? This answered everything about her changing moods. She must live in constant fear. "Before Napoleon's defeat, how could keeping such a secret be wise when Miss Hart has accompanied you out into Society? At any moment, she might have been discovered."

"My dear boy, secrets are not always a bad thing, as you will learn in your diplomatic career." Her casual demeanor showed he had not insulted her. "Have no fear. One day all will be revealed. In the meantime, do not delay in claiming her hand, if that is your intention. Once her identity is known, she will be besieged by suitors."

Remembering how Lord Melton had admired Miss Hart, Winston was now filled with a sense of urgency. "Yes, of course." His pulse began to race, and he glanced toward the door, wishing the object of his pursuit would put in an appearance. "May I have the honor of taking her for an outing this afternoon, if it pleases her? Mrs. Parton mentioned a tea garden, the White Rose."

The countess gave him a broad smile. "Of course. The White Rose has lovely flowers, gardens and entertainments, and their crumpets are beyond delicious. Perfectly reputable, I assure you." She patted his hand. "Do promise you will say nothing to Miss Hart about what I have told you."

"As difficult as it will be, I will not."

"Very good. You will do well in diplomacy." She stood and started toward the door. "I shall fetch her straightaway."

"Wait. Please." Winston jumped to his feet as a new concern filled his mind. "Is there someone I should speak to before I reveal my interest to her?"

Lady Blakemore laughed. "No, my dear. Blakemore and I have served as her guardians, whether she knew it or not, and we approve of you without reservation." She patted his cheek and then strode toward the door as if the future of England depended upon her mission.

Winston paced across the red-and-gold Wilton carpet, noticing for the first time how bright and airy this drawing room was. The light colors not only made it appear larger, but also more welcoming. His town house should have that same atmosphere. He had given Mother leave to redecorate, but if Miss Hart became his wife, she must have that honor. Should the ladies disagree, he would have a sticky matter to sort out. Had he inherited his mother's impulsiveness after all? He chuckled to himself. What did it matter if he had? Life was growing increasingly bright, and nothing could quash his happy temperament.

"Well, well, Winston." He turned to find Edgar behind

him, seemingly out of nowhere. "Or should I say Lord Dearbourn?"

"Edgar." Every cheerful thought vanished. "Where did you come from?" Had he used the servants' entrance?

"Never mind me, Dearbourn. You are to be congratulated on your advancement." Edgar beamed and held out a hand to Winston.

He reluctantly shook it. "I thank you, but I will not be Dearbourn, if I choose that name, until my investiture."

"Ah, but that is a mere formality." Edgar's grin grew wider, if that was possible. "The Prince Regent has signed the letters of patent. No one can take the title from you now."

"I suppose not." Winston's chest tightened again. "Just as no one can displace you as my heir." He had not meant for his words to sound peevish, but somehow they did.

Edgar wilted like a weed in the sun. "Only a son of your own, which I would welcome as surely as I welcomed my own son's birth. Why do you think I look forward to your marriage?"

"Forgive me, cousin." Winston said the words, but found he did not mean them, not after Edgar's insinuations about Mother…and his disparaging remarks about his son, Marcus, in the past.

"Oh, no matter." He waved a hand carelessly in the air, then waggled his eyebrows in a significant way. "I wish you happiness in regard to Miss Hart. Do enjoy your outing to the White Rose."

"So now you approve of the lady?" He narrowed his eyes. "How did you know about the outing?"

"Lord Winston." The object of his pursuit entered the room and walked toward him with a grace that stole his breath. Her beautiful dark brown hair was swept up into an elegant profusion of curls, and her rose-colored walking gown brought a blush to her ivory complexion. "How nice to see you." She extended a gloved hand, and he bowed over it.

"Miss Hart." His words came in a whisper. "You are a vision. Isn't she?"

He turned back to Edgar, but his cousin was nowhere to be seen. Anger and uncertainty cut through his joy. Where had the man gone?

"To whom were you speaking?" Miss Hart eyed him playfully. "Lord Blakemore's ivory figurines?" She tilted her pretty head toward the display on a side table.

The mystery would have to be solved later. He would not permit Edgar to ruin this day. Instead, he bowed again to Miss Hart and laughed. "Only to myself, dear lady. Would you do me the honor of accompanying me for a carriage ride?"

"The honor is all mine."

As he escorted her toward the door, he glanced back to see if Edgar had hidden behind a settee or large chair. But the room was utterly devoid of other occupants. With no little difficulty, Winston shook off the peculiar feelings churning through him and forced himself to look forward to his day with Miss Hart.

At the front door, Catherine donned her bonnet with the help of her new lady's maid, hired just this morning. The woman had accomplished what no one ever had, curling her straight hair. Once the task was completed, Catherine had gazed in wonder at her reflection in her bedchamber mirror. What an artful abundance of curls. At the time, she had decided that if this new style did not win Lord Winston's affection, nothing would. When she had walked into the drawing room, his admiring gaze suggested she was well on her way to victory.

Unfortunately, that delightful moment was interrupted when Mr. Radcliff slipped out of the room through the secret door so cleverly hidden in the fence lines of the floral wallpaper. The confusion on the baron's face caused by his cousin's disappearance should have amused her, but she found she did not like to see him discomfited. It was not in her nature to wish ill to anyone. How difficult it had been not to tell him what had happened behind his back.

"I hope you do not object to a phaeton. I borrowed it from Mrs. Parton." Lord Winston indicated the small black carriage in front of the mansion. "As you can see, it is brand-new."

"Oh, it is lovely." As Catherine accepted his assistance into the pretty little conveyance, she could not help but notice his youthful eagerness. Her heart sank as she considered what she was about to do. Tempted to jump out, run back into the house and abandon her plans, she nonetheless forced her attention to the phaeton. "You must tell Mrs. Parton how much I admire it."

Drawn by one horse, the doorless vehicle was more intimate than the four-horse landau, but no less grand in its appointments. Gold filigree patterns adorned the black sides, and the interior was upholstered in red. The four shiny black wheels had a fine red band circling the spokes. Brass-and-glass lanterns at the four corners held candles ready to be lit for evening travel. The black canvas top was down, but Catherine could see that it was lined with red velvet matching the seat, very grand for a sporting carriage. Behind the two-passenger bench was a small jump seat for the red-liveried groom, who now stood at the horse's head awaiting the baron's instructions.

Lord Winston climbed in beside her, took hold of the reins and nodded to the groom, a slender, brown-haired youth who sprang into place as eagerly as if he were a guest, not a servant.

"I see that you will drive us." Catherine cringed inwardly. What a silly, unnecessary remark.

"Unless you would prefer to." He gave her a mischievous grin and offered the reins.

Relieved at his response, she returned a similar smile. "You would be surprised at my driving skill."

"My lady, these days I would not be surprised at anything." He slapped the reins on the horse's haunches and directed it toward the gate. "Is there some particular place you would like to visit?"

"Oh, no." She forced herself to slip one arm around his nearest one, a bold gesture, to be sure, and one she was not the slightest bit comfortable making. It earned her a generous smile, so the baron must not think it too awfully bold. "This is a lovely day to be out, and I would not mind just a drive about the city, as long as—" She gasped softly. She had almost said as long as she was in his company, which would strain propriety more than she was willing to. "As long as the weather stays pleasant." She removed her arm from his and raised her parasol.

If he noticed her embarrassment, he was too kind to mention it. "Then perhaps you will not object if we go to a tea garden both Lady Blakemore and Mrs. Parton have recommended."

"A tea garden. How lovely. That is just the thing." Just the thing to give her plenty of time to question him. But perhaps she would do well to begin now. "Lord Winston, I understand that you will soon be elevated to an earldom."

His modest shrug surprised her. "I should have known Blakemore would tell you."

"But is it not something to boast about?"

He spared her a brief glance, then looked back at the

busy traffic as they turned onto Great Marlborough Street. "Perhaps if I had done something worthy of advancement. But this is an honor my father deserved for heroic service to His Majesty some years ago."

"Ah." With no little difficulty, Catherine refused to acknowledge his lack of pride. "But have you not done something heroic yourself? Did I not hear Lord Blakemore speaking of some letters you discovered regarding an attempt on the French king's life?"

The baron frowned and glanced over his shoulder at the groom, yet maintained his calm as he slowly wended his way along the avenue. "I cannot be credited with that." His well-formed lips quirked to one side in a charmingly worried expression. "Nor am I free to discuss it." He eyed her and gave her a sober smile. "I do not mean to rebuke you for asking about it."

"No, of course not." How frustrating he was, denying any part in forging those letters! "And I did not mean to pry—"

"Milord!" The groom cried out. "The wagon!"

Catherine watched in horror as a large wagon drawn by two giant dray horses plunged toward them at great speed. The driver clearly intended harm, for he struck the beasts with a cracking whip and urged them to increase their pace. In the busy traffic, Lord Winston had few choices that did not require injuring someone.

"Jump, Billy!" he cried to the groom. He stood and with one arm gripped Catherine and flung her from the phaeton to the safety of a grassy lawn.

She landed painfully on her hands and knees and spun around just in time to witness the disaster. While Lord Winston tried to drive his horse to safety, the great wagon turned sharply and slammed into the little carriage. Canvas, velvet and leather tangled with splintered wood as it flew in all directions. The poor smaller horse screamed in fear and pain and stumbled to its knees. Amid the rubble, Lord Winston lay facedown on the cobbled street, with Billy the groom wailing above him.

Chapter Seventeen

As the fog began to clear from him mind, Winston first became aware of a horrid keening sound. Facedown in the street, he hoped it was not Miss Hart's voice, for it was dreadfully common and grated on his nerves like nothing he had ever heard. Before he could renounce his affection for her for such a silly reason, his entire body began its own screaming, and his own voice bellowed out in pain.

"Ahhhh!" Shame forbade him to continue his cry, for it would only serve to further frighten Miss Hart. Gasping in deep breaths that racked his midsection, he managed to roll over on the bumpy cobblestones and saw to his relief that Billy was producing the screeching. The lady stood behind him, her bonnet missing and her glorious curls a shambles around her lovely, pale face, her pink lips set in a firm line. Through his pain he thanked God that she appeared uninjured.

"Lord Winston." She knelt beside Billy, and now he could see her tears through the haze of his own watering eyes. "Thank the Lord you are not...that you are—" As she reached down to touch his face, a sob escaped her.

Despite his agony, an odd bit of joy tickled his insides. At the same moment he rejoiced in her concern for him, his pain resurged with a vengeance, and it required all his willpower not to cry out again. But where to search first for a broken bone, a torn bit of flesh?

"Thank the Lord is right, milord." Billy swiped a red satin sleeve under his nose, making a mess of his livery. "What would Toby say if I lost me boss me first time out w' 'im?"

Winston tried not to laugh at the boy's innocently foolish remark, but a chuckle escaped him, causing his ribs to protest violently. "Oh. Mmm." He permitted himself that small groan. "Help me up, lad. Your boss must look rather like a ragbag beside the road."

"More in the middle than on the side," Billy said on a choking laugh. He reached under Winston's back and, with Miss Hart's assistance, helped him to a sitting position.

"You saved us, of course." The lady's words held a cross tone, though he could not imagine why. "Why do you suppose that man was trying to kill us?" She turned in the direction the dray had gone, but a crowd had gathered, blocking their view.

What Winston could see were the splinters of Mrs. Parton's brand-new phaeton spread across the ground, mingled with reins and canvas. He let out another groan, this time for his dear cousin's ruined carriage.

"The horse." He tried to stand, but knives of pain ripped through him. He settled back and found himself resting against Miss Hart's shoulder.

"Shh. Try not to move." Her tone had softened, as though she were talking to a child. Dizzy now from trying not to cry out, Winston rather liked the change. "Billy, see to the horse," she said in a calm voice.

As the young groom rushed away, Miss Hart continued to take charge, addressing the crowd in an authoritative voice. "Would you please move back and let Lord Winston breathe? Is there a surgeon or physician among you?"

Most of the crowd appeared to be working-class folk, but one or two well-dressed upper-class people stood about.

"Winston?" A dapper middle-aged gentleman in a blue jacket moved to the front. "Good gracious, what in the world happened here?" Winston recognized the Marquess of Pierpoint. "Do sit still, sir, until my carriage is brought around. I shall see you home."

"I saw the whole thing." Another man wearing a stained butcher's apron stepped forward. "You'd think that daft driver was out to kill 'im."

"Aye," said another man who was out of Winston's view. "Nobody drives like that in this 'ere neighborhood. Aimed right at his lordship, 'e did."

"You must give me a description." Pierpoint took the two men aside and began to record their words on a small notepad.

"'Ere, now, let us through." Leading the horse, Billy shoved his way between two bystanders who watched the goings-on as if it were a boxing match. "See, milord? 'E's gonna be fine."

Winston forced his attention to the limping, shaking beast. A ribbon of blood was already caking on its foreleg, and it snorted and bobbed its head as if disturbed by the crowd.

"You may see to the horse," Pierpoint ordered Billy. "Take him home and tend his leg. But first tell Lord Winston's butler that I shall bring your master straightaway, so he is to send for a physician."

Billy gave Winston a questioning look, and Winston returned a shallow nod. The boy and horse again disappeared through the crowd.

"Do stand back, won't you?" A man in green livery approached the marquess. "Milord, I've brought your carriage."

"Good." Pierpoint focused on Winston. "I say, my boy, an unpleasant business, this. Can you stand?" He eyed Miss Hart with a frown. "You are free to go, young lady. I am certain Lord Winston appreciated your assistance." He reached into his waistcoat as if to produce a coin.

"How dare you?" She clung to Winston's arm until he winced, and she quickly loosened her hold. Still, he could see she would not entirely release him. "I am Lady Blakemore's guest, and Lord Winston was escorting me on an outing."

"Indeed?" Pierpoint now eyed her up and down. "Well, I must say—"

"Miss Hart," Winston managed to croak out. "May I present the Marquess of Pierpoint? Pierpoint, Miss Hart." The marquess would understand that first presenting him to the lady, rather than her to him, was a declaration of her worthiness to be in Society.

"Ah, forgive me, Miss Hart." Now the perfect gentleman, the marquess tipped his tall black hat to her. "If you can manage, do help me to lift the baron into my carriage."

As they stood on either side of him and helped him to his feet, Winston forced his attention to her. "You were very brave, Miss Hart. You leaped from the carriage as if— Ah!" His left leg refused to support him. Fortunately, Pierpoint was on that side and supported his near fall.

"Oh, do be still." She seemed to be angry again, doubtless because of Pierpoint's initial insulting manner.

"You have lost your bonnet," he whispered, but would say nothing about her soiled clothes.

She gasped and cast a quick glance toward the grassy spot where he had thrown her. Large streaks of that same grass now stained her new gown. He could not ignore how ably and fearlessly she had leaped to the ground and appeared to have sustained no injuries. What a truly remarkable young lady.

"Here we are." Pierpoint and his footman took several minutes to complete the task of settling Winston somewhat comfortably in the elegant silver carriage. "I say, where did the young lady go?"

Miss Hart dashed back at that moment, bonnet in hand, and accepted their help to climb in beside Winston. "My parasol is missing, but at least my bonnet was still on the grass."

"Good gracious." Pierpoint settled on the opposite side, facing front. "What is this world coming to when lords and ladies are attacked in the streets? Why, those witnesses said the driver seemed intent upon doing you great harm." He exhaled an explosive breath. "By the by, Winston, I ordered those witnesses to gather the wreckage and deliver it to your home. There may be something to salvage."

"I thank you, sir." Winston leaned back into the plush upholstery to assess the damage to his body. He could not decide which part of him ached more, his entire left leg or his ribs. Other pains had subsided as these grew worse, and the left side of his face burned, no doubt scraped or bruised. He touched his cheek with his gray glove. Only a small amount of blood stained the leather palm. None of the splintered wood had pierced him. That was a mercy. His insides offered no complaint other than to hint at hunger, which only made him angry.

They should be enjoying tea and crumpets at the White Rose. He should have already asked Miss Hart whether she would accept his courtship. Yet here he was, returning home like a soldier wounded in the battlefield. And now he must consider the obvious questions: Who wanted him dead? Or was the mysterious Miss Hart the target?

Trembling almost as badly as the poor horse that had drawn the phaeton, Catherine struggled to reclaim her calm, her good sense. When she had seen Lord Winston lying still in the street, she had feared he was dead. More than feared. She had been beside herself with terror. She tried to convince herself that her fear was due to anger. If he were dead, she could not force him to tell her why he had falsely accused Papa. But her heart would not listen to such nonsense.

She must face the truth. She loved the baron, at least as he presented himself to the world, and she had no idea how to uncover the real man. What she did know was that he, her enemy, had heroically saved her life by shoving her from the phaeton. She would not be so ungrateful as to deny that. He had even managed to save the groom and the horse from the worst of the wagon's onslaught.

Now she must consider who would devise such a scheme so clearly intended to cause them injury, and why. Had the baron set himself against someone else, as he had Papa? Was that person seeking revenge?

Lord Winston shifted beside her and groaned in a soft, strangled voice, clearly not wishing to be heard. The marquess ignored the sound, probably to avoid embarrassing the baron. Too bad he had not granted her the same courtesy. The very idea that he should assume the worst of her simply because she was disheveled and grass-stained from her fall.

Yet she must admit to herself that much of her dislike of the marquess stemmed from the officious manner in which he had taken charge of the situation, one that she'd had well in hand before he arrived. Instead, he had practically shoved her aside to take control, while she wanted very much to be the one to help Lord Winston in his pain. Now, under the watchful eye of the marquess, she dared not even give Lord Winston a comforting pat on the arm. A sympathetic smile was all she could offer.

The short, quiet drive back to his Grosvenor Square town house took less than ten minutes. Once they arrived, the marquess dispatched one of his footmen to alert the household that their wounded master had arrived. The butler and Lady Winston were the first ones out of the door.

Catherine had expected the dowager baroness to become hysterical at the sight of her son's bloody face. But the lady stoically took charge of the situation and had already ordered footmen to bring an old invalid chair down from the attic.

"The late Lord Winston frequently required it," she whispered to Catherine, as if they were old friends.

Catherine once again felt that terrible pang of guilt over her plans to expose Lord Winston's lies, for it would deeply grieve this sweet lady.

"Bring it here." The baroness beckoned to the footmen who had the chair, then waved this way and that to the butler and other footmen to indicate who was to do what. "Dearest James." Once he was seated, she patted his scraped cheek. "We shall have you good as new in no time."

"I know you will." He gave her a smile that was more of a grimace, but the affection beaming from his fine green eyes caused another sharp pang in Catherine's heart. How she missed her own loved ones.

Lady Winston turned next to the marquess. "I thank you, sir, for your generosity." Her pleasant tone nonetheless held a hint of dismissal. "We are so grateful."

"Your servant, madam." The look he gave her could only be described as admiring.

The baroness's eyes widened briefly, and her cheeks grew pink. Then she glanced at his carriage, another clear sign of dismissal. "Good day, sir."

"Very well, madam. I shall return the young lady to Lady Blakemore." The marquess offered an arm to Catherine and gave her an expectant look.

"I—I…" How could she decline without insulting this generous nobleman?

"I thank you, but no." Lady Winston took Catherine's arm and tugged her toward the door. "I require Miss Hart's assistance. We shall see that she gets back to Blakemore House."

"Very well, madam." Fortunately, the marquess did not appear insulted. "I shall see what I can learn about this wretched business—perhaps engage the services of a Bow Street Runner—and bring a report to Winston at his convenience." He doffed his tall black hat. "I bid you all a good day."

Nodding her thanks, Lady Winston ushered Catherine into the house while the butler and footmen moved Lord Winston into the large entry hall and closed the door.

"Miss Hart." Once again she whispered in an intimate manner. "We are of course grateful to the marquess for bringing James home, but I could not send you back to Lady Blakemore until I am certain you are well. I hope you do not mind."

"We are of the same mind, madam. I could not leave without knowing the extent of Lord Winston's injuries."

"I must warn you, my dear," the baroness said. "He will deny their severity and refuse to let us dote upon him."

"I heard that. And you are right, of course." Lord Winston's soft grin at his mother seemed to hold some special meaning between the two of them, probably like the understanding looks Catherine shared with her family members.

The thought should have made her angry, for she would like nothing more than to see them all, especially Papa, and know that all was well with them. Instead she found herself appreciating the bond between this mother and son.

"Llewellyn," said the baroness, "take Lord Winston up to his bedchamber."

"No, Mother." He struggled to straighten in the invalid chair, flinching in pain as he did.

Catherine winced on his behalf, then noticed her own mild discomfort in her knees and hands from landing so hard on the ground. Her white kid gloves had been ruined, but the flesh on her hands had been spared.

"I should like to go up to the drawing room." The baron spoke through clenched teeth. Despite his mother's objections, he had his way, although Catherine noticed that the butler seemed none too pleased. Nevertheless, two hardy young footmen carried the baron, invalid chair and all, up the graceful curved staircase. Soon the baron and his mother were sitting in the room Lord Winston preferred, with Catherine comfortably seated across from them.

The baroness ordered water and towels, and tea, of course. Before they could be brought, Miss Beaumont rushed into the room carrying a large golden cat. "Oh, James, dearest." She hurried to his chair and plopped the feline into his lap, then flung her arms around his shoulders. "Are you all right?"

"Ahh!" His handsome face contorted with pain. "Sophia!" His protest frightened the cat, who jumped to the floor.

"Sophia!" Lady Winston scolded. "Darling, he is injured." She scurried to his side, stepping on the cat's tail.

While Miss Beaumont squealed her regret over hurting

her brother, the creature howled its complaint and dashed toward the door as Lady Winston cried out, "Oh, you poor thing."

"'Ere, now, wee beastie." The footman on duty grabbed for the cat, but he spun around and dashed toward Catherine's chair.

Experienced with catching her own pets, Catherine scooped up the rascal and secured him in a firm embrace. Oddly, he settled instantly in her arms, as though he knew they were a place of refuge.

"Well, now, Goldie," she said, "you must settle down and let your master be the center of attention."

"Crumpet." Lord Winston laughed and winced at the same time.

"Crumpet?" Was the baron calling for crumpets? Catherine wondered if he was as hungry as she was.

"His name is Crumpet." He ground out the words between clenched teeth, but his eyes shone with merriment.

More than pleased to see his happy mood, Catherine laughed, too. "Oh, I see. How very…different." She snuggled the cat up under her chin and was rewarded with a soft purr. "With this coloring, one would think his name should be Tiger." With a gentle touch of her finger, she traced the brownish lines amid the rich orange of his fur and gazed into his black-and-yellow eyes.

The cat placed one front paw on her chin in a friendly gesture, and Catherine petted the leg. "Why, it appears to be bent." Surely Lady Winston had not injured the poor thing just now, for it would surely be howling in pain.

"Father despised cats," Miss Beaumont said peevishly. "He threw poor Crumpet—"

"Shh." Lady Winston scolded her daughter with a look.

A sick feeling stirred in Catherine's stomach. How could anyone be cruel to such a sweet cat? "Crumpet, I think I shall take you home with me." How very interesting that *this* Lord Winston seemed to like cats as much as she did. She looked at the baron, who now watched her with nothing short of tenderness. Was he falling in love with her? She would be more than pleased if he was. But perhaps she had already fallen in love with him.

The night they had first dined together at the Marquess of Drayton's ball, she had remarked that she believed only evil could come from a person who did not like cats. It was a silly remark spoken to alleviate an awkward situation, yet she almost believed it. Had the late Lord Winston been evil, despite Lord Blakemore's praise of his character? Was that why his son could be so good and kind to his friends, even his cat, and yet think nothing of destroying a stranger?

And just exactly how would she go about making him pay for it when her heart seemed determined to get in her way?

Chapter Eighteen

Winston watched Crumpet burrow beneath Miss Hart's chin as if he were her pet. The sweet expression on the lady's face revealed a true love for cats, something Winston could only admire. While not in itself reason enough to fall in love with her, it did draw him to her even more.

"Where is he?" Blakemore's voice bellowed in the front hallway, and he bustled into the drawing room without waiting to be announced. Behind him came Lady Blakemore and Mrs. Parton. Edgar, whose face was even paler than usual, followed the others.

"There you are, Winston. Thank the good Lord you are not—" Blakemore stopped as he noticed the others. "Lady Winston, Miss Beaumont, Miss Hart." He made do with a single bow for them all, but his attention returned to Winston. "Are you badly injured, my boy? Has my physician arrived yet? Great mercy, look at your clothes."

For the first time since the accident, Winston looked down at his torn, filthy suit. In his resolve to be placed in the drawing room so he could remain in Miss Hart's company, he had paid no attention to his ruined garments. Then the business with Crumpet occurred, and he had forgotten his pain for a few moments of hilarity.

Dudley chose that moment to arrive through the side door carrying a bowl, a pitcher and several towels. He made a quick perusal of the inhabitants, but charged across the room. "My lord, do permit me to tend your wounds."

"Oh, yes, James," Mother said. "We shall not mind at all."

All formal manners seemed to have been dispensed with as Lady Blakemore and Mrs. Parton crowded around Winston with the others, leaving Dudley little room to work. Only Miss Hart remained in her chair, soothing Crumpet. Edgar hung back near the hearth, worry clouding his pale eyes.

"My dear Winston," Mrs. Parton said. "You must not dare to apologize to me for the loss of my new phaeton. This is a sign from the Almighty. My entire family, not to mention Lord and Lady Greystone, have urged me not to drive myself anymore, and I will take this as a sign from above that I must follow that advice. I only grieve that you suffered in my place. What happened, dear boy? Did an axle break? I shall call the wheelwright to account for it, you may depend upon it."

"No, it was—"

"Cannot depend upon workmen these days," Blakemore blustered. "You might have been killed—"

"Hush, my dear." Lady Blakemore tugged at the earl's arm. "Do not mention it." She gasped. "Why, where is my Miss Hart?" Turning, she gasped again. "Oh, my dear girl."

She and Mrs. Parton hurried over to the young lady, who stared at Winston, looking delightfully bemused. He was tempted to shut them all down and say they were both quite well, thank you very much. But he had not yet had a chance to ask Miss Hart whether she was entirely well. How could she not have sustained even the slightest injury after being so rudely thrust from the carriage? Yet what else could he have done to save her?

"If you please!" Mother's raised voice instantly silenced the room. "There, now, do be quiet, all of you. James, what did you wish to say?"

He took a deep breath, and then paid for it when knife-like pains shot through his ribs and abdomen. Neither did it help that Dudley was applying some sort of ointment to Winston's face that was anything but soothing.

"Miss Hart," he managed to say as he winced. "Would you kindly give an account of our little incident?"

She blinked charmingly and seemed to hold Crumpet tighter. In protest, the cat squirmed out of her arms and dashed straight toward Edgar.

"Get that beast away from me." Edgar kicked at Crumpet, and Crumpet returned a bare-fanged hiss and swiped at Edgar's leg, its claws catching on his stocking and ripping a hole. "My new stockings!" He raised a hand to strike, but Sophia rescued both cat and cousin and set the beast free to scamper away beneath a corner chair.

During this little drama, Miss Hart apparently composed herself, for now she glanced around the room with a serene expression. "It was not a broken axle, Mrs. Parton, but rather a careless drayman who caused the accident. He was driving rather too fast for the crowded street and crashed into the phaeton. You will all be proud of Lord Winston, for he was nothing short of heroic in saving all our lives at the risk of his own, very much like the chivalrous knights of old. Before the wagon could hit us, he helped me to jump safely from the carriage, shouted to Billy to jump and drove the horse out of the way. Both horse and groom survived with minor injuries, and I suffered only a ruined gown and gloves. Oh, and a lost parasol."

"You jumped? Goodness gracious." Mrs. Parton gasped and stared wide-eyed at Catherine. "Why, my dear, do you realize that had you been in a closed coach or a landau instead of an open phaeton, you would not have been able to jump free that way?"

"W-why, no." Miss Hart blanched. "I had not considered it."

While hums of agreement sounded throughout the room, Winston experienced a stirring of nausea over his kinswoman's observation. Dear Miss Hart—all of them, in fact—might have been killed, and yet she reported the event as if it were a mere accident instead of attempted murder. Perhaps she hoped to spare the older ladies further concern.

Winston would have to tell everything to Blakemore, of course. If Pierpoint did not discover who had devised the mischief, perhaps the earl could help to determine who would wish either of them harm and why. In the meantime, he lifted a silent prayer of thanks that Miss Hart was not only uninjured, but strong and brave and generous and wise…and exceedingly beautiful. How could he not love such a magnificent lady?

"Dear cousin." Edgar peered over Dudley's shoulder at Winston, apparently recovered from his battle with Crumpet. "I am almost faint with relief that you were not killed." His voice wavered with fear, confirming his words, "My, my, you look dreadful. Will this delay your investiture?"

Catherine had never seen Mr. Radcliff so completely undone. Although the cat had certainly caused some of his misery, his love for his cousin was evident, despite Lord Winston's evil actions. And of course her friend must ingratiate himself to the baron, as one always must do with the nobility. Would he now cease to help her in her quest for revenge?

No, not revenge. Something had shifted in her thinking today. Lord Winston's brush with death had frightened her in a way she did not entirely understand. No doubt it was merely her heart, which constantly betrayed her and obstructed her thinking. Yet now all she wanted to do was discover why Lord Winston had plotted against Papa. She would be willing to hear him explain that it had all been a mistake, that the letters he forged had been directed at someone other than Papa, perhaps even a joke or a wager that went awry. Perhaps pride kept the baron from apologizing for his mistake.

The only way she would ever know the truth would be to persuade him to talk about the letters. The only way he would discuss them with her would be if he loved her enough to trust her with his deepest secrets, even state secrets, as Lord Blakemore confided in Lady Blakemore.

What could she do in this moment to work toward securing his affections? While the conversation and hubbub went on around them, she gazed across the twelve or so feet that separated them and found him peering around his valet at her. In that strangely mystical moment, everyone else seemed to disappear, leaving the two of them the only inhabitants of the room. Was that love she detected in his eyes? Or was she only deceiving herself into believing what she hoped, even longed for?

After a miserable and sleepless night, Winston endured the painful ministrations of the physician, all the while trying to focus his thoughts on Miss Hart. Yesterday he had not been able to arrange a private moment with her before the Blakemores whisked her away. Now the memory of the way she had gazed at him across the room proved a helpful distraction. Had that warm expression in her lovely dark eyes meant more than a compassionate concern for his health?

"Ahh!" His pleasant reverie was interrupted when Dr. Horton prodded his ribs too firmly.

"Forgive me, my lord." The young black-clad physician winced in sympathy. "I do not mean to cause you further discomfort, but my diagnosis should encourage you. While your ribs are bruised, they do not appear to be broken. I will rewrap them, but you will need to avoid strenuous activity for a while."

Still trying to manage his pain, Winston exhaled a sharp breath. "And my leg?" A needle-point pain still jabbed him inside his hip joint.

"Wrenched badly, as I said yesterday. The only remedy is to pull it back into place, and the sooner the better." He frowned thoughtfully. "However, it requires at least two other men, and I fear the pain will be quite severe and could even cause further injury to your ribs. That is why I did not prescribe the treatment yesterday. I wanted to be certain your ribs could bear the jolt."

Winston swallowed hard. "Best to get it over with. Dudley." He beckoned to his valet, who stood slightly behind the physician, wringing his hands.

"Yes, my lord."

"Fetch that strapping bodyguard Blakemore sent over early this morning. He should be strong enough to help."

The brawny fellow must have been six and a half feet tall, for he easily towered over Winston's almost six-foot height. Blakemore had sent a note that Ajax was a bit simple but utterly incorruptible. Something unnerved Winston in the tone of the missive and even the fact that the earl thought he required a bodyguard. What had Blakemore discovered about the attack?

At Dr. Horton's instruction, Winston lay on his back on the floor. The giant held his shoulders down while Dudley braced him at the waist. The physician then gripped the left leg and yanked. A thousand knives seemed to pierce the injured joint, and then the room went black.

Chapter Nineteen

For the next two weeks, Catherine tried without success to meet alone with Mr. Radcliff. However, Lord Blakemore had at last heard his secretary's complaints about having too much work and hired him an assistant. Now the tall, muscular young man could always be seen hovering over Mr. Radcliff's shoulder, whether the secretary was seated at a desk or striding down a hallway as if intent upon losing his shadow.

Lord Blakemore had even given Mr. Fleming a bedchamber in the mansion until he could find proper accommodations of his own, an amenity Mr. Radcliff found extravagant, even radical. Because the room was across the hall from Catherine's, she met Mr. Fleming each morning on her way downstairs to breakfast. His company was a pleasant diversion on the long walk. Quiet and serious, but with a pleasant mien and intelligent, watchful eyes, the new black-suited undersecretary reminded Catherine more of the red-coated soldiers she had seen returning triumphant from the war than a man of letters.

"What shall we do today, Miss Hart?" In the sunny breakfast room, Lady Blakemore had already filled her plate with her usual eggs, sausage and rolls and now stirred a lump of sugar into her morning coffee. "I would suggest a visit to Winston, but Blakemore advises that the poor dear requires more time for recuperation before receiving guests."

This morning, Catherine had prepared an answer for the question the countess had posed every day for the past two weeks. "May we visit Lady Winston and Miss Beaumont?"

Lady Blakemore arched her eyebrows thoughtfully. "Why, I suppose so. Ah!" She set down her cup. "A better idea would be to send for the ladies, and we shall all go to the White Rose Tea Garden. What do you think?"

Since coming to London more than three months ago, Catherine had attempted to subdue any opinion that was contrary to the countess's. After all, the lady was her employer and might not receive contradictions well from someone she believed to be of lower rank. Yet Catherine had found herself dreaming of the day when she and Lord Winston could complete their excursion to the tea garden, which she had come to regard as their special destination.

"You are frowning, my dear." The countess offered a smile in return. "Perhaps you are afraid of another accident along the way."

"Oh, no, my lady." How could she be afraid when four footmen accompanied their every outing? She could not be certain, but she thought the men carried pistols concealed beneath their livery. "As always, I am at your disposal."

"Ah, what a sweet, accommodating girl you are." Lady Blakemore dug into her eggs with a singular vigor not lacking in gracefulness. "We shall go shopping and save the tea garden for another day."

Her change of plans did not surprise Catherine, but it did please her. These days, the countess never failed to order something new for Catherine on every outing to her favorite Bond Street modiste. While she had never before cared much for shopping, it was fast becoming a favorite diversion. And one day soon, she would repay Lady Blakemore for her many kindnesses.

"Mr. Grenville to see you, my lord. Will you receive him?" Llewellyn spoke from the doorway of Winston's bedchamber. He had yet to fully enter the room since the assault, nor had his cold tone changed when he spoke to Winston.

Already peevish from having to remain in bed for these past two weeks, Winston did not try to subdue his irritation. The time had come for a confrontation.

"Llewellyn, did my father ever speak to you about a pension or arrange some form of retirement for you?"

The butler's pale blue eyes widened, and his jaw dropped. He stepped into the room and closed the door. "Why, uh, no, my lord. At only three and fifty years, I am in the best of health."

He took a step toward the bed, where Winston lay, but stopped when Dudley coughed assertively from the other side of the room. Since the assault, the valet had insisted upon acting as a second bodyguard, and Llewellyn now glanced in confusion at him.

"If my lord finds something lacking in the performance of my duties, I beg you, in light of my long service, to condescend to explain it to me."

Winston glared at him through narrowed eyes. "You perform your duties to perfection." The butler relaxed only a little. He could easily demand that Llewellyn simply improve his attitude, but that would not explain why he'd had the effrontery to be so rude. "If you are to remain in my employ, you must give me a satisfactory reason for your arrogance, which began shortly after my father's death and only increased when Lady Winston arrived here." He would not mention the constant censure he had felt from Llewellyn since childhood.

Now the older man wilted. "It would be difficult to explain, my lord."

"Well, then." Winston inhaled a deep breath to steady his voice. He had always disliked confrontation, and unlike Father, had never dismissed any employee. "I know you never married, but perhaps you have family you can live with. I shall of course provide an adequate pension."

Llewellyn's pale face grew whiter. "My lord, I beg you… Very well, an explanation." He wiped a white cotton glove over his damp brow. "One does not lightly speak ill of the dead."

A chill went down Winston's spine. "Yes?"

"May I simply say that a certain, um, peer treated his lady wife most unkindly, and utterly without cause. One observed that the son followed in the father's footsteps." The butler swallowed hard. "Of course, it is not for the servant to correct the master, but—" He swallowed again and gave Winston a pleading look.

How completely he had misjudged the situation. All those years when he thought the butler was just like his father in condemning him, instead the man had been disapproving of the old baron for his treatment of Mother. Father had never paid attention to his servants any more than he noticed a chair that was doing its duty, so he never noticed anything amiss in Llewellyn's behavior. And after Father's death, until Winston had learned by accident the cause of his unkindness toward Mother, he had treated her just as badly. Now *he* was the one who must explain the matter to this worthy servant, at least in part.

"Yes, well, as I have been bedridden these past weeks, you had no chance to observe that a certain lady and her son have sorted out the matter and have established a new and felicitous friendship."

"Oh, my lord—" All arrogance gone, Llewellyn brandished a smile so broad that his lined face seemed in danger of cracking. "I thank the Lord for answered prayers."

"Prayers, eh?" Winston had spoken to the Almighty without ceasing these past weeks. "Speaking of such, do send Mr. Grenville up."

Llewellyn resumed his flawless formal posture. "Yes, my lord." He turned toward the door, then cast a doubtful glance back at Winston. "Shall I write to my family, then, my lord?"

Winston smothered a laugh. "Only to tell them you are in the best of health and will be in London as long as it pleases your master."

Llewellyn exited the room, but Winston could hear his uncharacteristic explosive sigh of relief through the door.

"No, no, not that one, Giselle." Lady Blakemore studied the fabric draped around Catherine's shoulder. "I much prefer the blue."

"Mais non, madame." The little modiste placed her hands on her hips. "Can you not see how zees glorious rose color brings ze appealing blush to ze young lady's cheeks?" She waved a hand in the air. "Every gentleman weel fall madly in love with Mees Hart if she wear zees color."

Lady Blakemore thumped the tip of her folded parasol on the parquet floor of the dressmaker's shop. "Every gentleman will fall in love with her *in the blue*."

Catherine did not know whether to laugh or cry. She was grateful to Lady Blakemore for all this attention, but she adored the soft rose silk material. Mama had always said this was her best color, and she preferred it, as well. Yet how could she contradict the countess?

"Maintenant!" The modiste had no such compunctions. "Giselle will not make ze blue." She crossed her arms and rapidly tapped one foot on the floor as if she had given the final word on the subject. Catherine was reminded of one of her governesses, a strict and implacable woman.

The bell above the door of the Bond Street shop tinkled charmingly, and Mrs. Parton bustled in, the new Lady Greystone in her wake. "Hello, hello, ladies."

"Madame Par*ton*." Giselle hurried over to greet her. "How may I assist you? Ah, Lady Greystone, I am honored by your patronage."

"But, my dear," Mrs. Parton said, "you must finish with Lady Blakemore first."

"Non." Giselle sniffed. "She refuse to see ze reason and—"

"Why, Miss Hart." Lady Greystone, exquisite in a sky-blue walking gown, approached Catherine, her bright blue eyes reflecting the color of the dress. "How divine you look in this pretty pink fabric. It is the perfect shade for you. Will you have a gown made of it to wear to Lord Winston's ball?"

"Ha!" Giselle sniffed again. "You see?"

"Oh, very well." Lady Blakemore did not appear the slightest offended by the turn of events *or* the modiste's insolence. "Hello, my dear. Marriage has made you even more beautiful. If Lady Greystone prefers the pink, then pink it shall be."

"Bon!" Giselle gave a victorious clap of her hands, summoning her assistants to take measurements and order accessories. The lace trim, satin ribbons and kid slippers would be dyed a slightly darker shade of rose to comple-

ment the pink silk, and a new pair of over-the-elbow white satin gloves would complete the ensemble.

While the older ladies discussed the transaction—for Mrs. Parton always lent her advice on everything—Lady Greystone took Catherine aside.

"I have missed seeing you at the theatre, Miss Hart, but it is clear that you are enjoying a fine Season." The young viscountess's blond curls peeked out from the fluted lining of her blue bonnet, enhancing her beauty. But Catherine suspected, as Lady Blakemore had said, that marriage was the cause of the glow in her ivory complexion.

She laughed softly. "I hardly know how to account for it, Lady Greystone. Since I last saw you, the countess has begun to treat me more as a ward than a companion."

The viscountess peered around her at the others. "Just as Mrs. Parton did for me. My brother, Lord Melton, had no money to pay for my Season, and yet she treated me more like a daughter instead of her paid companion. Lady Blakemore must realize you are worthy of such an honor, or she would not make the expenditure."

"But she has no idea who—" Catherine gasped softly. She had almost said *who I am,* which would have drawn unwanted questions. "Who my family is." She gave a careless laugh that rang hollow in her ears. If she lied to this sweet lady, who more than once had offered her friendship, how could she ever repair the damage? "Or perhaps I should say, who they are not."

Lady Greystone's smile invited Catherine to continue.

"Of course, they are not so base as to keep me from entering Society's drawing rooms." Now she was babbling... and digging a very deep well into which she would surely fall. Oh, where was Mr. Radcliff when she needed him?

"Of course not." Lady Greystone inquired no more,

but simply squeezed Catherine's hand. "Lady Blakemore would have seen to that, I am sure."

The thought startled Catherine. Even though Mr. Radcliff had assured her that he had forged adequate recommendations, exactly why had the countess hired her?

"Forgive me for not coming sooner." Mr. Grenville sat in a chair beside Winston's bed and offered an apologetic smile. "Please be assured that I have not ceased to inquire after your health and pray for you. My brother Greystone assured me that if your injuries had threatened your life, I would have been sent for straightaway."

"Indeed you would have." Winston regarded the minister for several moments. Although they had not been acquainted for long, the man's serene demeanor invited the utmost confidence.

They spent several moments exchanging pleasantries about various matters until the most important one pressed down on Winston's heart. He confessed his error of judgment about Mother and extolled her lifelong exemplary behavior. "Even my butler rose up in defense of her." He chuckled as he described Llewellyn's righteous indignation. Then he sobered. "After our carriage accident, Miss Hart likened me to the heroic knights of old, yet I did not even defend my own mother from those who would impugn her character."

"Have you asked her forgiveness?" Mr. Grenville inquired.

"I did think to do so, but would not such a request reveal my misjudgments and cause her terrible pain?" He clutched his counterpane to his chest like a shield. "She has no idea what I was thinking."

"You may be surprised. Perhaps she knew." The minister shrugged. "But I do see your point. No need to stir up strife."

"My physician has insisted that I stay abed these two weeks." Every day Winston had fought the urge to disobey his orders. "I had more than enough time to consider your words about God's forgiving nature."

"Ah, very good. Did you reach any conclusions?"

"Yes." Winston hesitated to speak disparagingly of Father, but to whom could he bare his soul if not this minister? "All my life, I have looked to my father to show me the character of God. However, his somber, unforgiving, even spiteful nature contradicts your view of a forgiving Savior."

"Hmm." Mr. Grenville's eyes were lit with interest, inviting Winston to continue.

"Although I have read the Holy Scriptures all my life and repeated the liturgical passages regarding God's grace every Sunday in church, I have let my father's image overshadow the light of Christ." He thought again of his father's cruel treatment of Mother and of the way he withheld approval from Winston, even suggesting that God would never approve of him, either. "John Newton's hymn 'Amazing Grace' has been much in my thoughts these days. I find that it perfectly describes the God of Scripture, the Father I wish to emulate from now on."

A sublime smile on his lips, Mr. Grenville nodded. "I believe you have found the key to peace, sir. Our heavenly Father desires for His children to know His love. We are accepted in His Beloved Son, not because we have done righteous acts, but because of His great mercy. Our only work is to accept His free salvation given through Christ."

Winston's heart swelled with joy at this affirmation of his own conclusions. "How could I not wish to serve such a generous Father?"

In the silence that followed, the minister eyed Winston with a teasing look. "Recalling our last conversation, did you ask Lady Blakemore about Miss Hart's family connections?"

"Yes, and I am confident she comes from a respectable family. However, I find that after nearly being killed alongside her, such connections have lost their importance for me."

"Ah, then you have formed an attachment?"

"If only on my part." Yet how else could he interpret the tender looks she had given him across the drawing room the afternoon of their near tragedy? A sudden longing to see her swept over him, and without thinking, he flung back the counterpane and rose from his bed. "Enough of this. The time has come to discover whether Miss Hart returns my regard."

Mr. Grenville jumped to his feet and barely had time to catch Winston before dizziness sent him spiraling to the floor.

Chapter Twenty

Catherine stood on one aching foot and then the other in the crowded viewing area in the House of Lords. Separated from the House floor by a wooden railing, the small space had only a few chairs, which had been placed there for Lady Winston, Lady Blakemore and several other peeresses. No seats were left for individuals of unknown rank like Catherine. Fortunately, her height made it possible for her to see most of the proceedings in this second ceremony that elevated the baron to his new title.

Because ladies did not attend levees, Catherine had not been invited to the earlier event at St. James's Palace during which the Prince Regent had named Lord Winston the new Lord Hartley. Only those who had been presented at Court could attend such a function. She would not complain, however, for this was by far the more exciting affair, at least in her opinion.

Marching into the hallowed hall behind several officials and Lord Bennington, and followed by Lord Blakemore, Lord Hartley was resplendent in his crimson-and-ermine robes and cocked black hat. Catherine's heart hammered in her chest to see him go through the various stations of the ritual. When he easily knelt on one knee before the

Lord Chancellor to present his letters of patent signed by the Prince Regent, she hoped that was a sign his leg had healed.

The Reading Clerk read the Writ of Summons that authorized Lord Hartley to sit in this august company. But before doing so, he signed the Oath of Allegiance and the rolls that listed every peer who had graced these halls since 1695. Next, Lords Bennington, Blakemore and Hartley doffed their hats to the Cloth of Estate, and Lord Hartley shook hands with the Lord Chancellor. Finally, after the three earls had exited to remove their ceremonial robes, they slipped back into the chamber and sat in their assigned places. Then the business of Parliament proceeded as usual.

"Well." Lady Blakemore stood and turned to Catherine. "What did you think, my dear?"

"Quite impressive." And quite wonderful to see Lord Winston—no, Lord *Hartley*—again, although he did seem a little pale.

His recovery had required several weeks, during which time he had not received visitors. Catherine's eagerness to see him almost made her forget what he had done to Papa. Almost.

She had managed at last to see Mr. Radcliff, who had assured her that his cousin would survive. Mr. Fleming had been in the room, so they had been forced to speak indirectly. In vague allusions, Mr. Radcliff encouraged Catherine to renew her plans to expose his cousin's evil deeds by securing his affections.

Yet how could she? Lady Blakemore had insisted they must permit the gentleman to recuperate before his investiture as Lord Hartley. That day could not come soon enough for Catherine. Or rather, that evening, for Lady Blakemore had planned a ball in his honor. At last her new lady's maid had slipped her a note from Mr. Radcliff saying she must not believe him to be the humble gentleman he seemed, for it was merely a pose. This very evening, she must entice the new Lord Hartley to declare himself.

Lady Blakemore seemed to have a similar goal for the evening, something more than celebrating Lord Hartley's advancement, for she had spared no expense in the purchase of Catherine's exquisite new silk gown. With her hair upswept in a profusion of curls and a string of tiny pink silk roses woven throughout, Catherine had never felt so beautiful or confident. Surely Lord Hartley would admire her appearance, if nothing else.

Her confidence held strong until she entered the Blakemores' ballroom to find the new earl at the center of no fewer than seven giggling heiresses, all of whom seemed determined to latch onto their quarry and not let go. Who on earth had taught these young ladies their manners?

Even more a curiosity was Lord Hartley's new ensemble. Instead of the somber black he had worn every time she had seen him, tonight he wore an emerald-green satin jacket embellished with gold piping, a dark gold waistcoat, gold satin breeches and velvet shoes that matched his jacket. How exquisitely handsome he looked. But what chance did she have to win his heart when he had no idea that she possessed a rank qualifying her to stand in the company of all those admirers?

"Lord Hartley," pretty Miss Waddington simpered, "you will permit me, will you not, the privilege of an old friend to inquire whether all your dances are spoken for?"

Still not used to his new title, Hartley looked around to see whom she was addressing. All of the young ladies giggled, and he felt heat rushing up his neck. Where were those red-uniformed war heroes when a gentleman needed them to take some of these girls off his hands? As to Miss Waddington being an old friend, he had met her at the first of the Season, and she had refused to dance with him at one of Drayton's balls, claiming tiredness, then promptly accepted a dance with a duke's heir.

"I, ahem, well." He tugged at his cravat to loosen it, but Dudley had secured it well. "Of course, Lady Blakemore and I will open the ball."

"And who will be your next partner?" The younger Miss Waddington—Amelia, if he was not mistaken—moved a little too close for his comfort, but her lavender perfume was pleasant enough. At her question, all seven girls crowded closer, their faces bright with hope.

Agreeing to be the honoree at this ball had been a mistake. After being on his feet all day, his formerly disjointed hip protested and his ribs ached. If he'd had more experience with young ladies, he would have some charming response to their flirtations, but their behavior only made him uncomfortable. *Lord, if You pay any attention to such things, could You please help me out of this?* Prayer had been his constant companion during his convalescence, and he found the practice more and more comforting, especially after his conversation with Mr. Grenville.

"How could I choose one flower from such a beautiful garden?" Where had that come from? He had never succeeded at poetry.

"Ohhh."

"How sweet."

"Such a flatterer."

The girls chorused their approval of his answer.

"But you will have to make a choice, Lord Hartley," said a blond girl in green. He had met this heiress at St. James's Palace this afternoon, but could not recall her name.

He searched the ballroom for someone to help him.

Lady Blakemore? Mrs. Parton? Mother? Someone? His eyes lit upon the fairest flower of them all: Miss Hart, dressed in a glorious pink gown with a riot of curls and flowers adorning her regal head. "Yes, I will, madam, and I have already chosen. Now, if you will excuse me?"

With no little difficulty, he disentangled himself from the group, all of whom voiced their complaints with sighs, whines and a host of other objections not without strong notes of indignation.

Forbidding himself to falter despite his aching joint, he strode across the room and sketched a deep bow that did not hurt him in the slightest.

"Miss Hart." *My heart.* "How wonderful to see you." His pulse pounded in his ears as he kissed her gloved hand and then looked up into her flawless countenance. A soft blush brightened her cheeks, and her dark eyes betrayed some high feeling that seemed to bode well for him. "I have missed you." He breathed out the words so softly that he could not be certain she heard him over the string quartet playing on the dais.

"And I have missed you." Her hand trembled in his, and her eyes brightened. "Are you well? I should say, you *look* well, and I pray that you are—I should say, I have prayed continuously since our, um, accident." Her blush deepened in the most charming way. She seemed as nervous as he.

If only they could find a place to sit and talk without having to go through the formalities of this ridiculous ball.

"Ah, there you are, Hartley." Lady Blakemore descended upon them and wrapped an arm around his. "Shall we open the ball? I know you have not entirely regained your strength, especially after your relapse, so I shall make your excuses for you, should you not wish to dance again." She leaned close to him and spoke in a whisper. "While no one other than Pierpoint and our closest friends know the extent of your injuries, we can claim weariness from your long day. You will forgive us, Miss Hart?"

Miss Hart had no chance to respond. Just as Lady Blakemore had dragged him to the young lady at Drayton's ball, she now dragged him away from her. But what a difference just over seven weeks could make. That first night he had condescended to dance with her. Now he wanted only to be in her company. The lingering pain in his body was nothing compared to the discomfort of being separated from her now.

"Do not sulk, Hartley." Lady Blakemore patted his cheek. "I shall return you to her soon."

As the music for the minuet began and other couples lined up behind them, he laughed. "Very well, madam. But I shall hold you to your promise. This is my only dance of the evening. I leave it to you to make my excuses, as you promised."

Somehow he managed to endure the ten-minute set. In fact, he was surprised to find that the exercise of the various steps actually helped him to regain his balance. Even when he risked a glance around the room to see who had come to celebrate his advancement, his dizziness did not return. Further, at each turn around the floor, he saw Miss Hart standing where he had left her by the wall. That dandy Melton hovered near her and apparently had presented several other gentlemen to her. She looked like a rose among thorns.

"Do pay attention, Hartley." Lady Blakemore waved her hand impatiently to indicate he should make his way around the gentlemen's line for the final promenade. "She will be there when we have finished here."

"Forgive me, madam." He should have known the countess was supporting his interests. She and Blakemore had proven themselves the best of friends.

None too soon they completed the set, and the countess led Hartley to a chair behind a row of decorative potted plants and near the dowagers, where Mrs. Parton was holding court. His cousin straightaway left her friends and moved to sit beside him behind a bushy shrub.

"One would never know you suffered an injury, dear boy." The plump, red-haired lady wore her usual purple colors with an orange paisley scarf draped across one shoulder and secured at the waist. As always, she sported a purple turban adorned with a peacock feather. The headpiece kept slipping over her forehead. "How are you feeling?"

"A bit winded from trying not to show my discomfort." Indeed, it had cost him much effort. "After nearly three weeks abed, including my relapse, I am all too pleased to sit down."

"Well, never mind. Grace and I will see to it that no one disturbs you." She patted his hand. "Ah, here she is."

Looking up, he expected to see Grace, Lady Blakemore, but found Miss Hart instead. He jumped to his feet, paying for it with a needlelike pain in his hip. "Miss Hart, do sit down." Somehow he managed to sound at ease as he offered his chair to her.

"Not at all," Mrs. Parton said. "Take mine, my dear." She stood to make way for the younger lady. "I shall be close by, so all will be proper." With that, she bustled back to her friends, leaving them alone.

"Well." Miss Hart gave him an uncertain smile.

"Yes. Well." He did not know what else to say, but his damaged joint gave him a suggestion. "Shall we sit?"

For several minutes they watched from their hiding place as couples lined up for the next dance. Melton spied them and made it halfway across the floor before Lady Blakemore accosted him and led him directly to Miss

Waddington. If the young lady had been holding out for an earl, Melton should make her happy. His title, her wealth: a perfect match. Was that not what this silly courting game was all about?

"Miss Hart, may I—"

"Lord Hartley, your new—"

They began at the same time, and both stopped.

"You must go first." Hartley encouraged her with a smile.

"Very well." She hesitated before continuing, "I have never seen you in anything other than black. This green suits you. It brightens your eyes in the most remarkable way." Her blush deepened. "I do hope it is not improper to say such a thing."

"If such compliments are improper, no one has ever informed me." He touched her hand to reassure her. "May I return the favor? You are the most beautiful lady in this room. I do not mean that as flattery. It is simply the truth, and I find myself wishing never to leave your side."

To his horror, her dark brown eyes filled with tears. "You must not say such things, Lord Hartley. Such a statement is—"

"Is my declaration to you." And clearly he was bungling the whole affair. "I should say, it is my wish to court you, Miss Catherine Hart. Will you accept my suit?" There. He had gotten through it without stammering.

She stared down at her gloved hands, which were tightly clasped in her lap. "That would please me very much." Her choked whisper did not convey the same feeling as her words. Nor did her demeanor recall their more felicitous times together before the assault. If she did not welcome his courtship, why would she agree to it?

Catherine's head ached, and she could hardly breathe for trying not to sob in front of Lord Hartley. She had achieved her goal. He was in love with her. She should be plotting how to take advantage of the situation, but all she could think of was how much she loved him in return.

"I-if I have offended you—" The dismay in his voice broke her heart, but she dared not look at him.

"No." She touched his hand to reassure him, as he had done for her seconds ago. "I am honored by your interest in me."

His soft laugh held a note of irony. "*Interest* does not begin to describe my feelings for you, Miss Hart."

She steeled herself to look into his face, into those emerald eyes, trying without success to control her racing heart. She should be happy, but all she felt was guilt. Why could she not just reveal her identity to him and ask him why he had plotted against Papa? Mr. Radcliff's words came back in answer, charging her not to give herself away, lest she be used to trap Papa, who would surely be tried and executed for a crime he had not committed. Shoving away her guilt, she considered how to redeem this moment so she could proceed with her plan.

"You must forgive my tears." She dabbed at them with her linen handkerchief. "I am not usually so emotional, especially when I am happy."

"If you are happy, that is all that matters." Lord Hartley gave her a crooked grin. "I am beyond happy. I am transported with joy."

Pasting on a smirk, she gave an artificial sniff. "If you are transported, I am on the moon."

Now his laughter rang out so loudly that even the guests who were dancing the Sir Roger de Coverley turned to look in their direction. "My dear Miss Hart, when it comes to wordplay, I refuse to duel with you. You will surely win."

She managed a demure smile. "You have made a wise

decision not to cross swords with me, Lord Hartley, for I would have every intention of winning the duel." The double meaning behind her words should have made her feel clever. All it did was increase her guilt.

Lord Blakemore strode across the room toward them, a broad grin on his round face. "Ah, there you are, my boy." Lord Hartley stood to greet him, and the earl pumped his hand vigorously. "Good news, good news. I have spoken to the Foreign Office, and we are to leave next week for Paris."

"Very good, sir." The boyish happiness on Lord Hartley's face did not match his calm response.

Catherine forced a smile to her lips, but black dread spread through her. If he was to leave for Paris that soon, she must make all haste to ensnare and expose him.

Chapter Twenty-One

The carriage rumbled over the rutted roads toward Dover, but Hartley barely felt the bumps. Since his elevation and celebratory ball the previous week, he had begun to feel increasingly better. Even in the flurry of preparations, he had not suffered another relapse. Perhaps Dr. Horton should revise his treatment of invalids to include exercise instead of constant bed rest.

He had left Mother in charge of the town house with instructions that her decorating must stay within the budget he had arranged with his steward. Sophia was more than a little annoyed at being left behind. She forgave Hartley when he assigned her the care of Crumpet and left her a clothing allowance from his own coffers so Mother would not have to use funds from the miserly annuity Father had left her.

Like Sophia, Edgar had come close to pouting over being left behind, yet Hartley thought his complaint did not ring true. His cousin despised the French, so it was just as well that Blakemore would not bring him along on a diplomatic endeavor.

The nearly seventy-mile journey to Dover would take at least three days, easily borne in such good company.

Blakemore sat beside Hartley, their backs to the front, and Lady Blakemore and dear Miss Hart faced them. He had feared his departure from London would threaten the future of his courtship. However, Lady Blakemore had dispensed with her social calendar, saying they could celebrate Napoleon's defeat just as well in Paris as in London. She would join her husband for the journey, which meant, of course, that Miss Hart must also accompany them.

Some fifteen miles out of London, the young lady appeared to doze in the over-warm carriage. He longed to brush back the damp strands of hair that had escaped her straw bonnet to drape across her flawless ivory cheeks. More than that, he had felt an increasing temptation to kiss those fair lips, puckered as they were in her sleep.

No, he would not think of it. Such displays of affection must wait until the proper time, so he would not needlessly torture himself by dwelling on them. Still, it was a challenge to be so close without picturing some sort of future with her, especially when her rose perfume tickled his senses in the most delightful way. With some difficulty, he forced himself to evaluate Blakemore's convoy, for in the future he would be devising such expeditions of his own.

This coach embodied the height of luxury, with excellent springs and plush upholstery. Heavier than most such conveyances, it was well suited to the coming trip over the notoriously rough French roads, but the excess weight that made it so sturdy also required it to move more slowly.

The two coaches that followed them held their servants, including the young assistant secretary, whose inclusion had further irked Edgar. Behind the servants' coaches came a massive fourgon. Formerly used as an ammunition wagon in the war against Napoleon, it now served as a handy conveyance for the great amount of luggage required by so large a party.

The coach jolted suddenly and came to a stop, tilted toward the front. The ladies awoke with a start as they tumbled forward.

"What in the world?" Hartley caught Miss Hart by her shoulders and helped her back onto the seat. Blakemore likewise assisted his wife.

"Oh, my!" Miss Hart blushed charmingly.

"Good gracious." Lady Blakemore sat back and fanned herself furiously.

"What on earth?" Blakemore peered out through the window on his side.

Hartley looked from his side to see the coachman, tiger and footmen staring at the front of the carriage. The driver's bleak expression did not portend good news.

"What do you see over there?" Rubbing sleep from his eyes, Blakemore nudged Hartley.

"We shall have to get out." Hartley gave the ladies a reassuring smile, then opened the door to climb out, turning to offer Blakemore his assistance. Once on the ground, the older earl gaped at the damage.

"A broken axle!" He scowled at his liveried coachman. "How could this happen? This is a brand-new coach."

Stiffening under his employer's harsh tone, the burly middle-aged man tore off his tall black hat and swiped a hand through his thinning hair. "Milord, I checked every detail afore we took possession of it from Hatchett coachmakers. Wouldn'ta accepted it without it were perfect." He knelt down on the dusty road and peered beneath the coach. He uttered some unintelligible words, then stood to face Blakemore and whispered, "Milord, the axle's been sawed near in two since I last seen it."

"Sawed!" Blakemore's face reddened so fast, Hartley feared the earl would suffer an apoplexy. "Great mercy and thank the Lord we were not traveling at a gallop."

"What is it, my dear?" Lady Blakemore had scooted across the carriage to look out the window.

Miss Hart appeared beside her, her worried gaze focused on Hartley. It warmed his spirits considerably to see her look to him in this difficult time, and he sent her a reassuring smile.

"Help the ladies out," Blakemore barked at the footmen. "We shall have to go on in one of the servants' vehicles." He beckoned to Hartley. "Do not mention the deliberate damage to the ladies," he whispered.

"Of course not, sir."

"We have the misfortune of being on the road at a time when highwaymen have begun to ply their trade once again. Sadly, some of our returning soldiers are desperate enough to turn to such thievery in order to survive." The earl glanced again at the damaged vehicle. "Go to Mr. Fleming and instruct him to ride in the jump seat with Ajax on the carriage we take."

"Yes, sir." Hartley could not imagine why his mentor would send him on a footman's errand, but he respected the gentleman too much to refuse him. As to taking Fleming along, perhaps the earl felt the need to have a secretary with him at all times.

After completing the deed, he returned to the larger carriage, where Lady Blakemore stood beside her husband clutching a small valise to her bosom as if it held the crown jewels. He arrived in time to assist Miss Hart as she stepped down. In the fading daylight, he could see the color had left her face. "Are you well, madam?"

She clasped his hand like a lifeline, another endearing gesture. "Yes. But this is the second time a mishap has occurred while we two were riding in the same carriage. What can it mean?" Fear combined with confusion in her eyes.

"I cannot guess, dear lady. Axles break all the time. No doubt the wood was inferior." He prayed she would believe that simple explanation, but he would not rest until he found out exactly who had made one or both of them a target.

Until an hour ago, Catherine had been delighted to accompany this party to Paris, for it meant she would not have to rush Lord Hartley into revealing his scheme against Papa. But the broken axle changed everything. For one thing, this older, smaller carriage they now rode in hit every rut and bump in the road. Lady Blakemore seemed able to endure it, so Catherine would not complain. But the other matter consuming her thoughts was the damaged axle. Had it truly broken by accident, or had someone caused the calamity? In either case, she lifted a silent prayer of thanks that no one was hurt, as Lord Hartley had been the last time.

At last Lady Blakemore exhaled a long sigh. "Must the horses run so fast, my dear? It makes for such a bumpy ride, and we have entirely outrun the other coach. How can we manage without servants and baggage?"

"I should like to get you ladies to the inn before dark, my love." Lord Blakemore spoke through gritted teeth, but whether from the jarring ride or anxiety over the axle, Catherine could not discern.

She looked across the darkened coach at Lord Hartley. His mild expression gave her no indication of his assessment of the incident. Yet if someone had deliberately caused it, she had little doubt that he was the target. She had no enemies. No one even knew who she was.

"Hold!" a deep voice shouted outside.

A gun fired.

The coachman cried out, and the carriage came to a lurching stop.

"Everyone out! Now!"

Another gun fired. Another man cried out.

"Stay here." Lord Hartley's order seemed directed at all three other inhabitants of the carriage. He reached behind the seat, where he had earlier deposited a long, slender satchel, and pulled out a pistol and a rapier. Then he kicked open the door and sprang out.

Terror ripped through Catherine as she saw him aim at someone and fire, then charge away with rapier raised.

Lord Blakemore retrieved another rapier from behind the seat and jumped from the coach with a vigor that belied both his age and his bulky form.

"No, Blakemore!" The countess grabbed for her husband's jacket too late. "Blakemore!"

Catherine could not sit still. She searched for another rapier behind the seat to no avail. Lord Hartley had left his cane on the seat. If it was like the one he had brandished in Hyde Park, it would have a hidden sword. Though much shorter than a rapier, it would still provide a weapon with which she could defend Lady Blakemore. She found the cane's tiny latch, twisted it and pulled out the gleaming blade.

"What are you doing?" Lady Blakemore cried. "Put that away, foolish girl."

"They shall not have your jewels, my lady." Gathering her skirts, Catherine crouched in the door and surveyed the brawl.

The giant footman named Ajax was living up to his namesake, for he was fighting several ruffians with the valor of the mythical Greek warrior. Even the mild-mannered secretary, Mr. Fleming, had engaged a villain in a sword fight. In the dimming daylight, she sought the one person whose welfare she prayed for the most and located him, his rapier at a man's throat. But another sight caused her heart to stop.

Not ten feet from her, one of the ruffians aimed a musket directly at Lord Hartley.

"Stop!" Catherine sprang from the carriage, sword raised, and raced toward the villain. A tiny voice within her head whispered that she had never killed so much as an animal. Another voice shouted that Lord Hartley must not die.

She slammed the sword, blade downward, onto the man's raised arm an instant before the musket exploded. The shot blasted into the dirt. The man bellowed in pain. Blood poured through the gash in his sleeve.

"'Ere, now, missy." Another man rushed toward her, sword raised. "Best leave the fighting to yer gentlemen." With a leer, he postured in a mocking fashion, as if daring her to fight him.

His longer sword gave her pause, but at this moment, she was fully engaged in the conflict. "And you should send your womenfolk to fight in your stead, you coward."

He blinked in surprise. A mistake, for she took advantage and skewered his sword hand. He dropped the heavy weapon and clutched at his wound. Oddly, sickeningly, pride and satisfaction surged through Catherine as she pulled back the sword. What had she become?

"'E said it would be a easy job. I ain't takin' no more from a blasted woman." The man ran toward a thicket where horses were held by an accomplice.

Others of the gang made haste to disengage and flee. Only one remained, and Ajax held the much smaller man by the scruff of his neck while his arms flailed and his legs dangled in the air.

"Lord, help us!" Lord Hartley raced toward a figure on the ground.

"Blakemore!" The countess echoed his plaintive cry as she scrambled from the carriage to kneel beside her unconscious, bleeding husband.

Chapter Twenty-Two

The second coach rumbled to a stop, and the coachman and servants quickly disembarked. Blakemore's valet dashed to his master's side, where Lady Blakemore knelt and struggled to regain her composure. Although he was unconscious, the earl's injuries did not appear life-threatening, so Hartley took charge of the larger scene.

"We have no other option than to continue to the inn." He addressed Mr. Fleming. An employee rather than a servant, the secretary seemed to be the most appropriate person to help him make decisions. "Tell the servants to make ready to leave."

"Yes, my lord."

The hesitation in his voice unnerved Hartley. "What is it?"

"Nothing, sir." He shook his head, then strode over to the two coachmen to give the orders.

Ajax and the footmen gathered the pistols that had been flung aside once their single charge had been fired. Swords were returned to their scabbards, pistols and muskets reloaded, and the captured highwayman was trussed up like a roasted goose and tied to the top of the coach.

Hartley returned to Blakemore, where Miss Hart and

the valet knelt over the earl across from the countess. To his shock, he saw his short sword in Miss Hart's hand, and a memory surfaced. In the heat of the battle, he had seen her engage one of the highwaymen in a sword fight. Involved in his own skirmish, he'd not had wits to think of her danger, but now it came back to him full force. She could easily have been murdered by that ruffian, yet she bravely faced him, mocked him and won. Instead of admiration, fear poured over Hartley. How could he bear it if she had been killed? The thought paralyzed him.

"He is awakening." Lady Blakemore gently dabbed her handkerchief over the blood on her husband's head. "Oh, my love, do return to me. Hartley, we must get him into the coach and leave this place before those ruffians return."

"Yes, of course." He was failing his friends. He must shake off this madness and deal with the present.

"I say." Blakemore coughed and sputtered. "Do help me up."

Unruffled by the rebuke in his master's voice, Blakemore's valet murmured encouragement while he and the countess helped the earl to a sitting, then standing, position. Grimacing as he cradled one hand in the other, he wobbled between them as they led him to the coach. But, thank the good Lord, he would survive.

Likewise, Hartley helped Miss Hart to her feet, longing to pull her into a reassuring embrace. Instead, he patted her shoulder. "I see you are a lady of action."

"I beg your pardon?" She frowned and tilted her head.

He wanted to laugh at the pretty confusion in her eyes, but this was hardly the time for gaiety. "Um, my sword?"

She held it up and stared as if seeing its dripping red sheen for the first time. "Oh." She held it out to him, and tears sprang to her eyes. "I—I have never drawn blood before."

This time he could not resist teasing, "And do you often engage in swordplay, madam?"

She closed her eyes, sending those silver tears splashing down her cheeks. "We must go." Shoving the hilt of the sword into his hand, she strode toward the coach.

He should not have teased. Another failure. All he could do was follow her.

Once the party was tucked back into the coach and the valet wedged in with them, Hartley gave the order to continue the journey. In the morning, they would have to return to London, of course. Strangely, he felt not the slightest disappointment over the delay in his diplomatic career. These friends might have been murdered by the highwaymen, and that put everything into perspective.

He could not stop thinking about how fearless his lady had been. Something about her posture as she faced the highwayman stirred a memory, but he could not grasp the elusive thought.

The inn's ostlers helped the grooms with the horses and coaches while Mr. Fleming secured accommodations for everyone. Hartley helped his friends from the coach and sent them inside, then beckoned to Ajax. "Did you get anything out of the prisoner?"

"Aye, sir." The bodyguard's crooked grin and gleaming eyes revealed how much he had enjoyed the fray. "Says they wanted her ladyship's jewels. Ha. About like old Nappy wanted his vacation on Elba."

"What do you mean?"

"Milord, I ain't too smart, but I know a killer when I see one. 'Twas you they was all aimin' for with those guns. Had the young lady not struck down one fellow—near to cut off the blackguard's arm, she did—we'd be carryin' your body back to London right now."

This double shock almost undid him. If Miss Hart had

almost severed a man's arm, no wonder she was so overset by her actions. He had never known any female, especially one gently bred, who would engage in a man's fight, no matter the cause. Oddly, rather than repulse him, it made him love this remarkable lady all the more.

The other matter should not shock him at all, for somehow he knew it. Some instinct had warned him that he was the target of these attacks. But who would want to murder him?

Catherine listened to the soft patter of rain on the roof of the Red Rooster Inn. Her lady's maid and the other female servants had long ago fallen asleep in the room they shared, and the sounds of their breathing blended with the rain to compose a soothing melody. Still, she could not sleep.

Lady Blakemore insisted upon staying in a private bedchamber with her husband, and Catherine could not blame her. Would that she could remain in the company of the gentleman who had caused her such turmoil. If he had embraced her after helping her up, she would have been completely undone. But oh, how she had longed for the comfort of his arms after their terrible ordeal.

She had overheard the bodyguard telling Lord Hartley about her actions. What on earth must he think of her? Even now, the memory of feeling the blade slicing into human flesh made her stomach turn. She could never kill anyone, nor had she ever truly wanted to do harm to Lord Hartley. If only he would explain why he had schemed against Papa. If only this entire matter were finished so they could all go back to their ordinary lives, whatever ordinary might be.

Perhaps the time had come for her to confront him. She would have to wait until they returned to London, of course, for she would rather confess her duplicity to Lord and Lady Blakemore first and in private. They had been so kind to her. How would she ever make up for her lies?

Back in London late the next day, Hartley left Blakemore in the countess's care at their mansion. The earl had suffered a blow to the head, but no dizziness followed, which eased much of everyone's concerns. His right forearm appeared to be broken and caused the earl much pain, so they would send for Dr. Horton. Mr. Fleming promised to watch over Blakemore, and Hartley had every confidence that the man would do that job as well as he performed his duties as a secretary.

Although he wanted very much to have a private audience with Miss Hart, he could see how weary she was from their misadventures. Tomorrow when they were both fresh would be soon enough to tell her how much he loved her, how he would be honored if she would become his wife.

After instructing Ajax to deliver the highwayman to Newgate Prison, Hartley rode a borrowed horse back to his town house. Ajax was not pleased with being separated from him, but for this short time, with no one expecting him to be in town, Hartley had no fears for his life.

The house was dark, and only Crumpet greeted him at the front door. He remembered this was Llewellyn's day off, and no doubt Mother and Sophia were out visiting, making up for all the quiet years in the country. He chuckled to think of their delight when they came home and discovered he had not abandoned them after all. Sophia would demand an accounting of the adventure. Mother would be beside herself with worry. Of course, he must call it all an accident, but she might not accept that label this second time.

Carrying his pet up the stairs, he looked in vain for a

footman, but the house appeared deserted. Perhaps they were all in the kitchen enjoying some of Cook's pastries.

At his office, he found the door slightly ajar. Strange. Llewellyn could never abide an open door. Hartley peered through the small space, and his stomach tightened. Edgar sat writing at his desk, a smirk on his thin, lined face. He wrote with a flourish, shook sand over the letter to blot the ink, then sat back to study it.

"Read it aloud." Hartley nudged the door open and sauntered into the room. In his arms, Crumpet stiffened.

"Cousin!" Edgar gaped and jumped to his feet. "What are you doing here?" His pale face grew even whiter.

"No, *cousin*. The question is, what are *you* doing here at my desk?" He had always trusted Edgar, but his cousin had never had the nerve to usurp his office this way.

"Why, I am looking out for you, of course. You left things in quite a mess." Edgar fluttered a hand over the papers lying on the desk. "I assumed you would want me to organize all of this."

"If I wanted a secretary, I would hire one." Hartley set Crumpet on top of the papers and snatched up the vellum sheet Edgar had just written. A chill went down his spine. The script looked exactly like his own. "'Be advised that in my absence, my trusted representative, Mr. Edgar Radcliff, is to be the executor for all of my affairs.'" He clutched the page, crumpling the edge. "What is the meaning of this forgery, Edgar?"

"Forgery? How can you say that?" Edgar slumped into a servile posture, and his voice became a whimper. "I was merely looking out for you, as I said. Lady Winston has gone wild with spending, and I merely wanted to curtail her extravagance." He wilted even more, and his eyes took on the sad look of a hound. "I have always looked out for you, even when my uncle questioned whether or not you were actually his son."

"Silence." Hartley trembled where he stood, forbidding himself to leap across the desk and strangle his cousin. "You will never question Lady Winston's character again. Is that understood?"

"Well, you need not get all upset. I am merely reporting what happened." Oddly, he smiled, a snakelike expression that narrowed his eyes and sent another shiver down Hartley's spine. "By the by, you surely know by now that your Miss Hart is also not the lady everyone thought."

"What are you talking about?" He should not listen, should not let this man speak another lie.

"Why, Miss du Coeur, of course." Edgar's malevolent laughter echoed throughout the room. "Did you not know you were falling in love with the daughter of the French *comte* who conspired to assassinate the French king? The man you exposed? Do you really believe she loves you? Wake up, silly boy. The girl planned to murder you. She was the 'youth' you fought at Monsieur's academy." He emitted another evil laugh. "She was just testing you to discover your weaknesses. I do believe she has succeeded, has she not?"

Yes, she had. And yesterday her expert handling of his sword had reminded him of that boy, although the memory had not become clear until now. Why had he not seen it before? She used both hands with equal skill, whether in writing, eating or using a sword against him. What a fool he was.

"Get that beast away from me." Edgar backed away from the desk, where Crumpet was trying to snatch his silk watch fob with a bared claw. "If you do not get rid of it, I shall kill it."

This time Hartley did not try to stop himself. He strode

around the desk and grasped his cousin by the front of his shirt, cravat and all. "Get out of my house and never come back." He pulled Edgar around and shoved him toward the door.

Surprisingly agile for his age, Edgar whipped back around. "And what will you do with your pretty little assassin, *milord?* Marry her?"

Hartley raised a fist to strike, but again, better sense claimed him. "Get out."

Once Edgar had gone, he slumped at his desk and put his head in his hands. Indeed, what would he do with his pretty, ambidextrous little assassin?

Chapter Twenty-Three

After two days of traveling, Catherine could tolerate only a short lie down, so she put on a fresh gown and paced the hallways of Blakemore House. Mr. Fleming seemed as energetic as she, for he offered to accompany her down the long hallways and galleries of the vast mansion.

The return of their party had thrown the household into chaos. Nonetheless, upon learning of his lordship's injuries, all of the servants proved more than willing to forgo the leisure they had anticipated during his absence. The French cook had no difficulty pulling together a fine repast for supper. Lady Blakemore ate in her husband's bedchamber, so Catherine and Mr. Fleming were alone in the smaller dining room.

The young secretary seemed disinclined to engage in conversation, even though as employees they were considered equals. After a while, however, Catherine decided to satisfy her curiosity.

"Mr. Fleming, you acquitted yourself quite admirably during the attack. I was surprised to see your fighting skill."

He looked up from his soup, sorrow in his expression.

"As I was unable to successfully protect Lord Blakemore, Miss Hart, I cannot think myself all that skillful."

"Sir, you are a secretary. No one expects you to protect anyone, or even to fight. Yet you did."

"But I am…" He stopped speaking and returned to his soup.

Before she could question him further, Chetterly entered the room and approached her side of the table. "Miss Hart, Lord Hartley has asked to see you in the drawing room. Are you at home?"

Her heart leaped. She had expected to see him tomorrow and confess everything to him. Now she could clear her conscience before she went to bed.

"Yes." She glanced at Mr. Fleming. "You will excuse me?"

His furrowed brow stopped her for a moment. Then he shook his head. "I hope you find Lord Hartley has recovered from his ordeal."

She laughed. "As we all must." How sweet and protective the young man was.

Chetterly led the way and opened the drawing-room door. Her pulse racing, Catherine swept into the room, barely able to keep from throwing herself into Lord Hartley's strong arms.

"Good evening, sir. How nice of you to come. We did not expect you until tomorrow."

Instead of the smile she anticipated, he lifted his chin and looked down that very fine nose, just as he had the day they had dueled at the fencing academy and he had flaunted his supposed superiority. "Good evening, Miss du Coeur."

Her breath went out of her, and she grasped a nearby chair to keep from falling. "You know."

He emitted an unpleasant snort of disdain. "I do." The

sneer on his finely sculpted lips changed his entire bearing. No longer the humble peer who almost refused his earldom. No longer the aspiring diplomat who hoped to humbly serve his king and country. No longer the bumbling swain who tried to win her affection. *This* was the man who had destroyed Papa, this arrogant dissembler who had deceived everyone, even Lord and Lady Blakemore.

Anger swept through her like a brush fire. "Well, then." She scrambled for self-control, but could not stop her trembling rage. "If you know who I am, perhaps you will be so kind as to tell me why you destroyed a better man than you will ever be. Why?" Her voice had risen in volume. She paused to regain control. "My father, Comte du Coeur, is a good and godly gentleman, something you only pretend to be. Why did you forge letters accusing him of conspiring to assassinate his king? Why did you—"

"I forged no letters, madam." His green eyes blazed with cold fury. "A French royalist or some honest Englishman saw to it that the letters were delivered to my home so that your father's Bonapartist plot could be exposed." He barked out an ironic laugh. "And you, with your swordsmanship, are clearly a party to the intrigue. Did you plan to murder me yourself or have someone else do it? Ah, yes. Your hired assassins made several attempts to murder me. Unfortunately for you, all of your plots failed."

"Plots? Plots? You are the only one who plotted. And why? To advance your own interests. To somehow prove yourself worthy of your elevation, all the while acting the generous peer to lesser beings. You arrogant, undeserving bumbler."

"Your father plotted an assassination."

"You are a liar. You forged those letters."

Silence ruled in the vast drawing room for a full ten seconds.

"That is entirely enough." Lord Hartley slammed his fist against the back of a chair, knocking it over. "I am going straightaway to expose your deceptions to Blakemore."

She glared at him through narrowed eyes. "You do that, Lord Hartley. But do not fail to mention your own sin. If you think Lady Blakemore will not believe my accusations against you, just wait and see." Catherine owned no such assurance, but she could not permit him to have the last word.

"I shall, my lady." He sketched an elaborate, disingenuous bow. "I shall." He stormed past her, and the scent of his cologne lingered in the air around her.

She vowed to despise bay rum for the rest of her life.

Hartley felt sick to his stomach, but nonetheless he ran upstairs toward Blakemore's suite on the next floor.

The footman outside the door bowed. "My lord, you may go through." He opened the door inward.

Hartley nodded to the man, if only to prove Miss Hart... Miss du Cocur wrong. He was not arrogant. His consideration of others, even servants, was genuine.

The valet met him in the anteroom of the large suite. "How may I help you, Lord Hartley?"

Now was the true test. Would he insist upon exposing Miss du Coeur's lies straightaway? Or would he put his friend and mentor's interests before his own? With no little effort, he calmed himself.

"If Lord Blakemore is able to receive me, I would so much appreciate it." He punctuated his request with a smile that felt more like a grimace. But then, noblemen need not smile at servants. Why had he felt it necessary?

"Of course." The valet walked toward the bedchamber door just as Lady Blakemore emerged.

"Why, Hartley, what brings you here at this hour?" Her maternal tone proved his undoing.

"Madam," he choked out, "we have all been deceived by Miss Hart. She is Miss du Coeur, the daughter of the Bonapartist who conspired to assassinate the French king."

To his shock, the countess merely nodded. "You must speak with Blakemore. Do go through." She waved toward the door. "I will speak with the young lady." With that, she strode from the suite.

Good. She would give Miss du Coeur the set down she deserved.

To his dismay, the thought twisted in his belly. He shoved aside the mad desire to follow the countess and protect the girl.

Catherine righted the fallen chair, then slumped down into its comfortable upholstery. Her world had just been shattered, and she had no strength to stand. Just as she had always thought before her heart got in the way, Lord Hartley was a wicked, scheming man. The very idea that he would deny her charges made her sick with rage, but she would not surrender to tears.

"Ah, there you are, my dear." Lady Blakemore entered the room all warmth and smiles. "Why, whatever is wrong?"

Her generosity was more than Catherine could bear. She flung herself into the countess's arms and wept. "Forgive me, my lady. I have misrepresented myself to you. I am not a gentlewoman or whatever you thought me to be. I am the daughter of Comte du Coeur, whom that dastardly Lord Hartley has accused of plotting against King Louis. But his accusations are false, I swear to you by all that is h—"

"Now, now, my dear. No need to blaspheme." She

smoothed back Catherine's straight hair. "Of course you are Miss du Coeur. We knew it all along."

"Wha—" Catherine dropped down on the nearest settee. "What are you saying?"

"My husband is a jolly man, my dear, but he is no fool. When Lord Hartley—Lord Winston at the time—brought the letters to the Home Office, Blakemore straightaway knew something was wrong, so he launched an investigation."

"And found that Lord Hartley forged the letters for political advancement."

"Gracious no, my girl." She spoke in a whisper and looked around as if searching for eavesdroppers. "Hartley was too innocent, too naive ever to be a suspect, but there was someone else close to my husband who concerned him."

"But why did you hire me?" Catherine's head reeled. Hartley innocent? Naive?

The countess laughed softly. "Why, to protect you from yourself. We could not have Mademoiselle Catherine du Coeur gallivanting all over England trying to avenge her father when we all knew he was not in the slightest guilty."

"You knew?" A thousand thoughts rushed in upon her, but only one stood out. "If I had been honest with you from the beginning, so many things would be different now."

"Yes." Lady Blakemore sighed. "And if we had been honest with you… But we had to trap the villain… Oh, enough of that. We did what we did. Now, I shall send Hartley down so the two of you can get this all sorted out."

"Oh, no. I could not." All this time she had forced herself to despise an innocent man instead of listening to her heart. He would never forgive her for the cruel things she said only moments ago.

"Hmm. Well, then, he may be coming down the stairs

at any moment. If you do not wish to speak to him yet, perhaps you should wait here."

Catherine nodded mutely.

"There, there, my dear. Do not weep." The countess patted her cheek, then walked toward the door, where she turned back. "It will all work out in the end."

Catherine sat with hands folded in her lap, wondering how long she must wait before leaving the drawing room. Perhaps it would be better to face Lord Hartley and have done with it, whether for good or for ill. She had no doubt he would never forgive her, nor did she deserve forgiveness. Against everything she had ever been taught or believed in, she had lied and, yes, plotted against a good gentleman, refusing the evidence of Lord and Lady Blakemore's recommendations and her own eyes and heart.

Lord Hartley—had he chosen that name because he believed hers to be Hart? She had thought herself so clever with her wordplay. *Hart,* a play on *heart,* the translation of *du Coeur.* How close little Lord Westerly had come to exposing her in the park that day. What would have happened if he had?

Lord, forgive me for my lies. Why did I ever think ill of such a good man?

"Ah, there you are, my dear." Mr. Radcliff slipped into the room through the secret door. "I understand you had a little adventure these past two days."

The instant Catherine looked into his pale gray, soulless eyes, the truth slammed into her.

"You!" She stood and backed away from him toward the hearth, searching in vain for a poker or shovel.

"Oh, bother." He heaved a dramatic sigh. "Now I shall have to take drastic action. Ellis."

A large, roughly dressed man slipped into the room with a stealth that belied his size. "Aye, Cap'n?"

"Imbecile! I have told you to address me as *my lord*." Mr. Radcliff waved a hand toward Catherine. "Seize the girl. We have had a change of plans."

"No!" Catherine dashed toward the door, but the henchman was too quick. When she tried to scream, he threw a burlap bag over her head and flung her up on his shoulder. She kicked and writhed to get free to no avail. On the way out through what she assumed was the secret door, her head banged into the lintel, leaving her unable to think of anything but the pain.

"There is no way around it, my boy." Blakemore lay propped up against the pillows on his four-poster bed. "Miss du Coeur lied about her identity, and we permitted the deception because we were trying to ferret out the real purpose for Radcliff's scheme. You cannot imagine our relief when we discovered he did not mean to assassinate old Louis. He simply wished to take revenge upon those he felt had harmed him."

Hartley grasped for calm, not daring to challenge his mentor's wisdom in using a foolish young woman for such a dangerous operation. "So in addition to his desire to murder me and seize my title, he wants revenge against du Coeur?"

"Yes. All those years ago when a certain Miss Beecham married the Comte du Coeur, Radcliff was enraged. He had hoped to marry the young lady to advance his own prospects. You see, she was the great-niece of Lord Beckwith, a baron of some prominence at the time. Being a young man, Radcliff made a cake of himself over the matter, which took him down a peg in Society's opinion and set him back considerably. No young lady would have him, so he had to settle for a woman of no fortune or consequence. He waited more than twenty years to destroy du Coeur and very nearly succeeded."

That explained Edgar's antipathy toward his own wife and son. The man had no capacity for love or even decent familial affections. Poor Emily and Marcus. Further, Hartley had missed several opportunities to learn the truth about Miss du Coeur. When doddering Lady Beckwith recognized her at Drayton's supper, he should have paid attention instead of dismissing the elderly lady as senile.

"And I do not have to guess why Edgar wanted me dead." The thought sickened him. "He could have had me murdered at any time over the past twenty-three years. I suppose he waited until he would inherit an earldom along with the barony."

"Yes, but do not discount your father. Whatever coldness he exhibited to others, he did protect his own. Before leaving London that last time, he asked me to watch over you. I believe he knew he would never be well enough to return to Parliament."

For all of his coldness and censure, Father must have cared for him, but Hartley would have to sort that out later. For now he still could not reconcile himself to Miss du Coeur's lies. Had she ever loved him? Or had it all been a pose to trap him into a confession of his supposed forgery?

"I do not understand how you could permit Edgar to have free access to your home." Hartley had made the same mistake, but Edgar was his relative. "Were you not concerned for your safety?"

Blakemore chuckled. "You know the saying 'Keep your friends close and your enemies closer'? Radcliff had no quarrel with us. Like most villains, he thought himself much more intelligent than an old codger like me." He shifted in his bed and frowned, obviously uncomfortable. "We hoped, Lady Blakemore and I, that you and Miss du

Coeur would recognize the true character in each other, perhaps even fall in love." The earl winced and grasped his broken forearm, then turned to Dr. Horton. "Hurts like the plague." His weary sigh prompted Hartley.

"Forgive me, sir. I shall leave you to your rest." He moved toward the door.

"And you forgive *her,* Hartley. Is there anything you would not do to save your family?"

His words rang in Hartley's ears as he exited the bed-chamber. Yes, he would do anything for Mother and Sophia. And yes, he must forgive Miss du Coeur and pray she would forgive him. He thanked the Lord he had not said every hurtful thing in his thoughts during their argument.

"Did your discussion go well?" Awaiting him in the anteroom, Lady Blakemore gave him a sweet, sly, maternal smile.

Hartley could only laugh. These two were like benevolent puppeteers, and he and Miss du Coeur had been dancing on their strings the whole time. Somehow, he did not mind in the least. "Where is your lovely companion?"

"Why, if you refer to our Miss Hart, I believe she may still be down in the drawing room."

Hartley started to give the countess a playful bow, then decided to plant a kiss on her cheek.

"Hartley!" The grand old lady blushed, just as he hoped.

He hastened down the stairs to find Mr. Fleming emerging from the drawing room.

"My lord, have you seen Miss Hart?" The young man's stricken face seemed at odds with his position. Did the secretary have a *tendre* for Miss du Coeur?

"Is she not in the drawing room?"

"No, sir. Her lady's maid tells me she has not returned to her room, and none of the footmen have seen her."

"Forgive me, Fleming, but what business have you with the young lady?"

"Surely you know by now, my lord. I have been her secret bodyguard since the phaeton accident."

His disclosure sent shock and fear knifing through Hartley's chest. Of course Blakemore would have hired a bodyguard for her, just as he had sent Ajax to protect Hartley. "And you say she is not in the drawing room?" He opened the door and strode into the chamber to see for himself. "How could she have vanished?"

"My lord." Fleming knelt by the inner wall. "The wallpaper has been damaged." He stood and ran his hand up the design. "A door." He pried open the aperture, letting in a blast of stale air.

"So that explains it." The day Edgar had vanished from this very room, Hartley had questioned his own sanity. Did no one else know of this door but his scheming, murderous cousin?

"I fear, Lord Hartley, that Mr. Radcliff has kidnapped your lady, and I am to blame."

Chapter Twenty-Four

"What will you do with me?" Catherine surveyed the small, dark enclosure, searching for a way to escape. Moving even an inch was impossible, for her wrists had been tied to her ankles, and she had been shoved to the floor between two of the crates that crowded the room. In the glow of a single candle, she could make out a small window on the opposite wall, but no light filtered in through the dirt. No doubt it was still night. Outside the thin wall behind her, water slapped against wood. Were they near the Thames? If she could undo the ropes and get outside, she could swim to safety.

"No need to attempt escape, my dear." Mr. Radcliff sat above her on a crate, looking down his nose at her, just as Lord Hartley had at their last meeting. How strange that the same handsomely shaped nose could look so unalike on two men of the same family.

"You have not answered my question." Catherine summoned every ounce of her waning self-possession to appear calm. "What will you do with me? Throw me in the river?"

"Now, now, Miss du Coeur, I am not a murderer. At least not of women." He studied his well-manicured fingernails and brushed them across his lapel. "I have decided to sell you to a ship's captain who travels to China. A pretty creature like you will bring a handsome sum in the Orient. Your exceptional height will make you all the more attractive to some wealthy mandarin."

Bile rose up in her throat, but again she forbade herself to react. "You are finished in England, of course, so you should go to China yourself. Why not simply demand a ransom for me to fund the trip?"

His eyes had flared maniacally, then took on that snake-like appearance she should have noticed long ago. "But you have utterly missed the point. If I delivered you safely back to your dear parents and that insufferable Hartley, how could I ensure their endless suffering?" He regarded her with a smirk. "In any event, I have plenty of money. I've been gathering it from numerous enterprises and saving it for years just in case I did need to flee the country." He jumped down from the crate and leaned against the wall, arms crossed. "Although I do like your suggestion that I go to China. Perhaps you and I could travel there together."

For once, she did not let herself be fooled by his light tone. Still, if she went along with the idea, it could provide more opportunities for escape. "I have always adored chinoiserie, especially Mama's lacquered jewel case and silk folding screen." She stared off to feign a wistful mood. "Perhaps..." She let her words trail off.

"Do not regard me as a fool, young lady. I know you too well."

She clamped down on a retort. "If you knew me all that well, then you would know I have a hearty appetite. Do you plan to feed me, or must I wait until I arrive in Shanghai?"

"Oh, do forgive me, my dear. I shall call for a footman

to bring your supper." To her surprise, he opened the door and walked out.

In the silence that ensued, Catherine rested her head back against the wall. Skittering sounds among the crates sent a shiver up her spine. Rats! Too bad Crumpet was not here to keep them away from her. Too bad his master was not here to save her. She had no doubt that gentleman was glad to be rid of her and her lies. If she could do it all again... No, regrets would not save her. All she could do was pray. While she could not reconcile with Lord Hartley, she could reconcile with the Lord of lords.

"Father in heaven," she whispered, "please forgive me for not listening to your still, small voice urging me not to be a Delilah. Please watch over my dear family." Her voice broke, and she swallowed hard, only to discover how thirsty she was. "If I am taken away, please grant peace to them all, including Lord Hartley. Please help him to forgive me. Please—"

The door swung inward and a slatternly older woman entered, carrying a tray. "'Ere's yer supper, girl. I brung the best I could." She knelt down and frowned. "'Ow's she supposed to eat all bound up? 'At's what I'd like to know."

The woman's kind tone ignited a flicker of hope in Catherine. "If I promise to be good, will you untie my hands? My wrists are terribly sore."

"Well..." The woman glanced over her shoulder. "'E's gone off fer a bit, so maybe 'e'll never know." She set the tray down and with some difficulty untied the tightly knotted cords.

"Thank you, mum." Catherine mimicked her lady's maid's accent, which fell somewhat short of Society's elocution. "I'm Catherine. What's your name?"

"Bess." She sat back on her heels to watch Catherine eat. Or rather, choke down the slimy fish soup. But she forced a smile. "It's good." Not entirely a lie. The warm liquid did feel good in her empty stomach. "Did you fix it?"

Bess nodded, then leaned toward Catherine, sending a strong smell of whiskey into her nostrils. "The last time I kept prisoners fer my old man, two little boys, it was, Lord Greystone hisself came along and set 'em free. 'Course, he gave me a gold florin and a fancy hankie with his initial on it. That made up considerable for the beating I took from my man after." She eyed Catherine. "You got any blunt?"

"Blunt?"

"Money. Gold is best, but I'll take wha'ever ya got."

Catherine shook her head. "I fear that Mr. Radcliff did not give me time to fetch my reticule." Her own silly remark made her giggle, though she hardly felt merry.

Bess laughed with her. "'At's the spirit, girl. Be brave. Don't do no good to cry." She collected the bowl and spoon and set them aside, then tied the rope back around Catherine's wrists. "I ain't the best at knots, miss." She winked. "If ya know what I mean." She stood and walked to the door. "Just remember ol' Bess if yer ever down this way again."

After she left, Catherine counted to ten, then tore at her bonds until a sound outside warned her. She clutched the ropes, trying to make them appear tied. She pulled her knees up to her chin and lolled her head to the side against the crate. Keeping her eyes open only a little, she watched Mr. Radcliff enter, study the scene, then leave. Before she could anticipate an escape, she heard the unmistakable metallic click of a key turning in a padlock on the door.

"If you will not give me the names of your accomplices, you will hang alone right outside these walls." Hartley hovered over the small man who had taken part in the attack on the coach. The clamor of inmates in Newgate Prison was nothing to the clamor in Hartley's chest. When the man refused to answer, he nodded to Ajax.

From behind, the giant gripped the prisoner's shirt and lifted him off the cell floor, a foreshadowing of his execution.

"If you tell me where I can find them," Hartley said, "I shall see that you are transported rather than hanged."

The man, little more than a youth, blustered a bit, but his bravado was beginning to fail him. "I don't know where they are, gov'nor."

"'Ere now." Ajax gave him a shake. "That's *milord* to you, weasel."

"Awright, awright. Make the ape put me down… milord."

"Put him down, Ajax." Hartley wanted to strangle the man himself, but that would not save Miss du Coeur. "Where does Edgar Radcliff meet with his henchmen?"

"A tavern down in the Sanctuary. Sharp's the name." The man had the audacity to smirk. "Fer a few shillings, I'll take ya there myself."

Hartley had hoped never to return to the Sanctuary, an ironically named area of poverty and crime. He beckoned to the keeper. "Put him back in the ward. Come, Ajax." As he walked toward the maze of hallways leading out of the prison, the man cried out.

"You promised to let me go."

"Only if your information is correct."

They rode back to his town house, where Mother and Sophia confronted him in his office and demanded to know of his progress. With no little difficulty, he calmed them with half-truths.

"Have no fear. I shall find our Miss Hart." *His* Miss

du Coeur. His heart. "Now, run along and go shopping or something while Ajax and I make our plans."

Sophia protested, but Mother seemed to understand that female hysterics would not help the situation, for she led Sophia away with promises of new bonnets and slippers.

"Send a footman for Fleming," Hartley said to Ajax as he strapped on a sword. "Tell him to make all haste."

"Aye, milord." The giant left for a few minutes. When he came back, another man followed him into the room.

"Greystone." The viscount's arrival dampened Hartley's spirits considerably. He had no time for socializing. "What are you doing here?"

"Good to see you, too, Hartley." The viscount snickered.

"Sorry. It's just that I am in the middle of a mess that requires sorting out straightaway."

"And you do not call upon your friends to help?" Greystone settled his fists at his waist, brushing back his jacket. Only then did Hartley see a brace of pistols across his chest and a sword sheathed at his side.

"Ahh," Hartley breathed out. Help from an unexpected corner. "How did you know?"

From inside his brown jacket, Greystone whipped a dingy monogrammed handkerchief no self-respecting gentleman would carry. "I owe you for helping me rescue my two little climbing boys."

Hartley grew more encouraged. "What does that handkerchief have to do with it?"

"I left it as a gift for the woman who was guarding the boys. She just sent it back with a note that I might be interested in purchasing another bit of cargo left in her care." Greystone waggled his dark eyebrows and smirked. "She urged me to bring along the pretty boy with the curly blond hair who backed down a dozen wharf rats. I could only assume she meant you."

Hartley would have rolled his eyes at the woman's description of him, but there was little time for such antics.

"Shall we go, then?"

Saddled horses were brought around from the mews, and they mounted just as Mr. Fleming arrived.

"Best let me lead, my lord," the former secretary said. "I know the Sanctuary all too well."

Hartley glanced at Greystone for approval. The viscount nodded.

"Lead on, then."

The quartet rode through central London toward the parish of Westminster as quickly as traffic permitted. Passing the Houses of Parliament and Westminster Abbey, they reached Old Pye Street, then headed into the labyrinth of dark lanes and courts that comprised the Sanctuary. The last time he had come this way, Hartley had followed Jeremy Slate, the excellent Bow Street Runner who had led them through a dense night fog. Today the morning sun tried in vain to illuminate the garbage-strewn alleys, but at least they could see where they were going.

The closer they traveled toward the Thames, the stronger the stink from garbage, waste and animal carcasses floating in its currents. Hartley had a sudden longing for his country estate, where the river ran free of refuse and smelled of spring. Once this was all over, he would take Miss du Coeur there—if she would marry him. But why should she when he had played into Edgar's hands so easily? And how could he have thought he would make a competent diplomat, someone who could discern the motives of foreign powers, when he had not even discerned the evil in his own cousin?

"That must be the stable where we left our horses."

Greystone pointed his riding crop at an unpainted shed that looked as if it might topple at any moment.

"Can we trust the ostler?" Hartley directed his question to Fleming.

"Aye, milord," Fleming said. "He's an honest man despite his location."

"Very well, then, proceed." Hartley once again fell in behind the erstwhile secretary.

Once the horses had been secured, they made their way to Sharp's Tavern, another building that appeared unlikely to survive the next winter's winds.

"Ah, memories," Greystone quipped.

Hartley snorted. "Does your new bride know you are risking your life on this undertaking?"

"Of course not." The viscount snorted. "I have learned the hard way that one never tells the ladies anything until the danger is over."

Now Hartley snorted. His friend's bride was a lovely, refined lady, but she had not been challenged quite like Miss du Coeur, who had been in the thick of the fight on the road to Dover. While he would not like to see her in such danger again, she was well equipped to face it without hysterics.

The memory of her handing him the bloody sword blasted into his mind. How on earth could he have accused her of trying to murder him? She had gone against every feminine instinct and saved his life by striking down one of the would-be assassins. He stopped suddenly, unable to comprehend his own absurdity.

Ajax bumped into him from behind, almost knocking him to the ground, and knocking some sense into him in the process. "Sorry, milord. Is everything awright?"

"Yes." The urgent need to save her displaced his self-reproach and spurred him once again to action. "Let's go."

Last time, because it had been dark, they had worn black capes and tried to blend in with the sordid types who inhabited the area. In daylight this time, they marched into the tavern, making no attempt to disguise themselves or their intentions.

The weasel-like tavern keeper, who previously had been the first one to flee Hartley's sword, now cowered behind the counter that held abandoned drinks and bottles.

"Where is everyone?" Fleming said in a conversational tone. "We thought there would be a party."

Hartley liked this man. He would have to hire him when all this was over.

"M-milord, it's just that…they was… We heard— "

Fleming vaulted over the counter and snatched the stout man up by the collar. "Where is the lady? Do not dare to lie, or they will be the last words you ever speak."

The man pointed a trembling hand toward the back wall. "A shed. Second one over."

"Let us make haste." Hartley dashed from the tavern with the others on his heels.

They found several sheds and approached the second one. An open padlock hung from the door. Inside they found a small pile of ropes.

"Look here." Greystone pointed to the side of a crate, where delicate pink threads clung to the rough wood as if fine fabric had brushed against it and snagged.

"She was here." Hartley could smell her rose perfume even above the stink of the river. While the others searched for clues, he looked up at the small window. More torn pink material festooned the rough wood like signal flags. "She escaped." He could not keep the laughter from his voice. "My lady is a wonder."

Fleming and Ajax traded worried looks.

"That she is, milord," the giant said. "The thing of it

is, sir, this ain't the best part of London for a decent lady
to be out and about."

"And on foot," Fleming added.

A sick feeling swept away Hartley's momentary op-
timism.

"Let's go find the woman." Greystone headed out the
door. "She knew we would be coming."

Back at the tavern, the proprietor was nowhere to be
found. Fleming and Greystone searched the upstairs and
returned just as the old slattern walked in the front door.
Her face sported a recent injury.

"There's the pretty boy." She grinned at Hartley, revealing a bloody front tooth. "And Lord Greystone hisself."
She sauntered across the room as if they were old friends,
then turned serious. "The girl got out, milord, but the
fancy gentleman what locked her up followed. I can't say
where she went, 'cause I don't know." She hung her head
and sniffed. "If I'd a-known when she was gonna get out, I
woulda got her to a safe place, but she left afore daylight."

Greystone patted her shoulder. "I believe you, Bess." He
fished a gold coin from his waistcoat and his old handkerchief from a pocket. "Here, take these. Why not find someplace else to live? Someplace where no one will beat you?"

She swiped the handkerchief under her nose. "Maybe
I will, milord."

"Where to now, milord?" Ajax chewed his lip like an
anxious child.

Panic threatened to envelop Hartley. Where indeed?

"Let me go! Help!" A scream split the air, sending them
all back out into the open. On the wharf by the river, his
beautiful Miss du Coeur was struggling with two thugs
who could not manage to subdue her. Her glorious brown
hair was entirely undone and blew in the wind like a ban-
ner. Racing toward her, Hartley pulled out a pistol but

feared to discharge the unreliable weapon lest he hit his beloved. The others reached the scene with him and drove off the ruffians, who fled like the cowards they were into the labyrinth of vice and depravity.

Flung aside by the criminals, Miss du Coeur reeled toward the edge of the wharf.

Chapter Twenty-Five

Terror ripped through Catherine as she slid across the muddy wharf, unable to gain a foothold with her tattered satin shoes. What a fool she had been. Now she would die without ever telling Lord Hartley that she loved him. His last memory of her would be words filled with misguided hatred.

In the slimy muck below her, she saw her own reflection move closer. Something clenched her around the waist. An arm, a very strong arm!

"My lady." Lord Hartley's unmistakable voice breathed into her awareness, and for a moment, she knew nothing but awe and relief.

"Hart—" *Thank You, God!*

"My heart!" He pulled her into his arms a half second before she could plunge into the murky, disease-ridden depths.

"Cowards, the lot of them." Mr. Fleming's voice reached her consciousness. "Shall we pursue them, my lord?"

"No." Lord Greystone stared off in the direction they had gone. "No use going any deeper into this den of iniquity. Do you not agree, Hartley?"

Lord Hartley was entirely too busy to answer, for he

was holding Catherine and brushing her hair back from her face. She gazed up at him with love overflowing from her heart. And from the love and joy she saw in his eyes, she had not the slightest doubt that he returned the sentiment.

Catherine rested her head on Lord Hartley's shoulder, ignoring the discomfort of the saddle. Seated in front of him on his horse, she would not tell him she could ride more easily behind him, for that would mean his arms would not encompass her like a warm blanket, as they now did.

They had said little at the wharf. In spite of their angry duel of words at their last meeting, nothing seemed more important than just holding each other in an almost desperate embrace. And now getting safely out of this horrid place called the Sanctuary took precedence over explanations and pleas for forgiveness. Yet Catherine knew she must make those pleas a priority as soon as possible.

As they wended their way through the filthy, crowded streets, several disreputable sorts shouted vulgar comments in their direction, calling her attention to her tattered clothing and unbound hair. When she looked up into Lord Hartley's eyes, he gave her a rueful smile. "We shall find a hackney as soon as possible."

"Never mind this lot." Lord Greystone rode up beside them. "They have no idea who we are and will have no opportunity to besmirch our names."

Nevertheless, Catherine bowed her head and let her hair cover her face like a shield. Through the uncombed strands, she saw Mr. Fleming riding ahead, making a way for them through the crowds. When this adventure was over and done with, she would have to tease him and suggest he become an actor. Still, although he had posed as a secretary, somehow she had always felt safe in his presence. Now she understood why.

Once they left Old Pye Street and neared Westminster Abbey, Greystone hailed a hackney, and Catherine was handed down into its cloistered interior. She looked up at Lord Hartley, aching to be back in his arms again. His green eyes reflected that same sentiment, or so she liked to think.

"Do not look so bereft, Miss Hart." Lord Greystone gave her a fraternal grin. "If Hartley wishes to ride with you, I shall be your chaperone."

The driver eyed her suspiciously, and in that moment the entire wretched business caused her face to flame. Without answering the viscount, she shrank back into the darkest part of the two-passenger carriage to hide her embarrassment.

Disappointment clouded Lord Hartley's eyes. "To Blakemore House," he said to the driver, then directed his horse to proceed down the street.

Within the half hour, the small procession arrived at the mansion. Lady Blakemore whisked Catherine away to her bedchamber before anyone had a chance to say anything more. The countess ordered a bath and a light repast and demanded an accounting of the past sixteen hours.

After telling her story, Catherine succumbed to exhaustion and slept far into the next afternoon. When she awoke, it all seemed like a bad dream, except for a few scrapes, the painful ache in her heart and the warm memory of Lord Hartley's strong arms clutching her before she could fall into the foul waters of the Thames.

Hartley paced Lady Blakemore's drawing room until he feared he would wear a hole in the red-and-gold Wilton carpet that lay in front of the hearth. He had counted the earl's ivory figurines—there were twenty-seven—counted the seating and concluded that forty-one individuals could be accommodated comfortably in the five groupings of chairs and settees. He then examined the repaired wallpaper that hid the secret door.

Blakemore explained that he had not used the door since he was a boy and never gave it a thought. Nor could he guess how Edgar ever found it. They decided that a man intent upon evil would have no compunction about searching his employer's home for any convenient device to use in his malicious schemes.

Just hours after they had rescued Miss du Coeur, Edgar had been apprehended boarding a ship about to set sail for China. He now waited in Newgate Prison for his trial. After Blakemore explained the extent of his cousin's murderous plans, Hartley could not bring himself to visit him. He did manage to send a note promising to take care of Emily and Marcus; however, Edgar had responded that he had never cared much for his wife and son and was pleased to be rid of them. Such a man deserved no mercy, but Hartley still could find no satisfaction in the idea of his cousin's execution. Perhaps he should be sent to Bedlam rather than hanged, for surely some sort of madness had driven him all these years.

These activities and musings did nothing to alleviate his impatience as he waited to learn whether Miss du Coeur would receive him. He had paced this room for over two hours, and still she did not appear.

At long last, the door opened, and she entered. Actually, she peered around it as if checking to see whether it was safe to come in. She looked so beautiful in her pink walking gown, so shy, so utterly appealing, that he laughed for joy over seeing her at last.

"My dearest heart, do come in." Startled by his own

words, he wished them back. What if she did not love him in return?

"Dearest Hartley." She ran into his arms, sobbing. "How can you ever forgive me for all of my lies? How could I have been so foolish?"

He held her for a moment, savoring the scent of her rose perfume, the nearness of her being, the joy of her returning his love. "Which question would you like me to answer first?"

She laughed and cried at the same time. "You choose."

"My darling, of course I forgive you." He took her hand and led her to a settee. "We were both puppets dancing to Blakemore's tune." A minor chord resonated within his heart. "I am grieved to think he could not trust me enough to explain everything to me from the beginning."

"I asked the same question about my own situation. Lady Blakemore told me the Home Office was testing both of us *and* my father. An assassination plot against a king has greater consequences than a grievance between two families. Had it turned out to be genuine, Louis might never have made it back to France, and war might have erupted again between our two countries." She dabbed at her tears with a silk handkerchief. "But I believe Mr. Radcliff was the puppeteer. How cleverly he used us both against each other, and all for revenge."

Hartley sighed. "Not so entirely clever, was he?"

She shook her head and gazed off thoughtfully.

"Well." He touched her chin and returned her gaze to himself. "Enough of that. We have something else to discuss."

"Oh?"

He slipped down on one knee and gripped both of her hands. "My dearest heart, would you do me the honor of becoming my wife?"

Bursting into tears, she pulled back her hands and covered her face.

"I—I am…" How could he have so completely misjudged her feelings? "Please forgive me—"

"No, no." She hiccoughed another sob. "I mean, yes, yes. I will marry you. Though after all I did, how can you want—"

"Shh." He placed a finger on her lips. "Do not say another word about it. I forgive you." To seal the matter, he bent forward and at last succumbed to the temptation to place a kiss on her sweet, soft lips.

Catherine had never felt more beautiful. Her lady's maid had once again coiffed her hair into a thousand elegant curls with tiny white silk roses woven throughout. Her bridal gown, a white brocade creation with dark pink lace and ribbons around the square neckline, and short, similarly trimmed puffy sleeves, had taken Giselle three weeks to make. Fortunately, the wedding could not take place until the banns had been cried for those same three weeks. Lady Blakemore had insisted upon being the hostess for the wedding breakfast, and she had invited Mama and Lady Winston to assist her. But first came the wedding.

Catherine stood at the back of St. George's Church with Papa at her side. At the front, Lord Hartley stood with Lords Greystone and Blakemore, awaiting her arrival. The music began, Papa squeezed her hand and they proceeded down the aisle. She was so grateful to have him to support her, for no matter how happy she was this day, her knees insisted upon trembling.

As her gaze settled upon Lord Hartley, whom she had decided to call Hart, all nervousness subsided. How handsome he looked in his green velvet jacket, sparkling white shirt and cravat, and green satin breeches. His gray-green eyes caught the colors and sparkled brilliantly in the sunny church sanctuary. His untamable curly blond hair gave him that youthful look that she so adored. But it was his warm, welcoming smile that melted her heart and brought a tear to her eyes.

Reading from the church's prayer book, Mr. Richard Grenville conducted the wedding ceremony, and Catherine had every confidence that he and she and Hart said all the right words. But in the end, all she heard was the final phrase, which was followed by "in the Name of the Father and of the Son and of the Holy Ghost. Amen."

One day soon she must read the ritual over again and perhaps even memorize the wonderful holy words. For now, "I pronounce that they be man and wife together" was all she needed to hear. When Hart placed the gentlest, sweetest kiss upon her lips, she knew she was utterly and completely happily married.

Epilogue

"En garde." Catherine positioned herself for a duel, feet set apart and one hand lifted behind her for balance, her slender walking stick raised in a challenge to Hart.

After a long winter, the fresh spring air of Surrey invited them out for daily walks over the hills surrounding their country home. When they had come from London last August, she had been surprised to see not a recently built manor house but a beautiful, ancient castle where she would live with her beloved the rest of her days.

Now delicate violets and exquisite pink primroses filled the April air with their lovely scents, while countless birdsongs sounded in the nearby woods. A few feet away, Crumpet chased a butterfly, only to land in the clear spring bubbling out from a small mound of rocks on the hill. These merry signs of spring sparked in Catherine this bit of dueling mischief.

"Mais non, madame." Hart's green eyes twinkled in the sunlight as he lifted his cane—this one without a hidden sword. *"Vous en garde."*

So he meant to launch the first attack. Catherine smirked. *"Très bien, monsieur.* Proceed." Expecting a direct lunge, she prepared to deflect his assault. Instead, he pointed his make-believe sword at her and circled it in the air so she could not guess his next move.

With a giggle, she backed away but tripped on a protruding root. As she staggered to keep from falling, alarm shot through her. She must not fall! Hart dropped his cane and caught her around the waist just in time, rolling onto the soft grass so she would land on top of him.

"Oof!" He flung his arms wide, then lay limp on the ground, obviously feigning injury.

Catherine rolled off him and placed her head upon his shoulder. "I shall lie here until you awaken."

He exhaled a deep sigh of contentment. "That may not be until August."

She sat up and nudged his side. "What? And miss an entire session of Parliament? An entire Season?" Not that she cared at all for Society, but she would like to see her friends again after all these months.

"If I never had to participate in another parliamentary debate, I would be pleased beyond measure."

She sat up, plucked a blade of grass and tickled his upper lip. "You do not mean that."

"Only a little." He sat up and snatched the blade to return the favor, then gave her a peck of a kiss. Later she would demand much more from him. "I may have rejected my father's harsh view of God, but I still take my responsibilities seriously. All of them."

She sobered. "I know you do. You have been so good to Emily and Marcus since Mr. Radcliff died." She could not think of that man without a shudder.

Hart pulled her into his arms and kissed her forehead. "I will always grieve over his death." The haunted look in his eyes hinted at a deep remorse.

"It was not your fault. We are told that these horrible

fevers often sweep through prisons. He did not have a strong constitution."

Hart waved a dismissive hand, perhaps still wrestling with his unnecessary guilt. "I must make certain to spend time with young Marcus before he goes to Eton. I want him to know he will always have a special place in our family." Hart plucked another blade of grass and chewed on its end. "Perhaps I can influence him for the good. As my heir, he—"

"Well, I do agree we should continue to support his mother and him." She gave him a sly look. "But, as to his being your heir, it is entirely possible that he will soon be supplanted by a little Lord Winston. Shall we say, before All Saints' Day?"

"What?" Hart's eyes grew round, and his jaw dropped. "Are you... Will we... I am going to be a father?" The excitement in his countenance gave him that adorable youthful look she loved so much, but not without a decided infusion of maturity he had sported of late.

Catherine laughed for joy. "Indeed you are, my dearest Hart."

"*My* dearest heart." He gently pushed her back down on the grass for a celebratory kiss.

As delicious warmth swept over her entire being, she lifted a prayer of thanks to God for the path he had brought them on. Not a path of hate and revenge, but of love and forgiveness and a grace that promised never to end.

* * * * *

*If you enjoyed this story by Louise M. Gouge,
be sure to check out the other books this month
from Love Inspired Historical!*

Dear Reader,

Thank you for choosing *A Lady of Quality,* the third book in my Ladies in Waiting series. I hope you've enjoyed this journey back to Regency England. I love to write stories about this unique and fascinating era, the setting for Jane Austen's timeless novels. One of the most appealing things about it is that everyone knew exactly what was expected for someone in her or his station in life, and diligent people strove to play their roles well. Still, love could always find a way to overcome the rules of Society, at least in fiction!

My stories take place in 1814, at the end of the war with Napoleon. It was a time of great upheaval in England, but also a time when ambitious men could take advantage of the changes. King George III had gone mad, and his eldest son, the heir to the throne, had been designated Prince Regent by Parliament. That empowered him to do everything a king could do, including the signing of a writ of patent creating a new peer or elevating a peer to a higher level of the nobility. When I learn such an interesting historical fact, I love to incorporate it into my stories.

Getting the details right, however, is one of the tricky things about writing historical fiction. The social structures of the Regency era were quite strict and confining, so if you're a die-hard Regency fan and find an error, please let me know! And please know that I tried to get it right!

As with all of my stories, beyond the romance, I hope to inspire my readers always to seek God's guidance, no matter what trials may come their way.

I love to hear from readers, so if you have a comment, please contact me through my website: http://blog.Louisemgouge.com.

Blessings,

Louise M. Gouge

Questions for Discussion

1. In the beginning of the story, Lord Winston is searching for a suitable wife to enhance his diplomatic career. What makes him change his mind and begin looking for a wife to love?

2. From the instant Winston sees Catherine Hart, he is smitten by her beauty and grace. Why does he try not to become too attached to her? Do you think he is justified in that response, considering the expectations of the era? How do you think this reflects upon his character? What causes him to change his opinion over time?

3. Catherine had grown up in a loving Christian home and, as the oldest child, has always felt responsible for protecting her younger brother and sister and setting a good example for them. What causes her to go against everything she believes in order to get revenge? Is this consistent with her character? Have you ever suffered loss and felt as Catherine did?

4. After meeting Winston at the ball and finding him to be a kind, thoughtful gentleman, Catherine struggles not to fall in love with him. What forces work against her natural inclinations and poison the evidence of her eyes and heart? Have you ever misjudged a person because of some previous prejudice or misinformation?

5. Winston also grew up in a home where Christian principles were taught. How did his family differ from Catherine's? How did this affect the development of

his character? How did he come to reject his father's example? Who helped him? Have you ever sought help from a spiritual advisor in understanding the character of God?

6. Both Winston and Catherine are Christians. Which one changes the most in the story? In what ways does each one mature and become stronger? In what ways do they stay the same?

7. Sometimes Winston seems a little naive. Why hasn't he had an opportunity to learn about romance? Does he fit your definition of a hero? Why or why not?

8. Have you ever been certain you knew the truth about a person or situation, only to find that your sources were incorrect? How did you react? What did you learn?

9. Well-bred young ladies of the Regency era were expected to be more ornamental than assertive, but Catherine has gone against the expectations of her era in learning to fence and ride. How does this serve to make her a stronger character? Do you find her a compelling heroine? Why or why not?

10. What sort of people arc Lord and Lady Blakemore? Why do you suppose they involve themselves in the lives of Winston and Catherine? Have you ever had a mentor? How did this person help you choose your path in life? Have you ever mentored someone else?

11. The overarching themes of this story are revenge and forgiveness, two sides of the same coin. How

did Catherine and Winston work through their own issues? How could each one of them have taken an easier path to resolving their issues?

12. This was an age in which the aristocracy ruled and held all of the privileges. As much as we romanticize the era, would you like to travel back in time for a visit? At what level of Society did your ancestors live?

COMING NEXT MONTH
from Love Inspired® Historical
AVAILABLE AUGUST 6, 2013

THE BABY BEQUEST
Wilderness Brides
Lyn Cote
When a baby is abandoned on her doorstep, schoolteacher Ellen Thurston fights to keep the child despite the community's protests. Her only ally is handsome newcomer Kurt Lang—but can these two outsiders make a family?

THE COURTING CAMPAIGN
The Master Matchmakers
Regina Scott
Emma Pyrmont hopes to convince single father Sir Nicholas Rotherford that there's more to life than calculations and chemistry. As she draws him closer to his young daughter, Nicholas sees his daughter—and her nanny—with new eyes.

ROPING THE WRANGLER
Wyoming Legacy
Lacy Williams
To save three young girls, schoolmarm Sarah Hansen teams up with her childhood rival. But is Oscar White still the reckless horseman she remembers, or has he become the compassionate cowboy she needs?

HEALING THE SOLDIER'S HEART
Lily George
After his experiences at Waterloo, Ensign James Rowland finds healing through governess Lucy Williams's tender encouragement. However, their different social stations threaten to ruin their happily ever after.

Look for these and other Love Inspired books wherever books are sold, including most bookstores, supermarkets, discount stores and drugstores.

REQUEST YOUR FREE BOOKS!

2 FREE INSPIRATIONAL NOVELS
PLUS 2
FREE
MYSTERY GIFTS

Love Inspired
HISTORICAL
INSPIRATIONAL HISTORICAL ROMANCE

YES! Please send me 2 FREE Love Inspired® Historical novels and my 2 FREE mystery gifts (gifts are worth about $10). After receiving them, if I don't wish to receive any more books, I can return the shipping statement marked "cancel." If I don't cancel, I will receive 4 brand-new novels every month and be billed just $4.74 per book in the U.S. or $5.24 per book in Canada. That's a saving of at least 21% off the cover price. It's quite a bargain! Shipping and handling is just 50¢ per book in the U.S. and 75¢ per book in Canada.* I understand that accepting the 2 free books and gifts places me under no obligation to buy anything. I can always return a shipment and cancel at any time. Even if I never buy another book, the two free books and gifts are mine to keep forever.

102/302 IDN F5CN

Name		
	(PLEASE PRINT)	

Address		Apt. #

City	State/Prov.	Zip/Postal Code

Signature (if under 18, a parent or guardian must sign)

Mail to the Harlequin® Reader Service:
IN U.S.A.: P.O. Box 1867, Buffalo, NY 14240-1867
IN CANADA: P.O. Box 609, Fort Erie, Ontario L2A 5X3

Want to try two free books from another series?
Call 1-800-873-8635 or visit www.ReaderService.com.

*Oscar White has come to town to tame a horse,
but finds love in the most unexpected of places.*

*Read on for a sneak peek at
ROPING THE WRANGLER by Lacy Williams,
available August 2013 from Love Inspired Historical.*

"They say he's magic with the long reins—"

"I saw him ride once in an exhibition down by Cheyenne…."

Sarah clutched her schoolbooks until her knuckles turned white. The men of Lost Hollow were no better than little boys, excited over a wild cowboy! Unfortunately, her boss, the chairman of the school board and the reason Oscar White was here, had insisted that as the schoolteacher, she should come along as part of the welcoming committee. And because they'd known each other in Bear Creek.

But she hadn't known Oscar White well and hadn't liked what she had known.

And now she just wanted to get this "welcome" over with. Her thoughts wandered until the train came to a hissing stop at the platform.

The man who strode off with a confident gait bore a resemblance to the Oscar White she'd known, but *this* man was assuredly different. With his Stetson tilted back rakishly to reveal brown eyes, his face no longer bore the slight roundness of youth. No, those lean, craggy features belonged to a man, without question. Broad shoulders easily parted the small crowd on the platform, and he headed straight for their group.

Sarah turned away, alarmed by the pulse pounding frantically in her temples. Why this reaction now, *to this man?*

Through the rhythmic beating in her ears—too fast!—she heard the men exchange greetings, and then Mr. Allen cleared his throat.

"And I believe you already know our schoolteacher…"

Obediently she turned and their gazes collided—his brown eyes curious until he glimpsed her face.

"…Miss Sarah Hansen."

His eyes instantly cooled. He quickly looked back to the other men. "I've got to get my horses from the stock car. I'll catch up with you gentlemen in a moment. Miss Hansen." He tipped his hat before rushing off down the line of train cars.

Sarah found herself watching him and forced her eyes away. Obviously he remembered her, and perhaps what had passed between them seven years ago.

That was just fine with her. She had no use for reckless cowboys. She was looking for a responsible man for a husband….

Don't miss ROPING THE WRANGLER
by Lacy Williams,
on sale August 2013 wherever
Love Inspired Historical books are sold!

LIHEXP0713

The Master Matchmakers

Emma Pyrmont hopes to convince single father
Sir Nicholas Rotherford that there's more to life than calculations
and chemistry. As she draws him closer to his young daughter,
Nicholas sees his daughter—and her nanny—with new eyes.

The Courting Campaign

by

REGINA SCOTT

Available August 2013 wherever
Love Inspired Historical books are sold.

www.LoveInspiredBooks.com

LIH82976

Love Inspired

CARING Canines

Both Abbey Harris and Dominic Winters long for a second chance at love, and it'll take two adorable dogs and a sweet little girl to bring them together.

Healing Hearts
by Margaret Daley

Available August 2013
wherever Love Inspired books are sold.

www.LoveInspiredBooks.com

LI87830